Kamal is a by-the-book mercenary and hitman who keeps to himself, dealing with the brutal politics of the Bosnian underworld. He has very few ties to the world around him since the war that left him broken and betrayed by his lover. An encounter with a fellow mercenary, whose job it is to kidnap the son of the only man Kamal ever loved, leads Kamal to do something irrational. In an isolated cabin in the mountains of Bosnia with his hostage, Kamal follows the well laid-out plan of his predecessor, but somewhere along the way things get personal. The boy in his care becomes more than just a stand-in for his father, but a job is a job and Kamal is a professional. When questions and tensions begin to mount, Kamal begins to put the pieces together for himself, and doesn't like what he finds. Can Kamal get his revenge and the boy or will he have to settle for one or the other?

Also recommended...

You may also enjoy these other ForbiddenFiction works:

The Brig by **Mason Powell**

This classic gay BDSM novel, set near the end of the Viet Nam war, has been out of print for almost 20 years. The Brig is a brutally dark erotic drama of a young sailor confined to a military prison where he tortured with pain, fear, sexuality, and mind games to force changes in his psyche and break his spirit. The sailor learns things about himself and his captors that will transform him and challenge those who hold him. (M/M)

Don't by **Jack L. Pyke**

"Don't... open me." Three simple words that tease Jack, taking him places from his dark past. For Jack, BDSM is a way to resist his worst impulses. Yet, the stranger calling himself The Unknown seeks to use that to seduce him. As Jack slips further down into the abyss, two men hold the power to save him. Will it be Gray, the Master who knows Jack's every secret? Or Jan, the first man to give Jack a reason to hope? With deadly ghosts coming out to play, Jack may lose everything, even his life. (M/M)

Backdoor Politics

C.L. Mustafic

ForbiddenFiction
www.forbiddenfiction.com

an imprint of

Fantastic Fiction Publishing
www.fantasticfictionpublishing.com

BACKDOOR POLITICS

A ForbiddenFiction book

Fantastic Fiction Publishing
Hayward, California

© C.L. Mustafic, 2017

CREDITS
Editor: Rylan Hunter and D.M. Atkins
Cover Design: Siolnatine
Cover Art: Adapted from photos © Konstantin Tavrov and © Pablo Hidalgo at Dreamstime.com
Production Editor: Kaye O'Malley
Proofreading: Ava Verdugo
Font: Wellrock Slab, by Manfred Klein

SKU: CLM-1.000304-01 FFP
ISBN: 978-1-62234-336-2

Published in the United States of America

DISCLAIMER

Dedication

To Pippa Brook,
who listened to me go crazy with ideas
that would scare most people
but never told me no.

Contents

Chapter 1:
Prologue – Just Another Job

It was dark. With the clouds obscuring the moon and stars, it was darker than most nights in the small mountain village, but that only aided Kamal in his endeavor. Even though he was sweating, he pulled the black ski mask down to cover his face as he reached the edge of the thick pine forest that butted up to the back of the small compound he'd been watching for days. There was no noise coming from behind the high stone wall. Kamal knew his window of opportunity was open but only for a short period of time while the inhabitants slept and the inept guards met for their nightly game of Rummy and shots of strong homemade *rakia*. They'd become complacent in their jobs, lulled into a false sense of security by the routine and serenity of the simple country life in a small *etno selo*.

He used the natural hand and foot holds the rustic design of the fence allowed for to easily scale the wall. Dropping down amid a wilting flower bed, he crouched for a moment to listen. When no alarms sounded, he silently crept across the well-manicured back lawn, making use of the many topiaries to hide his movements. Once he'd made it to the back of the house, he used the trellis to climb to the balcony of the room he'd pinned down as the one he wanted. The balcony door stood wide open making it almost too easy for him to gain entry. He shook his head at the lack of security, or maybe it was at the arrogance of the man inside that left him vulnerable to the approaching threat; either way Kamal had expected a much more challenging job when he'd accepted the assignment.

He edged his way along the wall to the door, halfway expecting there to be a trap. In his experience, it was never as simple as it seemed when presented with such easy access to a target. There were no hulking bodyguards there to meet him as he stepped gingerly over the threshold into the large bedroom, so he made his way unhindered to the side of the massive bed centered along the far wall of the room. Pulling both his guns out, he then clicked on the bedside table lamp to alert the sleeping couple of his presence.

The woman roused first, and after a brief moment of confusion her eyes flew open wide, but the gun pointed at her head combined with Kamal putting a finger to his lips, in the universal sign for *shut the hell up*, kept her from making even the smallest of peeps. Her hand reached across the bed to touch the still slumbering man's arm, bringing him to wakefulness and full awareness much quicker than the woman had previously achieved it. The man's brow furrowed as he took in the intruder and the guns pointing at his wife's and his own forehead. It wasn't until he reached between them that Kamal noticed the small lump in the middle of the bed.

The woman's eyes widened in terror when a small voice questioned, "Mama, *Babo*?" before a small tousled head of blond hair emerged from beneath the light blanket. Little hands rubbed sleepy eyes as the child yawned and then, upon dropping his hands, opened his cupid's bow of a mouth as if to scream in fright at the sight that greeted him. The man's quick reflexes stopped the boy from making the situation worse for the family and Kamal when he slapped a hand over the child's mouth, cutting off any sound the boy thought to make.

"Shh, *sine*," the man whispered as he looked at Kamal with pleading eyes.

Kamal gave the man the slightest of nods and the man visibly relaxed. He wasn't there for the child, at least not this time. Kamal swallowed and in a steady voice recited the words he'd memorized, "Koslov isn't happy with the way things are going. You were given a choice and you have made the wrong one. I'm here to assure that the next time you are presented with the same set of options, that you make the right one."

"I will, I couldn't — "

"No excuses, next time you will make the right choice or he will be next," Kamal said as he moved the gun he had pointed at the man to aim at the center of the child's forehead.

The woman made a little terrified squeak as a wet spot spread across the blanket over the child's lap. Kamal pulled the trigger on the gun. The silencer did its job. There was little sound from the muzzle of the weapon, which left only the splattering sound of brain matter and bone fragments landing across the headboard of the bed and its other two occupants, as the bullet left an exit wound ten times that of the point of entry before it lodged itself in the wall. The woman's figure slumped back against the pillows as the man stared in wide-eyed astonishment at Kamal. Only the hand he had pressed tightly against the child's face kept the screams of distressed anguish from alerting the guards to what had just taken place right under their noses.

"Let this serve as a warning to you, Gospodine Izetbegović, and pray that you never see me again," Kamal said, keeping his voice even to show he wouldn't hesitate to carry out his earlier threat to return.

The man nodded causing a large glob of gelatinous red goo to drop from his chin onto the top of the, now silently staring, child's head. Kamal gave a curt nod before turning quickly on his heel as he holstered the guns. He was out the patio door and over the railing when the man shouted for the guards and the high-pitched keening wails of the child started.

Kamal ignored the trellis in favor of just dropping to the ground. Landing hard, he rolled into a forward tumble and regained his feet on a sprint that took him headlong towards the wall. He was up and over--he was sure--before the guards would even make it up the stairs to check what the commotion was about. Kamal ran, holding nothing back, knowing he needed to put as much distance between himself and the scene in as short an amount of time as he could. The thick pine forest that surrounded him would hinder the clumsy guards once they got their shit together and started to try to track the man who had showed them to be as ineffectual as a band of untrained monkeys when it came to safeguarding the influential family.

Kamal had no problem making his way through the maze of trees as he'd spent the previous week walking through them to get a feel for the forest floor. Now, he traversed the uneven terrain with sure-footed ease, slowing only when he started down the steep slope that would lead him into the little ravine where he'd left the provisions he'd use to make his way back to the city undetected. The small creek that ran through the bottom of the ravine was fed by the springs further up the mountain and was cold even in the heat of the summer. Kamal ran another five hundred meters through the quickly moving water, soaking his pants up past the knees and leaving his legs tingling with the cold when he stepped out on the bank next to a small rocky overhang.

His pack was sitting right where he'd left it. Quickly pulling off his ski mask and gloves before digging through the pack, he found the dark garbage bags he'd stowed within and opened one. He placed both guns in the bag before sitting and stripping off his boots; they joined the guns in the bag. He stripped out of his dark clothing and placed them in another one of the bags. When he was sitting in only a pair of boxer briefs, he stopped to take a deep breath and listen to the sounds of the forest around him. He heard nothing unusual, which was good; he had time to make sure things were done properly.

He stood with the two bags and, barefooted, walked fifty meters away from the overhang to the first of two deep holes he'd dug days before. Placing the bundle of clothing in the hole and using his bare hands, he covered it with the displaced dirt. He made sure to use some of the leaves and sticks from the forest floor to cover the obviously freshly-turned soil. Another hundred meters away he repeated the process with the other tightly-wrapped package. He looked at the surrounding area and knew that within only days, maybe a week, the prickly *trnje* on the vines of the wild blackberries would reclaim the small patches of cleared ground leaving little evidence of his deeds to be found.

Walking back to where the creek flowed just meters away from his pack, he stepped into the water once again. He washed his face, bracing himself when the frigid water stole his breath as he washed his hands and arms of the dirt but didn't clean under his fingernails. When he was sure he didn't look like a wild animal that had just run headlong through the forest, he returned to his pack and used a small cloth to dry himself before donning a set of work clothes that had the name of one of the large factories in the city embroidered on the jacket.

Shouldering his pack, he looked to the east where the sky was starting to lighten. His timing was impeccable, as always. He made his way back up the steep slope but on the opposite side from which he'd came and headed down the barely perceptible path. After a brisk twenty minute walk, he emerged from the forest just meters from the bus stop that was already bustling with activity. He joined the group of men and women, dressed as he was, waiting there for the bus that would take them to the factory for their early morning shift.

Kamal pulled a pack of cigarettes from his pocket, offering one to the man standing next to him before taking one for himself. He let the man light him up and took a deep calming drag before nodding politely to the man who gave him a smile in return. The bus showed up right on time. Kamal took a seat near the back and settled in for the ride back into the city.

Chapter 2:
Meet the Fat Man

The streets were mostly deserted as Kamal made his way through the moist air that seemed almost too heavy to breathe. The heat, humidity, and signs of an oncoming storm conspired to keep the area free of late night strollers which Kamal found just fine for his purposes. He specialized in not being seen and it was much easier to accomplish when there was no one around to see him. He raked a hand through his hair before pulling the door to the small café open and stepping into the dim interior.

The young man behind the counter took a moment to acknowledge his presence with a slight tip of his head before going back to watching the football match silently playing on the flat screen hung at the back of the empty seating area. Kamal nodded back and then made his way to the sectioned-off area where the man he was looking for was seated at a small table. Kamal waited until the big man stood and extended his hand.

"Rodak, I didn't expect you so soon," he said in way of greeting.

"The job went faster than planned. You got the message," Kamal said as he shook the meaty hand and took the seat across from the man. The target of his last job had given into Kamal's employer's demands quickly after he'd watched a video of Kamal removing only one of his seven-year-old daughter's fingernails with a pair of pliers after having jabbed a hot needle into the nail bed to loosen it. The man had handed over the confidential documents right after he'd finished throwing up all over the front of his expensive suit.

Kamal pulled a pack of Drina's out of his pocket and offered them across the table. Fat fingers pulled one of the cigarettes out of the pack before Kamal took one for himself. He leaned forward and lit the other man's cigarette before putting the flame to his own and exhaling a large cloud of smoke on a sigh. "Tell me what's the reason for this meet, Demetri? You know how I prefer to make my transactions. Why are you changing things you know are better off left alone?" he asked, getting straight to the point.

Demetri shifted on his chair, making the old wood creak in protest. The boy from the counter appeared with a bottle of *rakia* and two glasses as well as a tray bearing two small coffee sets. Demetri took his time pouring his coffee from the small *džezva* into his cup before he looked up to meet Kamal's unwavering stare. "I have another job for you," he said quietly as his eyes shifted from side to side. He bit the sugar cube that had come on the side of his saucer in half and took a sip of the strong coffee while Kamal watched, not touching his own drink.

"You know that's not how I work." Kamal fingered the empty glass hoping Demetri would get the hint and pour him a shot of liquor.

"I know this is not how you do business but this isn't a usual situation. When you hear the details I think you may change the way you work." Demetri uncapped the bottle of *rakia* and poured them each a full shot-glass of the potent alcohol.

Kamal downed the shot, resisting the urge to hiss at the familiar burn as the libation made its way to his gut. He put his glass down and prepared his own coffee while mulling over what job could make him want to change how he'd done things for years; coming up with nothing he cocked his head to consider Demetri. The older man was sweating, but Kamal chalked that up to the fact that he was twenty-five kilos overweight combined with the heat of the season. Even though Demetri was acting much more nervous than normal, Kamal tried not to read anything into it.

"Do you have the package?" Kamal decided not to play the fat man's game but instead finish up their transaction so he could make it home before the storm hit.

"I have it and it's yours to take but please hear me out on this before you leave," Demetri said, letting just a hint of annoyance at Kamal's lack of interest in what he had to say show through.

Kamal drank his coffee in one large swallow before he stubbed out his cigarette. "I don't want to hear it, Demetri. If you have

C.L. Mustafic

something for me, you go through the proper channels," Kamal said before he pushed his chair back and made to stand.

Demetri's hand shot out and latched on to Kamal's wrist. From the look on the older man's face, he was just as surprised by his action as Kamal. Kamal looked down at the offending hand and then slowly raised his dark eyes to meet Demetri's light ones, his lips twisting in a snarl. Demetri snatched his hand back as though Kamal's skin had burnt him. "I'm sorry, Kamal, but this is important. You must listen to me," Demetri pleaded.

"Give me what's mine," Kamal said menacingly, seething at the man's disrespect. It was well known that nobody touched Kamal. It was rumored even his own mother had to ask permission to hug her son. Kamal did nothing to dispel the myth, preferring to let it fester and grow, making him that much more of a threat in the minds of those who had reason to fear him.

Reaching under the table, Demetri pulled out a small leather shoulder bag. It was as inconspicuous as any other a man might carry on any given day on the streets of the city. He handed it over but held the strap until Kamal tugged it loose. "Please, you don't know what you're — "

"I don't want to hear it. Our business is done." Kamal slung the bag across his chest. Demetri watched as Kamal strode to the door pausing only long enough to give the young man behind the counter a look that was returned with an almost imperceptible nod.

Kamal exited out onto the sidewalk, letting the heat hit him full on in the face, which did nothing to improve his mood. He was fuming that things had not gone as planned. He hated when the players tried to change the rules of the game on him. He walked briskly down the street before turning and doubling back through the narrow alley that ran between the large stone buildings. There was very little light shining through from the streets to either side of the alley, but there was enough for Kamal to pick out a silhouette leaning against the brick wall halfway down the narrow path. Good, he wouldn't have to wait this night when his patience was lacking.

He kept his pace steady as he walked up to the young man who was waiting for him. "Hamza," he said quietly.

The young man dropped the cigarette he'd been slowly smoking to put up the appearance of nonchalance as he waited for Kamal. "I don't have much time. I told him I was taking out the trash," Hamza

8

said when Kamal stopped, leaving only inches separating them. Hamza reached up toward Kamal but he grabbed Hamza's wrists and turned him so he could lean in the spot where the young man had been lounging. Letting go of Hamza's wrists, he pushed on the slight shoulders, making what he wanted the young man to do as clear as if he'd given him detailed instructions.

Hamza sank to his knees without so much as a muttered protest. He made fast work of the button and zipper on Kamal's tight jeans, revealing the unfettered arousal within the denim. Hamza licked his lips as he looked up at the man above him. "Go on, what are you waiting for?" Kamal urged him as he grabbed a fist full of silky hair and jerked him closer.

Hamza opened wide and took half of Kamal's cock into his mouth, but then he pulled back to suck slowly at the crown. Slow and drawn out wasn't what Kamal wanted. He pulled the hair in his hand and forced the mouth down his shaft, eliciting a gag from his unsuspecting partner. He held Hamza, impaled fully on the rigid length, as the smaller man struggled to pull back. Kamal bucked his hips, loving the sensation that the spasming of the unwilling throat he was buried in produced around his sensitive flesh. It had been too long since the last time he'd found release with something other than his own hand. Kamal found himself teetering on the edge so quickly he couldn't find it in himself to care that he was suffocating the poor boy trapped in his grasp. He needed an outlet for the anger that had built up over Demetri's earlier stunt and the quick brutal face-fucking he was administering to the kid would keep him from going back and shooting Demetri in his fat ugly face for putting him in such a mood.

Kamal's other hand joined the one on Hamza's head as the man's struggles increased the longer he went without air. Kamal pumped hard, feeling Hamza's nose hit his stomach on each forceful thrust. Hamza's fingernails dug painfully into Kamal's hips, but he ignored the sting as he let the feeling spooling at the base of his spine take over. With a grunt he shot his load down the hot tunnel of Hamza's convulsing throat and then held the young man's head in place through his orgasm. Just as soon as the last of his release left him, he finally let it go.

Hamza dropped onto the ground as he gasped for air. Heaving and retching while on his hands and knees, he left a small puddle on the dirty asphalt, as Kamal righted his clothing. Kamal waited until the other man got himself under some semblance of control, before he reached down and patted the damp cheek a little harder than a love tap but not so hard as to be misconstrued as a slap. The look he got would have usually pissed him off, but he understood he'd taken more than Hamza had wanted to give. Though he didn't feel the least bit bad about it, he understood what a hit it must have been to the other's pride at being used in such a way. He dug through his front pocket and fished out a bill, letting the fifty mark note fall at his feet in front of the kneeling boy who made no move to even acknowledge the money.

"Thanks, kid," Kamal said before turning and stalking off down the alley, ignoring the eyes that bore into his back.

He walked down the street until he hit the main thoroughfare that was better lit and had more foot traffic despite the lightning that lit up the hulking mountains surrounding the city, heralding the coming of a nasty storm. Kamal caught the tram which happened to arrive at the stop at the same time as he did. He entered the back car and stood at the rear of the tram, displacing a group of misfit youths with just a dark look. He let the gentle sway of the moving tram soothe his nerves as he waited through the stops from Alipasino Polje to the one he wanted at Skenderija.

He left the tram just as the rain started to fall. The fat drops were intermittent as he crossed the river and made his way up the winding road that led to his apartment building, but ten minutes later rain was pelting him as he pushed through the front door into the large nondescript concrete building that housed him and about three hundred other nameless strangers. He took the stairs to his fifth floor apartment without even a thought for the elevator that stood waiting on the ground floor. Once at his door he inspected the frame and lock and, finding nothing amiss, he pulled his key from his pocket and let himself in. Kamal shut the door behind him and secured the three inside locks before stopping to look around at his space.

His apartment was furnished with just the bare necessities. The living room held only a couch, a coffee table, and a small flat screen television, all covered in a layer of undisturbed dust; the kitchen remained unused since he'd moved in some five years before. One look around and even Kamal himself could tell the apartment was but a way-stop for someone who spent most of his time elsewhere. Stepping out of his shoes so he wouldn't leave wet footprints across the hardwood floors, he made his way to the one room in his apartment he actually used. He unlocked the heavy wooden door and stood at the threshold of his bedroom/office. The air was stale after being shut up for two weeks so he crossed the room and opened the door to the small covered balcony, the scent of rain instantly invading the space and chasing away the musty unused smell.

Kamal pulled the strap of the small bag over his head and dropped the pouch on his desk. Pulling his shirt over his head as he walked to the bathroom, he grabbed a towel to dry his dripping hair before he sat down half-naked in the chair at his desk. Using the remote, Kamal clicked on the small television that hung on the far wall. The channel never changed from N1 BiH where political news was repeated ad nauseam throughout the day. It was a presidential election year which Kamal knew was the reason he'd been so busy. The parties in the three factions were in the process of making their nominations for their candidates for one of the spots that would fill the rotating position of the most powerful man in Bosnia. This year the people in control would most likely decide the fate of a good portion of the country. Kamal had it on good authority that in the next year or so the *Republika Srpska* would be looking to secede from Bosnia to join Serbia. Kamal knew if that happened it would most likely trigger another war which he and most of the people who remembered the last one were in no hurry to do again.

He lit a cigarette from the pack on the desk and sat back with a sigh as he switched his attention from the screen to the bag which he contemplated with a heavy feeling hanging over him. He knew what he'd find within the small leather satchel and only the strangeness of his earlier meeting with Demetri stayed his hand from the zipper pull. The uneasiness he was feeling was something new to him. He'd done his job just like he'd done hundreds before and the bag held what was due him and nothing else. It made no sense that Kamal had to convince himself of this.

Taking another deep drag from the smoke he held between his fingers, he set it in the ashtray and pulled the bag across the desk, lifting it as if to test its weight. It didn't feel any different from his usual packages, but for some reason the small bag took on an enormous weight in Kamal's head. Demetri had been almost panicked in his quest to make Kamal listen to him which made him wonder what could make an aging gangster breach every protocol to talk to him. He took a moment to wonder if he should have listened to the man's pleas, but then he remembered why he stuck to his own set of laws when business was involved: it was too easy to get sucked into the drama of other people's lives and lose sight of the goals he'd set for himself. Kamal lived for himself and no one else.

He opened the bag and took out the thick envelope. It was the same as always, nothing different about the pile of Euros he held in his hand from all the other stacks he'd held over the years. He let out a breath and picked up his half-burned smoke. Whatever it had been that had Demetri acting strange hadn't been important enough for him to leave even a cryptic, hidden message for Kamal. He smoked the rest of his cigarette while he counted out his pay; it was habit, not because he thought anyone would ever try to short him.

When it was all accounted for, he got up and pushed the desk over to the right just enough to expose the floor board that hid the temporary holding spot for his money. It was cliché, he knew, to hide his money in such a spot but it had worked for him since he'd been a small boy; no sense in changing something that hadn't failed him. Pulling the board up, he took out the heavy metal box, entered the password on the electronic keypad and stashed away his latest payday within before putting it back in its hole. He took the gun out of the small holster on his ankle and deposited it alongside the box before covering everything back up.

Kamal decided to take a quick shower since the jeans he still wore were damp, making him feel a bit off, before resuming his post job ritual. Wrapped only in a towel when he took up his position at the desk once again, he opened his laptop and turned it on. His computer was the only thing of value in his apartment other than the contents of the box under the floor. The security on the machine was top notch, and he'd been assured by the best hacker in the business that nothing he accessed from the internet would ever be traced back to him and his accounts were all encrypted with the latest programs the teenage computer wiz could get his hands on.

He hunted out the keys he needed to type in his passwords that would allow him access to the deep, dark places of the internet where normal people wouldn't dare to tread. Logging into his account on one particular website that specialized in the type of work Kamal was looking for, he found he had only one alert. He opened the message from the familiar screen name and let a small, tight smile grace his thin lips.

> Smoker69
>
> *I have a job out your way. Drinks?*
>
> Mr_Happypants

Kamal checked the date on the message, it had been sent only days before so he pressed the button to reply.

> Mr_Happypants
>
> *Send me time and place.*
>
> Smoker69

Kamal logged out of his account and onto the private email server he used to correspond with the people he worked for in various capacities. Starting with the oldest of his emails, he began opening them. The first was from one of the legitimate businessmen he occasionally took jobs for to keep himself looking above board. A week as a personal security guard for an out-of-town businessman didn't sound all that appealing. He'd leave it until the last possible moment, and if nothing better came up he'd think about taking it. He clicked on the next and, not finding the prospect of holding a ten-year-old for ransom all that appealing after having just dealt with a seven-year-old for two days, went on to the next. He cleared his inbox without lining up anything definite for the near future before he logged back into his account to see if Mr_Happypants had responded.

The smile returned when the icon indicating that Mr_Happypants was online and available to chat was green. Kamal's English wasn't very good and communicating via the written word was even more challenging, but he threw his pride out the window in anticipation of setting up a meet with the other man.

> Smoker69: *Fancy to meet you here.*

C.L. Mustafic

Kamal waited to see if the other man would respond. He wasn't good at flirting and his lame come-on would probably get a dismissive snort from the more social man on the other end of the link, but he also knew the clumsy attempt was what was expected of him.

> Mr_Happypants: *Ah, you are online. I was just replying to your email.*
> Smoker69: *I am here.*
> Mr_Happypants: *I see that. Do you want me to send the email or should I tell you here?*
> Smoker69: *Here is OK.*
> Mr_Happypants: *Am I sensing some impatience?*
> Mr_Happypants: *Does someone miss me?*

Kamal knew the other man was joking with him but if he was honest with himself, he was looking forward to seeing him. It had been far too long since he'd indulged in the type of activity he knew they would engage in together. He wouldn't tell him that though; as with everything else in his life, Kamal would play his cards close to the vest.

> Smoker69: *Just busy. Tell me when and where.*
> Mr_Happypants: *Well, that wasn't much of an ego boost, you better be careful or I might change my mind about seeing you this trip.*

Once again, Kamal knew he was being played with and wouldn't let the other man know how eager he was for the meet by rising to the bait.

> Smoker69: *See me or not, I have not time for games.*

Mr_Happypants didn't answer right away. Kamal wondered if he'd offended the man; people were funny and Kamal had no way to judge if his actions would upset someone or not and usually he didn't care. He lit up a cigarette and sat back in his chair to wait, not giving the other man the satisfaction of asking him again for the time and place. He watched as the storm raged on outside his balcony door, the rumble of thunder was almost constant as the worst of the squall passed overhead. He passed a couple of minutes watching the news but when a familiar face popped up on the screen, one attached to too many memories, he clicked it off, not wanting to go down that road if he could avoid it. He'd just stubbed out his smoke when the next message popped up on his screen.

> Mr_Happypants: *I'll be in Neum two days from now. Hotel Sunce, you know how to find me.*
> Smoker69: *I do.*
> Mr_Happypants: *Until then, then...*

The light indicating that Mr_Happypants was available to chat blinked out as soon as Kamal received his last message. Though he understood the other man's need to connect, even if for a brief period of time, Kamal didn't have the social skills to pull off the idle chat that led up to what he was really after. He knew it wasn't easy to deal with his directness and wished he could skip the niceties and go straight to the sex. His life would be so much easier if everyone thought the same as he did.

After shutting down his computer, he got up to stretch before walking over and securing his balcony door and then going to pull the dust cover off his bed. Kamal locked the bedroom door, dropped the towel to the floor on his way to the bed, and settled down for the night. His mind was already planning out every aspect of his trip to the city by the sea even as he drifted off to sleep.

Chapter 3:
Old Friends

Kamal left Sarajevo just after lunch so he wouldn't have to stop along his way to eat, even if the roast lamb at the Zdrava Voda in Jablanica was calling to him. If he was being honest, he also didn't want to look too eager by showing up so early in the day for his meeting. He would still make good time if the traffic on M17 stayed the way it was once he left the city. Two hours at most and he'd be in Mostar, then it was just a little over another hour to Neum if he crossed into Croatia and then back into Bosnia. He made sure one of his passports was in his laptop bag in case he decided to take that route instead of the longer one which kept him in Bosnia but took him on a winding road through the mountains that was only wide enough for one car in most places. As he drove along the curvy road ahead of him, he weighed the options between the longer drive and using the passport which would make his whereabouts easy to track if anyone with the resources to do so had the mind to do exactly that. Since he wasn't actually on a job, there was no real reason for him to cover his tracks but one never knew what might come up. Kamal liked to keep his options open.

Kamal lit a cigarette – he smoked too much when he drove – as he hit Mostar's city limits. As he drove through the busy tourist destination, he got one of those strange feelings that made him nervous. He couldn't explain them, but they'd saved his life more than once, always causing his guard to go up automatically. When faced with the sign that pointed him either to the Croatian border or the small city of Stolac, Kamal suddenly turned left instead of going straight. The more scenic route through the mountains seemed to be what his instincts were telling him was the right way to go. He didn't question it. The mountains in Herzegovina were much rockier than those around Sarajevo and being that it had been a particularly dry year, what little vegetation there was had mostly turned brown in the arid heat. The long, slow drive up and down increasingly steep inclines was made that much longer by the static scenery of rocky cliff faces.

Almost two hours after leaving Mostar, Kamal pulled into the crowded city of Neum. It was the most popular destination for the natives who wished to vacation on the sea. The fifteen kilometers of Bosnian shoreline was packed with houses and hotels climbing up the hillside making it feel like the mountains were trying to push the city into the sea. The narrow, twisty roads were clogged with cars and hordes of people laden down with everything from umbrellas to flotation devices who were trying to make their way from their apartments to the sea on foot. Kamal was about out of patience by the time he turned into the hotel's gated parking area. He told the guard the fake name he'd used to make his reservation so he could call it in before instructing Kamal where to park.

With overnight and laptop bags in hand, Kamal locked his car. The hotel lobby was large and clean; the Hotel Grand was the newest and most modern hotel in Neum. Kamal had little choice but to pay the inflated price for one of the only rooms left available in the city even though it was a weekday. He checked in and took the stairs to his room on the top floor. Even though he'd paid a premium for his room, he didn't much care what his accommodations were. He didn't expect he'd be spending much time in the room.

He dropped his overnight bag on the bed and sat the laptop bag on the little desk in the corner of the room to open it and take out the machine so he could start it up. Forgoing the hotel's free wifi, he set up his own mobile hotspot device and signed in to check his emails. He'd asked for details on a job before he'd left and was waiting for the reply but there was nothing there from his prospective employer. It left his mind free to think only of scratching that seemingly insatiable itch that had brought him to the last place he wanted to be at the peak of the summer season. Kamal hated crowds.

Dressed in a pair of lightweight linen pants and a form-fitting t-shirt, Kamal made his way down the paved path that ran along the shore. His dark sunglasses hid the glares he aimed at the other pedestrians who always managed to somehow get in his way, as if they were all making a concerted effort to delay his progress. Even in his irritation, the slight smile stayed in place. Like a wolf in sheep's clothing so as to not alert the flock to its presence, Kamal kept up the happy tourist façade without even thinking about it. When he came upon a woman standing a few stairs above the path, obviously trying to figure out how to get the stroller containing her baby down on her own, Kamal grabbed the front of the conveyance and helped the lady out of her predicament. She thanked him and he smiled as he told her it was no problem and to have a nice day.

The area outside the Hotel Sunce was packed with a sea of sweaty, half-naked humanity making Kamal mentally shrink back as he approached the edge of it. He took a deep breath and wound his way through it to the lobby until he got to the less populated bar area of the restaurant. It took him only a moment to find the man he was there to meet. He was sitting in the corner with his tablet propped in front of him while he nursed a glass of red wine.

Kamal headed straight for the man, knowing he wouldn't take him by surprise no matter how he tried. He was sure his presence was noted the minute he stepped foot through the door. Walking right up to the table, he stopped, but before he could even say hello, the other man was up and out of his chair, embracing him. After a quick hug and kisses on both his cheeks, Kamal stepped back to take in the other man. Julien was a few centimeters shorter then Kamal's own height of one hundred and ninety but the man's body was all wiry muscle and he was every bit the match for Kamal's strength, a fact he knew very well.

"Julien, good to see you," he said as he took off his dark glasses and hung them on the collar of his shirt.

"Kamal, it's been too long, my friend, please sit," Julien invited. His English was perfect, unlike Kamal's own stilted attempts, even if it was heavily influenced by his native French. Kamal sat on the opposite side of the table, noticing Julien had picked the only one in the bar that allowed both of them full view of the room around them. Julien gestured to the waiter and ordered Kamal a whisky, neat, and another glass of wine for himself before turning back to his table companion. "I expected you to arrive a bit earlier than this." Julien's gaze took in every inch of Kamal that was visible to his steely gray eyes.

"You waited long?" Kamal asked with a raised eyebrow.

"Too long," Julien said, letting a hint of huskiness drop into his voice to get the double meaning across. He smiled easily at Kamal as he put his elbows on the table to lean in a bit closer. "If you'd gotten here a couple of hours earlier we would have had time for a bit of exercise before dinner, but now it must wait until I've eaten. There's this little place down the road a bit that serves fresh black sea bass and mussels that are only found off the shores of the coast here. I thought we might indulge our palates before we indulge other parts of our bodies." The twinkle in his eye belied his mischievous intentions, but Kamal only nodded his acceptance of the plan. He always went along with Julien's plans because he knew it was socially unacceptable to just demand they go back to Julien's room and fuck.

"Is early for evening meal, but if you are hungry…" Kamal said with a shrug, his brain busy retrieving the correct words in English.

Julien laughed. "You are unflappable as always. I wonder, what *would* it take to get a rise out of you?"

"Will not happen sitting in crowded bar," Kamal said, gesturing to their surroundings.

Julien cocked one well-manicured eyebrow and dropped his eyes to Kamal's lips. "No I suppose it won't," he said thoughtfully.

The waiter dropped off their drinks and Julien told him to put it on his tab. Kamal watched as Julien twirled the thin stem of the crystal wine glass between his thumb and forefinger. Picking up his heavy tumbler, he sipped at the strong amber drink as he tried to drown out the images that flitted through his mind of what those hands were capable of – both the pleasure and the pain. Instead he turned his attention to studying Julien's face. Kamal didn't know exactly how old the other man was, but going by how he talked – things he spoke of – if he had to guess, he'd put Julien around ten years his senior, but he didn't look it, only the touch of gray mixed in with the light brown at his temples hinted at his age. Julien was in fine shape for a man Kamal surmised was on the verge of fifty.

"How have you been then?" Julien asked when he realized that Kamal wouldn't be the one to keep the conversation going.

"Good, you?"

"I've been busy though I did manage to take a vacation this year. I went to the Canary Islands, ever been?" Kamal shook his head. "Well, then you should definitely plan to visit them one day."

Kamal sat back and let Julien regale him with stories of beautiful Spanish men in an island paradise the likes of which he'd never laid eyes upon before. He sipped his drink while Julien ordered another for himself and kept the narrative going for over forty minutes. Kamal had only to nod and ask the occasional question between drags of his ever present cigarette to keep the man talking. It wasn't that he enjoyed hearing Julien's stories, but he figured if he had to wait for the sex he may as well do so without revealing anything of his own life.

Julien was Kamal's polar opposite when it came to his personal affairs, not caring what details he shared with Kamal because he figured they were the same and no harm would come to him from someone in the same line of work unless a contract was put out on his head – honor among thieves and all that nonsense. Kamal, on the other hand, looked at everyone as a potential threat so he remained tight-lipped assuring his secrets would stay where they belonged, with the only person he could trust – himself.

"Well, shall we amble on down and see if we can fill our bellies? I have a feeling that I'll need to build up my strength for things to come," Julien said as he finished his last tale and his wine.

"Yes, let us go now." Kamal stood and waited for Julien to put his tablet into his shoulder bag.

They walked down the street in companionable silence. It took them only five minutes to reach their destination even though the streets were even more crowded as people returned from changing out of their beach clothes and into their night apparel before converging on the boardwalk in search of a good time. The restaurant wasn't as busy as it was still a good hour until normal people took their evening meal, so Kamal and Julien were seated in a prime spot on the wooden patio that hung onto the rocky cliff over the sea some fifty meters below. The sun had begun its descent towards the water and the two men were positioned just right to catch what was sure to be a spectacular sunset over the Adriatic.

Appetizers were the famed mussels Julien had mentioned, steamed and served in a sauce that tasted way too fishy for Kamal's liking, but the Frenchman practically kissed the waiter when he asked if they were enjoying the dish. While they waited on their main course of grilled black sea bass and asparagus, Julien began talking again but this time it was about the job he'd taken that had brought him to Kamal's little corner of the world. Kamal smoked while he listened, fairly disinterested until a familiar name popped into Julien's ramblings.

"So anyway this politico has been given multiple warnings but for some reason he refuses to go along with what Koslov wants," Julien said.

"You will lean on him?" Kamal asked, hoping to get a few more details about Julien's job now that he knew who it was for. He did a lot of work for Koslov, most of his dirty work in fact, and wondered why he hadn't been tapped for this job.

Julien's lips twisted into a cruel imitation of a smile. "Oh no, it's not the man himself I'm after, it's his son," Julien said with what seemed to Kamal to be more glee than snatching a snot-nosed brat and babysitting them for god knows how long should garner in any sane man.

"You look," Kamal started, but had to search for the word he wanted and then it came to him, "pleased."

"Well, you see, his son isn't a child but a young man." Julien paused to wink one of his wickedly gleaming eyes. "A handsome one at that and I've been instructed to use whatever means necessary to get our man to agree to Koslov's terms." Julien paused to let the information sink in. "I have some very inventive ways to make the young man scream for mercy which are guaranteed to make his papa roll over and give in."

The waiter placed their entrees in front of them, causing Julien to stop talking and Kamal had to wait until the other man tasted and then fawned over the food before he could prod him for more information. Kamal was familiar with most of the politicians of note in Bosnia and he had to wonder which one was the cause of so much ire to Koslov and again why he hadn't received... His thoughts drifted back to the meeting with Demetri; what if? Well, what was done was done, no changing the past, but he still liked to have information on the goings-on within the circles in which he moved.

21

He knew he was but a pawn in the overall game, but he liked to be as informed as possible about the impact his actions had on the world around him.

"What is politician's deal?" Kamal asked after he'd eaten half his portion of fish which was much more to his liking than the mussels had been; funny how fish could be less fishy tasting than mussels.

Julien finished chewing the bite he had in his mouth and took a drink of his white wine before he blotted his lips with his napkin. "Well, it seems he's a key member of the nominating party for the SDP and he's not inclined to throw his vote behind the guy who has been chosen by the powers that be," Julien said. "I guess he claims to have moral issues that preclude him from backing the nominee." Julien let out a little snort at the thought of any politician having a sense of right and wrong.

"That is problem." Kamal knew the Russians had spent a considerable amount of money to fix the election in the favor of the secession. They wanted war for whatever reason, and they were doing whatever they could to spark a fight.

Julien nodded. "Yes, it is, but it means I get to spend a month in your lovely country."

"Month is long time for job." Most kidnappings were fairly quick affairs; parents usually did anything to get the kid back which was why it was such an effective tool and also why Kamal thought anyone who ever aspired to be in the public eye should refrain from having offspring.

"Koslov has given me very specific orders and first contact won't be for two weeks after I snatch the young man. He wants this man to sweat for a bit. I have a list of things to occupy our time and I'm sure my guest will appreciate the detailed planning, as well as his father when he gets the pictures and video." Julien used a piece of bread to wipe his plate clean and popped it into his mouth. "Do you want coffee and dessert?"

Kamal knew the answer to that question, but he weighed it in his mind for a moment while trying to figure out the phrasing he should use to get his point across. "I think dessert in room is better." Okay, so he knew it wasn't exactly right but the smirk that graced the lips of the man across from him let him know his meaning had been received.

He called the waiter over and paid for their meal after arguing with Julien over it, of course. They walked in the dwindling light back to where they'd started and Kamal felt the anticipation building as he followed Julien in the side door of the hotel and up the stairs to his room. He clenched and unclenched his fists as the other man used his key card to unlock the door after he'd inspected it to make sure it hadn't been tampered with in his absence. Kamal barely let Julien step over the threshold before he made his move. Pushing the smaller man forcibly into the room, he kicked the door shut behind him. Julien grunted, but before he could regain his balance to turn on Kamal, he was pinned face-first to the wall.

Julien chuckled. "Oh, so that's how it's going to be tonight," he said, not sounding a bit surprised to find himself in his current position. He threw an elbow back, catching Kamal just below the ribs on his right side, stealing his breath. At the same time, Julien hooked his foot behind Kamal's leg and in one swift movement they were on the floor. The fall stunned Kamal when he landed hard on his back with all of Julien's weight on top of him, giving Julien the time he needed to twist around and straddle Kamal's prone form. In what seemed like a second, the tables had turned and now Julien was the one pinning Kamal to the floor.

It had been a much shorter struggle than their usual battles for dominance, and Kamal cursed himself for jumping too soon. He saw now that Julien had been expecting it and had planned for it accordingly. He noted the error he'd made, marked it down, mentally assuring he'd never make it again. Staring up into the gray eyes that darkened to a shade of charcoal, he saw the killer Julien truly was staring back at him and it only stoked the fire of arousal in Kamal.

"I do believe I won this one. Do you concede?" Julien asked. Kamal could only blink up at the other man whose forearm was pressed tightly against Kamal's neck, making it impossible to either nod or speak to his surrender. "I'll take that as a yes. Now, are you going to behave or do I have to get rough with you?" He lifted his arm just enough so Kamal could get a full breath to answer his question.

"You win," Kamal said, resigned to his fate.

Julien smiled wickedly down at him. "I promise that if you play nice, I may think about giving you a chance to drive."

C.L. Mustafic

Kamal pushed his hips up against the body holding him captive, letting Julien feel his thickening cock through the thin linen of his pants. Julien raised his eyebrows as he ground down against the evident lump. Hissing, Kamal internally cursed the fact that he wasn't going to get to stick his dick into the other man that night unless Julien was in an uncharacteristically charitable mood.

Julien's arm remained against Kamal's neck as he bent down so their faces were a mere centimeters apart. "I'm going to fuck you hard, but if you scream my name and beg for mercy, I might be persuaded to go easier on you," he said lowly before he smashed their lips together.

Kamal could taste the sharp tang of copper as his lower lip split against his teeth under the bruising pressure Julien exerted. He opened his mouth, but not in invitation – no, Kamal waited until Julien pressed the advantage, then clamped his teeth down on Julien's bottom lip. Julien tried to pull away but Kamal held him fast, and only a sharp jab to his kidney – like the key to the lock of Kamal's jaw – made him release Julien's lip.

"Fuck," he growled as he writhed in pain.

"You are just asking for it tonight, my young lover," Julien said as he sat up, rubbing the crimson droplets from his injured lip. "You surrendered, it is my right to do as I will and I want a kiss." Kamal gritted his teeth, kissing was his least favorite sexual act. It was fuel for the fight against Julien because he knew the other man would demand it of him if he was the one in charge. He despised that Julien knew his aversion to it, but pressed the issue every damn time.

When Julien bent to him once again, he accepted the light brush of lips without complaint. As the kiss deepened so did Kamal's need to lash out again, but he'd learned his lesson the first time, he'd probably be pissing blood in the morning. Instead of biting Julien once more, he turned the kiss into something more like fighting as he thrust his tongue deep into the moist cavity to gain control. From there it only got rougher as hands tore at clothing and when those were gone and Kamal had gained the upper ground, cradled in the vee of Julien's thighs, Julien used his hair as a handhold to pull him back. Kamal stopped the motion of his hips which had been causing little jolts of pleasure to shoot up his spine with the friction it produced as the two hard, fleshy rods rubbed together.

"Though I do enjoy a bit of frotting, I believe I'd like it better if I were buried inside you when I came," Julien said. When Kamal just stared at him uncomprehendingly, Julien let out a put-upon sigh. "I meant get your ass off me and on the bed so I can ream that tight ass of yours before I blow my load between our stomachs." Julien's more blunt statement got through the lusty haze that had befallen Kamal's mind. He got to his knees which allowed Julien to sit up. "The bed now."

Standing, Kamal walked over to the bed, eyeing the supplies laid out on the little bedside table. There were condoms, lube, and not too surprisingly a few lengths of satiny rope. He decided he'd behave, saving Julien the trouble of having to restrain him to make him obey this time. He climbed onto the bed, positioning himself on his hands and knees in the center of the large mattress. Letting his head hang between his shoulders, he tracked the other man's movements out of the corner of his eye. Julien fingered the ropes as if considering the need of them before he picked up one of the foil packages and the bottle of lube.

The bed dipped on Kamal's left as Julien's weight was added to it. "You look lovely like that, it's a shame you don't enjoy being in that position more often." Kamal heard the top of the lube being popped. Cold, slick fingers pressed between his ass cheeks, dancing over his entrance before Julien penetrated him with one finger, shoving it in past the second knuckle without hesitation. Kamal's breath caught, more at the thought of being touched so intimately by another person than from the slight bit of pain Julien had caused. Being forced by his own impatience to take another into his body was also not one of Kamal's favorite things. He didn't particularly enjoy anal when he was on the receiving end of things, but knew if he got through this humiliating bit of the evening, Julien would suck him dry and, before the night was over, Kamal hoped he'd get his chance to fuck his occasional lover senseless because, for all his posturing, Julien did like getting a good ass pounding.

Another finger joined its mate before Kamal had even had time to adjust to the first. "So tight, I guess it's not such a shame that you don't bottom often," Julien purred as he stretched Kamal's tight ring of muscles.

"*Šuti šupak i* fuck me," Kamal gritted out between clenched teeth.

C.L. Mustafic

Julien pulled his fingers free and slapped Kamal's ass. "Watch it or I will redden this fine ass before I fuck it." The bed jiggled as Julien positioned himself behind Kamal and Kamal couldn't help but shift away as a hand grasped his left hip and he felt the slimy rubber as it slid along his crack. "Oh, I do so love it when you struggle a bit, but remember what happened the last time I won this honor." Kamal looked at the ropes knowing Julien was trying to goad him into a fight so he'd have reason to bind him to the bed. "Ah, yes, I see that you do." Julien punctuated his sentence by shoving his cock into Kamal's hole, only stopping when he was fully sheathed.

"*Jebem ti u pićka materinu,*" Kamal uttered as the pain sliced through his bottom and he fought to hold still.

"Tut, tut, such language," Julien said but his voice wasn't steady enough for it to come out as the threat Kamal was sure it was meant to be. Kamal breathed in through his nose and out through his mouth, glad Julien was at least giving him a little time to adjust to the fullness. "You ready now or do you need more coddling to get through this?" Julien asked mockingly.

Kamal rocked his body forward and then pushed it back, giving Julien his silent answer. Julien's grasp on his hip tightened, with both hands now holding him steady as he began the brutal onslaught of short hard strokes that left Kamal panting. After a few minutes of that, Julien switched to long, slow, horribly drawn-out movements that only irritated Kamal, but when he tried to control the speed and depth, Julien put a hand between his shoulder blades and pushed him down onto the bed. Kamal had to turn his head to keep from being suffocated by the pillows he'd nearly landed on face-first. He put up a brief struggle that only ended with one of his arms being twisted up painfully behind his back.

"Always fun...to...fuck you..." Julien grunted as he picked up his pace. It didn't take long until Kamal felt the other man's hips start to take on an erratic rhythm. Kamal clenched his muscles to help him along and that was all it took. Julien groaned as he pounded through his orgasm, finally falling forward so his body draped over that of Kamal's awkwardly positioned one.

"Off," Kamal growled as he struggled to get his arm out from between their bodies so he could push Julien the fuck off. Julien listed to the side, giving Kamal the advantage he needed to dislodge Julien's cock from his ass and get out from under him. Julien snorted as he rolled to his back, but Kamal straddled him quickly and put his hands around Julien's neck, exerting enough pressure to cut off his air. Julien's eyes didn't lose their mirth as he looked up at Kamal. Kamal let his anger drain from him. This was all part of their game and he was being a sore loser. He let Julien go and flopped over on the bed next to him, throwing his arm across his eyes with a sigh. A hand almost gently stroking his limp dick drew a shuddery breath out of Kamal. No matter how much he hated Julien at these times, his body couldn't resist his touch, it was what kept him coming back time after time. Kamal felt the urge returning in full force as his cock plumped back up and this time when Julien's lips met his own, he let him steal a probing kiss without struggling. Julien murmured something in French when their mouths stopped moving against one another. He kissed his way down Kamal's body, avoiding the scars that littered the skin along the way. It was pure bliss when he swallowed Kamal's hard-on to the root and then proceeded to make him come until his vision blurred. It was worth it, this little game they played.

Chapter 4:
Unexpected Actions

It was during his post-coital cigarette that Kamal made a decision that would change his life. Julien had gotten up to use the bathroom, leaving Kamal with his smoke and tumbler of whiskey he'd poured from one of the tiny bottles in the mini-fridge before excusing himself. Kamal always found it strange that Julien felt the need to shower between rounds, but was relieved when he heard the sound of water running in the shower as it meant he'd have time to indulge his curiosity. He still wondered who Koslov was having problems with and why he hadn't given the contract for the kidnapping to Kamal. He put his cigarette in the ashtray on the nightstand before rolling to the side of the bed and then off onto his knees. He reached for the bag Julien had carried with him and pulled it to him.

After a quick glance at the bathroom door, he pulled the tab on the zipper and peered inside. Just as he'd expected, there was a small file folder tucked inside behind the tablet Kamal had seen Julien using at the bar. He pulled out and opened it to find photos of young men engaging in various activities, swimming, playing soccer, and drinking at a bar seemed to be popular pastimes for the group. Kamal thumbed through the stack until he found a picture that held the image of just one handsome young man. His breath caught in his chest when a pair of familiar blue eyes stared back at him from the young face in the photo.

"Orhan," Kamal breathed the name like a benediction.

He flipped through until he was certain the blue-eyed youth was Julien's intended target. Slapping the file shut when he heard the water shut off in the adjoining room, he quickly replaced it and the bag as close to the exact spot where he'd found it and climbed back on the bed to resume smoking and nursing his drink. He hid his racing mind behind a blank mask as Julien walked out rubbing his head with a towel. Kamal watched impassively as the other man walked naked across the room and poured a glass of wine from the open bottle on the dresser.

"So, a smoke and a drink and then more fucking, how does that sound?" Julien asked. He took a sip of his wine and turned to look at Kamal. "Though I do think I would prefer to switch places this time. I'm not in the mood to struggle with you because frankly, though it's fun at times, it does get a bit unpleasant to think about how you abhor my touch the way you do."

Kamal didn't recognize the look Julien was giving him as he made his way to the bed, so he ignored it along with the words he'd said, because it was no secret Kamal hadn't enjoyed what had transpired between them earlier. His body perked up, though, at the thought of getting to turn the tables on the other man and give as good as he'd gotten and then some. Kamal finished his drink and put his cigarette out. He let the back of his mind deal with figuring out what, if anything, he should do about the fact that Julien was going to kidnap and torture someone he knew, while the front part focused on the naked man next to him. Compartmentalizing his thoughts was something Kamal excelled at, making it easier to do what needed to be done.

Rolling onto his side, he ran a hand across Julien's chest, letting the sparse chest hair tickle his palm. Kamal surprised himself when he blurted, "What you want from me, Julien?"

Julien stilled under his touch. His steely gray eyes looked like they had storm clouds raging in them when he turned them on Kamal. "Would it be too much to ask for you to act like a human being for just a short time?"

"I am human." Kamal's brows furrowed, not understanding what Julien meant.

Julien rolled his eyes and shook his head. "I know you're human, Kamal. I meant could you maybe act more like a normal human acts toward another that they've had an intimate relationship with for over eight years?" When Kamal only looked back at him with a blank stare, he added, "Never mind, ignore me. I guess I'm getting a bit sentimental in my old age." He tried to smirk, but it came off looking more like a pained grimace to Kamal.

"Tell me how you want me to be, I will be," Kamal said. He could be almost anything if he knew what was expected of him, but this was the first time Julien had expressed a wish for him to be anything other than what he normally was and he was confused by it.

"I don't know how to explain how normal people act except to tell you to do the opposite of whatever you would normally do," Julien said as he started to roll away from Kamal.

Kamal grabbed Julien's arm, stopping him, which was exactly the opposite of what he would normally have done. He could follow instructions. "Show me what you want," Kamal ordered a little tersely.

"It's stupid because I know you don't want what I want, it's pointless to try to force you to be something you're not, even if it is only for one night." Julien stayed on the bed, but didn't look at Kamal as he spoke.

"Maybe I learn something new." Kamal wasn't sure what Julien wanted that *he* didn't want. Sex had always been what their meetings were about and they always managed that just fine even if it did take a bit of fighting to accomplish it. He was also willing to do almost anything to get to fuck Julien just then; a little play-acting if necessary was no deal breaker if that was what the other man needed.

Julien turned, letting his eyes scan Kamal's face, probably looking for some sort of trap or lie written there and when he seemed assured Kamal wasn't fucking with him, he sighed. "Okay but this will take a bit of restraint on your part, no biting or hitting when I do something you don't like."

"I cannot promise…" What if Julien tried to strangle him? Of course, he would hit or bite or whatever it took to fight the man off.

"I won't hurt you so you'll have no reason to do any of those things, just go along with it for a bit."

Kamal heard the pleading tone in the man's voice practically begging him to agree to his demands. Julien was acting strangely, and Kamal wondered what had prompted it. Was it his unexpected question about what the other man wanted that had set this deviation from their usual nights in motion? If so, Kamal would make sure to never make that mistake again, he only hoped he hadn't changed things between them forever.

"Okay," Kamal agreed, but reserved the right, in his own mind at least, to do whatever he saw fit if Julien crossed any of his boundaries. He could only trust so much and already he felt his limits being tested.

"Okay," Julien said breathlessly. He licked his lips and leaned in to kiss Kamal. At first Kamal just let him, but he could almost feel the other man's desire to be kissed back and in keeping with his new role he prepared to do just that. He huffed out a breath through his nose, leaving no doubt about how he felt about what he was about to do. Opening his lips, he let Julien sweep his tongue into his mouth, bringing with it the taste of the dry red wine he'd been sipping only moments before. Kamal kissed him back hesitantly at first, but then as he felt Julien's passion increase with every second he responded, Kamal's kiss turned into something ravenous and wanting, something so strong he had no choice but to see where it would lead him.

Julien pulled back and smiled at Kamal. "See, not so bad, right?" he murmured.

Kamal didn't answer, instead he claimed Julien's lips in a searing kiss that left them both breathless. He rolled on top of Julien and, remembering their earlier struggle, he started rocking their groins together to get that feeling once again. It was so good, that delicious friction they were producing between them, so when Julien pulled him down for more kisses he went willingly. Soon the pressure was too much and Kamal knew he needed to be inside of the man beneath him. He reached out and grabbed a condom and lube, then got to his knees to apply them. Julien started to roll, but Kamal stopped him.

"No, like this." Julien stared up at him with a puzzled look on his face, but he obeyed. They'd never done it like that, face to face, and Kamal wondered what it would be like so he was going to do it. It helped that Kamal could tell himself it seemed like the thing the person he was role-playing at being would do. He held up a finger and wiggled it. "You need?"

Julien shook his head no, that he didn't need any prep. "Kamal?"

"Being human," Kamal answered simply as he lined himself up with the entrance to Julien's body. He pushed forward until the head of his dick breached the other man. Unlike every other time they'd performed the act, Kamal stopped and let Julien's sounds and body movements guide his own as he pressed his way in more slowly than ever before. It was a new experience for him, turning sex with Julien into something more intimate than he'd ever done with anyone, other than that one man but he wasn't going to associate that with this. He wasn't sure he liked it, but at the same time was loathe to stop. When Julien started moving against him, he took that as his cue to start fucking him a little harder.

It was good. Being buried deeply in such a hot, almost suffocatingly tight, channel always reminded Kamal of what he was normally missing. His hand just wasn't the same nor the unwilling mouths of those he found to service him occasionally. Julien pulled him down for more mouth action and Kamal found himself cradling the other man's head in his right hand, fisting the back of Julien's hair to hold him there as if the man would try to escape him. When kissing became too much, and Kamal needed more oxygen to keep his body going, he pulled away from Julien's lips only to have the man kiss and suckle at his jaw and neck. It wasn't an unpleasant feeling so he let Julien do as he would while he concentrated on moving his hips in a way that he found most pleasing. Julien wrapped his strong legs around Kamal's waist and encouraged him with heels to his ass to go deeper. Kamal was lost in the sensations and he allowed his mind to float for just a moment.

It wasn't until Julien started saying his name over and over that Kamal's thoughts came back online, but then it wasn't the present they found upon return. Instead of the steely gray eyes he'd expected to find in the face reddened by lust and pleasure, he found that lipid pools of sky blue met his own dark-as-night gaze. The sound of his name changed in his ears as he heard a voice from the past screaming it in fright on a breathless terror-filled run through the trees. The image from the photo came back to him and he wasn't even aware of it when his left hand found the chin of the man beneath him. The eyes he was staring into changed back to the gray he was so familiar with and there was no fear in them when Kamal grasped Julien's chin.

Julien opened his mouth, perhaps expecting another of those claiming kisses Kamal had bestowed on him earlier. There wasn't even time for Julien to express shock when Kamal pushed his chin sharply to the left with the hand he had placed there while at the same time using his right which was still almost lovingly cradling the head, to jerk in the opposite direction. The sound of a neck snapping was one that still got to Kamal. A shiver ran down his spine while he watched intently as Julien's eyes lost focus and his breathing came to a halt upon one last exhale. The sudden clamping down of the muscles in Julien's dying body reminded Kamal that his dick was still inside the man and his natural instincts took over before he could stop himself. He made a few more quick hard thrusts inside the still fluttering tunnel and spilled inside the condom with a guttural moan while Julien's body slowly asphyxiated beneath him.

Kamal lay there, letting the aftershocks of his orgasm thrum through him before he rolled off to sit at the side of the bed. He stripped off the condom and put it in the glass that had held his whiskey. He looked over his shoulder and shook his head. Not good, not smart, big hassle, no time to waste, he thought to himself as his mind started making plans, so many plans, but first he knew he needed to make some calls. He reached over and felt for the pulse in Julien's wrist. Finding none, he dropped the limp arm back to the bed.

"*Jebi ga,*" Kamal uttered as he got up. He rubbed his face as he paced across the room and then looked back at the body on the bed, once again shaking his head at his stupidity. He bent and dug through the pile of clothes to find his pants and then from the pocket of those he pulled out his phone. There was only one person he wanted to call but knew that he shouldn't, no he couldn't call *him*. He needed to place two phone calls and that's what he'd do. He'd have to deal with the mess he'd created by letting his emotions overrule his common sense. He hit the one number in his contact list he'd never had to use before and then listened as it rang and rang and rang.

"*Šta?*" a sleepy yet obviously annoyed voice answered, just when Kamal was getting ready to disconnect.

"Why the fuck didn't you tell me that it was his kid, his fucking kid, Demetri!" Kamal couldn't help the rising of his angry voice as he questioned the fat man.

"I tried — "

"Fuck you tried! You should have just said it and not played games with me or better yet you could have told me weeks ago when the contract was put out." Kamal lowered his voice, remembering that he was likely to be overheard if he kept shouting. He didn't need to draw attention to the room with a cooling corpse lying in the middle of the bed. There was silence on the other end of the line for a moment and while he waited he compiled a list of things he'd need to take care of his most pressing problem, but unfortunately he'd have to wait until the shops opened in the morning to get most of what he'd use to dispose of the body.

"How did you find out?" Demetri asked. "As far as I know the grab wasn't scheduled until the day after tomorrow."

"I ran into an old friend."

"You don't have any old friends except the one that wouldn't know until it was too late."

"The man who was going to do the job has decided that he'd rather spend his time swimming," Kamal said cryptically.

Demetri snorted. "I can't believe you would do something so foolish. You realize the job has to be done; if not by him, someone else then."

"I'll do the job," Kamal said before he could think of what that would actually entail.

"Koslov didn't want you to have it, that's why I was trying to tell you about it the other day. He knows of your connection to the family and thinks that even you wouldn't have the stomach to do what needs to be done," Demetri said.

"He doesn't need to know it's me. I'll have access to everything the former employee had pertaining to the job. It will go off as planned." Kamal's mouth was working faster than his brain, but he was pretty confident that Almir, the computer geek he used, would be able to get him access to Julien's files.

"You don't know what you're in for, Kamal. Koslov is pissed and he had one of his experts devise the torture methods to be used on the kid. Even you are not cold and detached enough to be able to do these things to someone you know."

"Don't tell me what I can and cannot do, you have no idea what I am capable of," Kamal said. If it meant he'd be the one to control how the methods were administered, he'd take his chances because there was no way he could leave the kid in the hands of someone who could, and very likely would, cross the line and quite possibly maim or even kill him. Kamal owed the boy's father at least that much.

"It's not a good idea and it will end badly," Demetri said, but with no real conviction, probably deciding there was going to be no talking Kamal out of his insane idea.

"It's a chance I'll take, I just need you to keep your mouth shut to Koslov and to keep me in the loop," Kamal said. "I will pay you," he added as an afterthought.

"Fine, do what you will as long as you understand that if the shit hits the fan, it's your ass. I will deny any knowledge of your plans."

"That's fair." Kamal accepted the terms.

"I have a bad feeling about this," Demetri said before he hung up.

Kamal went through his contacts once more and found the number for Almir. It was late, but he knew the teenager was usually up most of the night doing things on his computer that would make governments shudder in fear for their national security if they ever found them out. This time the phone only rang twice in Kamal's ear before it was answered.

"Hey man, what's happening?" Almir answered in his usual way.

"I have a job for you, it's a rush job and I'll pay whatever it takes to get it done." Kamal wasted no time on greetings.

"Um, okay, hold on a sec," Almir said, and Kamal could hear him talking to someone before he came back on the line. "Dude, I'm sort of busy but since you're one of my best customers, tell me what you need and I'll see if I can fit you in."

"I need you to meet me in Mostar tomorrow as soon as you can get there, but I also need you to either catch a ride with someone or take the bus because I need you to drive a car back to Sarajevo." Kamal figured he could kill two birds with one teenaged stone. He needed to get rid of whatever vehicle Julien had planned on using for the job so it didn't sit taking up valuable space in a jam-packed parking lot. It would be sure to draw attention before too long.

"I can't. I got things to do tomorrow," Almir said.

"I'll pay double what I normally pay you," Kamal countered. He waited while listening to keys tapping in the background on the other end of the line.

"I don't know, you know I have a schedule to keep here and taking a whole day will put me seriously behind on things."

"Name your price."

"Five times the regular rate," Almir said quickly.

Normally Kamal would have countered again but he was in one motherfucker of a bind, a fact Almir had probably figured out since he'd had the balls enough to ask for such an outrageous amount. "Fine, how soon can you be in Mostar?" Once again only the clacking of keys broke the silence, and Kamal felt his patience wearing thin.

"I can leave in an hour so that would put me in Mostar at about six, depending on the traffic," Almir said. "Where do you want to meet?"

"The café at the Gazprom just as you hit Mostar. Make sure you are alone." Kamal assumed the kid would be getting a ride from someone and he didn't need any other witnesses who could place him anywhere near the area.

"Yeah, I get that you probably don't want an audience. I got a friend going to Neum to his parent's house. He'll drop me off on his way through," Almir said. "I have to go take care of a few things before I leave, catch you later."

"Wait, Almir," Kamal said, his mind catching up with his plans at last and finding holes where he'd been ready to act too quickly without proper planning. Kamal realized he was going to need a little time to focus on what he was actually doing, the drive to Mostar and back would give him that at least.

"Yeah?"

"How trustworthy is this friend of yours?"

"He's my right-hand man, man. He basically does the same thing I do, why?"

"I need a ride back to Neum, do you think he'd do it and could he forget he drove me there?"

"I'll ask him, but I'm sure he could for a price."

"Talk to him, but make sure he knows we'll have to take the back route so it will take longer. If he agrees, tell him to wait at the INA just down the road for me."

"Got it, see you in a few," Almir said before he disconnected.

Kamal put his phone on the dresser and surveyed the room around him. He only had an hour to get things done before he needed to leave for Mostar himself. He figured he'd start with the most pressing of his issues and went to the bed. Using the top sheet to wrap the body up, he hefted the weight to his shoulder to carry it into the bathroom where he deposited it in the tub. Pulling the shower curtain across to block out the sight, he turned to the toilet and relieved himself while running through his mental checklist of things he needed to do before he left.

Turning the air conditioner on to the lowest setting was number one and he did just that when he emerged from the bathroom. Second was to find everything Julien had brought with him to the hotel room. He quickly found all the man's electronics: phone, computer, tablet and camera were all placed in one of the bags Kamal found in the armoire. The keys, along with the rental papers for the SUV Julien was using, were in the desk drawer. The license plate number on the rental papers would make the vehicle that much easier to find, especially with the little stub from the parking garage where it was located. The file from the bag was added in with the electronics and then Kamal set about gathering the man's personal belongings and any other evidence of his time in the room with Julien to be disposed of somewhere along the way to Mostar. Third was to get himself dressed because a naked man seen pretty much anywhere in public would not go unnoticed.

By the time he was finished pulling his clothes on, it was time for him to leave. He slung the bag with the things he needed over his shoulder and carried the suitcase with Julien's non job-related items in his left hand. He locked the door behind him after putting the do not disturb sign on the door handle and made his way down the hall and stairs without meeting anyone. The side door to the hotel brought him out to a path that would take him straight to the parking garage he was looking for about two hundred meters up the hill. The first call to prayer resounded through the air just as Kamal pulled out of the garage. He was running late.

Chapter 5:
Chasing the Ghost

The plastic surrounding Kamal as he bent to the job of getting the body into small enough pieces so he could pack them into the four suitcases he'd bought that afternoon, made a crinkling noise. The sound was seriously getting on Kamal's nerves as he embarked on the third hour of toiling at his task. Having already removed the extremities, the head, and the innards, Kamal was left only with splitting the trunk of the corpse in half so it would fit into one of the seventy-six by fifty-one centimeter bags while also distributing the weight more evenly amongst them. He was running on fumes after not sleeping for more than thirty-six hours and, with no relief in the near future, he had to slow himself down to ensure he didn't make any mistakes. Dismembering a corpse was a painfully methodical process if one wanted to do it right.

He cut through the spinal column between the third and fourth lumbar vertebrae; after that was accomplished, cutting through the skin and muscle was the easy part. Sitting back on his heels, Kamal surveyed his work, nodding as he took in a job well done. The tub was filled with body parts but Kamal still turned the water on and washed his arms and chest and then dried his hands before pulling on a pair of latex gloves. He dug out a roll of heavy duty garbage bags he'd bought at the construction store and a roll of duct tape, then systematically packaged up all the pieces and wrapped them tightly with duct tape before placing them into the plastic-lined suitcases. When the tub was empty, he washed the tools he'd used and wrapped them in the soiled plastic before bundling it up into another of the garbage bags. With that done, he set about cleaning up the mess he'd made, knowing he would never get every trace of blood off the tiles but unless someone showed up with a black light he didn't have to worry too much.

Kamal stood under the hot spray from the shower, feeling his muscles relax as the water finally started to run clear. He lathered his hair and body and rinsed off before stepping out onto the gleaming floor to towel off, then checked to make sure his bags weren't leaking. He'd leave them in the tiled bathroom just in case. His original plan had been to make the dump into the sea, but then he'd run up against too many hurdles for that to be a viable option. Instead he decided he'd drive into the mountains to a spot he'd scouted on his drive to Mostar, but he was just too tired to get behind the wheel at that point. After a short nap, he'd load the cases into the trunk of his car under the cover of darkness.

He'd picked up his own belongings from his room before checking out so he had clean clothes and with the air conditioner still blasting an icy chill over Julien's room, he was glad of that. He pulled on a pair of track pants and a t-shirt before lying on the bed with Julien's computer and the file full of photos and hand-written notes he couldn't read. Thankfully, Almir had come to their meeting as prepared as ever and had been able to scan the notepad papers into the computer. Using a program he'd stolen from the American's Pentagon, he'd translated the notes in less than a minute and they now sat in a file on Julien's computer, ready for Kamal to read at his leisure, along with everything else Almir had cracked open for him on the hard drive.

Even though sleep was pulling at him, Kamal opened the file and stared at the photos within. The kid was the spitting image of his father at that age, a fact that tugged at parts of Kamal that had long been buried with carefully constructed layers. He'd only glimpsed most of the pictures before, but now he took his time and placed them in piles, dividing out the ones he thought would give him more clues as to who the kid he'd played with as a small child had become. After they were sorted, he picked up the stack that interested him most. The young man was in a dark *discoteche* seated next to a much larger boy who had his arm draped across the slighter boy's shoulders. To any passerby it would only appear to be the chumminess of two good friends, but Kamal could see the possessiveness in the way the big hand curled around the slim upper arm. The next photo of the two was taken in the dark hallway outside the restrooms and again the taller of the two used his size to his advantage as he loomed over the wide-eyed yet obviously enamored boy before him. The slight part to the little blond's lips just begged for a kiss, the next photo in the sequence proved he'd gotten just what he'd wanted. Kamal's stomach turned sour at the sight of someone who looked so much like *him* kissing another man and the urge to find the person who took such liberties and beat the life out of him flared brightly in Kamal's mind.

He threw the pictures down on the rumpled sheet of the bed and rolled to grab a smoke to calm his nerves. He wasn't used to feeling so many emotions anymore, it made him remember why he'd decided to stuff them away all those years ago when *he* had abandoned him. Taking a slow drag, he let the smoke settle in his lungs before blowing it out in an exasperated huff of blue smoke. His mind wanted to be dragged into the past, but that was a luxury he didn't have time for, a fact he was reminded of when he grabbed his phone and set an alarm to wake him in only a few short hours. He needed sleep so he could set about ridding himself of the slowly decaying packages before they started to stink and draw attention. After only half of the stick in his hand had burnt away, Kamal stubbed it out in the ashtray. He pushed his work to the far side of the bed and laid himself out with a blanket. He closed his eyes and after mentally chasing the images that tried to play on the back of his eyelids away, he sank into a deep and dreamless sleep.

Sweat poured down Kamal's face, droplets dripping from his nose in a quick staccato beat to land on the rocks he was arranging to cover the gray cases that were now emptied of their grisly contents – it took a much smaller hole to bury a butchered body than bulky suitcases. They would blend nicely into the pile he'd made. He stood, shirtless and slick in the moonlight, after he placed what he thought was the last of the stones he'd gathered before turning and nearly breaking his ankle on one he'd missed.

"*Jebem ti bogu,*" he cursed as he stumbled.

Turning and kicking the offending object only sent a sharp pain through his foot once again, he'd forgotten he was only wearing tennis shoes and not a pair of the steel-toed boots he favored when doing such work. He let out an inarticulate howl at his own stupidity before turning to make his way back to his car which he'd left alongside the small dirt track about a kilometer away. He was certain the place he'd chosen for Julien's final resting spot was secluded enough that no one would stumble upon it until after Kamal himself had forgotten where it was. He pulled the flashlight out of his pocket and turned to shine it on the impromptu burial ground once he was a few meters away. The stone piles, though newly formed, blended quite well with the existing ones that had been made years before when some intrepid family had settled there with sights set on farming the rocky land.

His trek took him down a slope and when he turned back to look from the path, he couldn't even see a hint that there was anything hidden away up on that little plateau. The fact that the abandoned track had taken him three kilometers from the actual road only added to Kamal's sense of rightness in his decision. He pulled his gloves off before opening his car door and grabbing his shirt. The material stuck to his skin and made him uncomfortable in the sticky heat, but he resisted the urge to dump the bottle of water he opened over his head; instead gulping it down quickly and throwing the crumpled plastic back into the car when he'd finished.

Driving let him switch his thoughts from the job he'd just finished to the one that faced him when he returned to Neum. He had little time until he would be forced to snatch the kid if he wanted to keep on schedule, making Julien's meticulous planning all the more valuable to him since he had no time to make his own. His next errand took him in the opposite direction from Neum because he needed to check out the hold house Julien had set up. The drive took him further from the seashore and had him turning onto a little used road just past the blink-and-you-miss-it village of Hutovo. Kamal was sure he'd end up somewhere that had no access to electricity or running water and immediately started running options through his head on where else he could hole up with his captive for up to a month. Coming up with nothing off the top of his head, he followed the barely maintained gravel road down until it came to a fork, then took the road less traveled, once again heading down for another five minutes until it ended abruptly in a small valley.

There were trees, but when Kamal looked harder he could see that they had not grown there naturally but had instead been planted. Set back from the end of the road was a small cabin that appeared to be well taken care of by whomever owned it. The absence of powerlines confirmed Kamal's suspicions about the electricity, though there was a small creek he could see running out on the side from somewhere behind the cabin, so there would be a water source even if there were no taps inside. Doubtful the isolated shack would serve his purposes, he made sure he had his flashlight and got out of his car to walk down the paved path to the front steps. He took the key out of his pocket and unlocked the door. At the same time he pushed it open, he reached in and grabbed the rope that was attached to the booby trap hooked up to it. Kamal knew the rope was attached to a shotgun that was aimed so a bullet would strike a grown man somewhere around the knee if he entered not knowing it was there. It was one of the many tricks Julien had shared with Kamal over the years. He untied the rope and let it drop to the floor as he stepped into the dark space.

Feeling around on the wall for a light switch, he was surprised to find one, but when he pushed it there was no light which didn't surprise him. He pulled out his flashlight and flicked it on. The cabin was one big room with only one far corner sectioned off that Kamal assumed was a bathroom. His beam swung across the room lighting up things he knew could only be Julien's handiwork. The man had obviously been in the country for quite some time before he messaged Kamal. That he'd contacted Kamal at all and had time for their dalliance showed he'd been confident his preparations were finished to his satisfaction. Kamal wondered if they'd be up to his own high standards.

He walked to the small kitchenette and found the cupboards overflowing with canned, bagged, and boxed foods. In a floor to ceiling pantry, he found drinks of every flavor including alcoholic ones. There was a fridge, which perplexed him with the lack of electricity, but then a light bulb went off in his head. He took a short trip out to the back of the cabin where he found a large generator in a small brick shed that appeared to be sound-proofed to cut down on the noise, and just outside there were large containers of petrol. Kamal's hopes for the place doubled at the discovery. Making his way back into the cabin, he inspected the bathroom to find it similarly stocked with ordinary toiletries but also with an abundance of medical supplies.

Once back into the main cabin, he studied the handcuffs that were linked to chains hooked to eyelet bolts embedded in the wall at Kamal's waist level and another set that hung from the ceiling. The thin mattress positioned under them left no doubt as to what the setup was intended for. Other than that there was a couch, a coffee table, and a trunk which Kamal opened to once again take an inventory. He didn't even bat an eye at the equipment he found, but thoughts and images he knew he shouldn't be thinking assaulted him, making him slam the lid closed a little harder than necessary. He stood and, with the decision that the cabin would work, he grabbed a few things he'd need and would have a hard time procuring on short notice before he headed back out. He still needed to pick up some supplies of his own, pack up the stuff he'd left at the hotel, maybe get another couple of hours of sleep if he had time and then the game would be afoot.

Julien's detailed notes of the boy's daily activities meant Kamal didn't have to search out his location. He stood on the concrete slab fifty meters from the sectioned off part of the sea where his prey was practicing water polo with a group of other young men. The sun was just touching the sea, meaning the session would end shortly and the boy would make his way back to the gated house located in the oldest and priciest section of town where Kamal had just come from. Kamal's shaded eyes scanned the people around him, stopping on one man, and he knew he was not the only one keeping an eye on his target. The muscle-bound security guard was sitting at a table in front of one of the little cafés that provided him with a view of the surrounding area while still letting him monitor the kid in the water. It wasn't a surprise, Julien had noted the presence of the two men tasked with keeping the boy safe. It was only the kid's own stupidity and willful flaunting of the rules put in place to keep him out of harm's way that would be his downfall.

Kamal had left the seashore before the kid and his babysitter so he could take up a position on the balcony of the house just above the one he was monitoring. He'd been in luck, finding an empty house in such a fortuitous spot at that time of year was something he would have thought impossible. He watched as the group of boisterous young men arrived and then grilled meat out on the large patio facing the sea; from his vantage point up on the hill he could see everything. The boys ate and then settled in with laptops and beer while the guards made themselves inconspicuous in the corner with a chess set. Kamal couldn't be sure, but he figured the young men were most likely playing some sort of game if the hollered protests and high fives were any indication. It lasted hours and Kamal was bored by the time the boys adjourned into the house, some of them stumbling more than walking.

It was Kamal's cue that the time had finally come. Making his way down to the road, he walked past the house about five hundred meters before he took a set of public stairs down. He stopped and stood a few stairs up from the bottom, letting the two large houses on either side conceal him. It took only a half hour until footsteps approached from the opposite direction of the house he'd been surveilling. Kamal took a chance and peeked out to make sure it was the person he'd been waiting on. The larger boy from the photos was strutting along the concrete slabs the owners of the houses had poured to make up for the lack of beach since the homes were built on the side of a mountain with only a shear drop off into the sea. He wasn't even looking in Kamal's direction and Kamal thought all his sneaking about was made unnecessary when people couldn't keep their eyes off their phones for even a second these days.

Kamal pulled back and waited until the young man was in front of him, then reached out and grabbed his arm, pulling the startled boy into the stairwell with him. Stepping up on the first step gave Kamal the height advantage he'd need to put the kid in a headlock. He applied just enough pressure with the bone in his forearm to the carotid artery below the thin skin of the boy's neck, cutting off the blood supply to his brain. Kamal waited until the body slumped back against him before lowering it to the stairs, positioning the legs so they were crossed at the ankle and visible from the path, making it appear as though the boy was sitting on the stairs waiting for his secret lover to arrive.

Kamal ventured a look and when he found the coast clear he stepped out, retrieved the dropped phone, and made his way a bit down to one of the private gated stairs in the direction the kid would be coming from. He had only to give the locked gate a good push to make it give and then he was secreted away behind it. The phone in his hand vibrated and the screen showed him a preview of a text message telling him he would not have to wait much longer. He pulled the small pistol from its holster and put the phone in his pocket while reminding himself to put it back on the sleeping young man before he left. After pondering the best way to get his victim to his car, he'd opted for scaring him shitless.

Footsteps drew his attention about five minutes later. He watched through the iron bars at the top of the gate as the kid came down the path. Kamal knew just when the kid caught sight of his lover's feet because he smiled softly and shook his head as if in disbelief of the way the boy was lounging as he waited. Kamal let the kid get about halfway between his stairway and the other before he stepped silently out behind him, catching up with his prey just as the boy turned to look at the one he was there to meet.

Kamal put his arm around the boy's shoulders, then covered his mouth cutting off the startled scream of his victim. He pushed the pistol into the boy's side right under his ribs, hard enough to hurt just the right amount so the boy would know it was no prank being pulled on him by a pal. The thin body pressed to Kamal's front stilled except for the slight trembling which the boy had no control over.

"I'm going to take my hand away from your mouth now," Kamal said after the boy had stopped trying to scream. "You're going to keep your mouth shut and do just what I say or your friend there won't just *look* like I killed him." The boy nodded a little more enthusiastically than needed in response to Kamal's command and Kamal knew he had the boy's number in threatening his lover. He slowly removed his hand, keeping it at the ready just in case.

"You're going to walk quietly and calmly with me up the stairs and down the road, you try to even make eye contact with anyone and I'll shoot you." Kamal dug the muzzle of the gun even further into the soft tissue of the boy's side to let him know he was serious. The boy nodded once again, but he drew in a watery breath and Kamal knew he'd already started to silently cry. "You do what I say and everything will be alright," Kamal lied, because he knew that was what every victim wanted to hear whether it was true or not.

He grabbed the boy's hair with his free hand so he could use the hand with the gun to dig out the cellphone while cursing himself for putting it in the wrong pocket. He dropped it on stair next to the kid's hand. "Your phone, drop it next to his," Kamal ordered. The kid did just what he was told and the small clattering noise jangled Kamal's nerves just a bit even though he knew it wasn't something that would draw attention. With the gun pressed back in, they made their way up the stairs.

The street was deserted except for a couple walking hand-in-hand about twenty meters down the road from where they emerged. Kamal turned the kid in the opposite direction and marched him to the small side street where he'd left his car. The kid didn't put up a fight until Kamal opened the door of the car, then he tried to smash his head back into Kamal's face. He underestimated Kamal's reflexes and the fact that he'd been waiting for him to do exactly that. Kamal put him in a headlock exactly as he'd done to the other young man earlier, only the kid was just the right height for him to execute the maneuver without needing the extra centimeters the stairs had given him. He didn't mind knocking the kid out in such a way, in his opinion it would only make what came next that much easier.

Kamal laid the limp body in the back seat of his car before pulling out a case that held a needle already prepped with a dose of Diazepam. It would hopefully keep the kid sleeping and, if not, he'd be too relaxed to do anything more than stare into space for the drive to the cabin. Squeezing the boy's bicep right above his elbow to make the veins stand out a bit, he uncapped the needle with his teeth. After feeling for the vein with a finger, he jabbed the needle in, pulled the plunger back, and knew he'd done it right when the fluid in the syringe turned pink with the back flow of blood. He pushed the plunger slowly, letting the steady pumping of the kid's heart take the medicine through his body.

Kamal arranged the boy to look like he was napping in the backseat and covered him with a light blanket even though it was hot outside; he'd blast the air conditioner if he had to for appearances. He stacked bags and a few beach related items around the sleeping young man, so if he was stopped by a policeman it would only look like a father driving home from vacation in the middle of the night with his exhausted son. Kamal got into the driver's seat and pulled out of his spot to begin the journey to the cabin.

"And so it begins," he muttered to himself before lighting a cigarette.

Chapter 6:
And So It Begins

"Be quiet and just follow where I step." Kamal nodded as he walked silently through the mined woods behind his older brother, Đemo, and Orhan Ferhatović, his best friend.

Kamal had one of his feelings and just knew they shouldn't have left the village, but the people were starving. They'd just buried his two-year-old cousin the day before, people were dying because there wasn't enough food to feed everyone who had taken shelter together. Kamal, his brother, and his best friend were the only young ones who'd volunteered to go out with the small party of older men who were going to raid the Serbian village on the other side of the mountain. They'd all heard the stories of how Serbia had sent a convoy of trucks with food and weapons to the area and now they were going to risk their lives to try to steal some of it in hopes of saving the lives of the people most in need; babies and old people were starting to die at an alarming rate. Hell, it had been over a month since Kamal had eaten anything other than a few grams of cornbread, chicken broth, and a little cheese for a meal and he and the other men who guarded the town were given almost double rations to keep up their strength.

Đemo stopped and raised his fist in the air, signaling the other men to stop. He stood there still and silent as he listened to the sounds of the forest around them. Đemo had been picked to lead because even though he was one of the youngest at just twenty-two, he was the most familiar with where the mines they had planted in that area of the mountain were. They didn't dare take the beaten paths that had linked the two villages before the war had divided the country. He knew soon they would cross the line into enemy territory and then only Đemo's knowledge of what to look for and where to step would keep them from dragging the wounded and dead back through the tangled vegetation. Đemo dropped his hand and started to once again walk slowly ahead.

Orhan dropped back and matched his step with Kamal's. Kamal gave him a sideways glance before once again turning his full attention to where his older brother was stepping. "You look scared," Orhan whispered so only Kamal could hear. Kamal nodded his head. Of course he was scared, you'd have to be an idiot not to be, he thought. "Want to hold my hand?" Orhan asked, holding out his hand to Kamal. Kamal knocked it away with a snort that earned him a glare from over Đemo's shoulder.

"*Odjebi peder*," Kamal hissed at Orhan. Orhan just smiled at the insult but made no attempt to bug Kamal after that.

They stood some five hundred meters uphill from the small Serbian village where only a year before, the people who lived in it had been their friends. It was dark since they had no electricity, only the flickering light of fires in a few barrels broke up the blackness.

"Over there is where they keep the supplies, Meho and I saw them unloading one of the trucks into that building," Đemo said as he pointed out what he was talking about. "We'll circle around and try to take out the guards quietly, no shooting if we don't have to, it will only draw attention and more men with guns."

Đemo split them up into groups, Orhan and Kamal would stay with him as he took the most direct route to the back of the small building. It was quiet and the lack of sound was what unnerved Kamal the most. It felt like they were walking into a trap, a feeling that got more intense when their little group easily subdued only two men who'd been charged with guarding the reserves of the entire town. They loaded up the backpacks and bags they'd brought with them with all manner of food stuffs, grabbing everything they could without a care for what it was.

Kamal watched as the men stuffed chunks of smoked meat into their mouths as they filled the bags. Kamal's stomach hurt but he accepted a hunk of the salty chewy meat when it was handed to him and took his own big bite. It was heaven to have something so substantive in his mouth after having gone so much time without.

Churning stomach or not, Kamal chewed quite happily before taking another bite.

When they had as much as they could carry and still there was no alarm raised, the men left the building and started the more arduous climb back out of the village. They were almost to the line where they would pass back into their own territory when the first shot rang out. Then there were too many to count.

"Run," Đemo hollered as he stopped and grabbed Kamal to push him ahead. "Run, Kamal."

Kamal started to run the best he could, burdened down by his heavy pack and the thorns that caught at his pants from the side of the path as if they had chosen a side and it wasn't his. He focused on Orhan's back as he ran for his life. The shots and screams from behind them got louder as the skirmish turned into a full-out battle. Kamal slowed and in a few moments Orhan turned to look at him.

"Come on, Kamal, we have to go," he urged, even taking a few steps back to where Kamal was standing to tug at him.

"We should go back and fight," Kamal said, but made no move to actually do it.

"No, remember what Đemo said before we left." Orhan reminded him that his older brother only wanted him to get back home alive.

"But he's back there and maybe he needs our help," Kamal argued. Orhan tugged at his arm once again, but Kamal stared back down the path where there were now more screams than shots ringing through the air. The trees rustled and a figure stumbled out just out of range of what Kamal's night vision allowed him to see.

"Run, Kamal!" Đemo screamed at him. "Orhan, do your job!" Another volley of shots and Kamal watched as his brother's body jerked and then dropped to its knees before falling face first in the dirt.

Kamal screamed as Orhan pulled him down the path. "Please, Kamal, run with me," Orhan begged him. Kamal's body did what it was told without his mind telling it to because he was in shock over watching his brother die before his eyes. Orhan was getting ahead of him but Kamal's legs had started to shake and his body felt like it was going to give out on him at any moment so he slowed, widening the gap between him and his friend. Then there was an ear-shattering sound and Kamal felt like he'd been hit by a bus. He was thrown; he didn't know how far, but his landing was the most painful thing he'd ever felt in his entire life – that was until his body started screaming in agony from what felt like hot pokers being shoved into his flesh all over the front of his body.

Kamal tried to scream, but he couldn't hear if he was making any sound or not. His body felt like it was on fire and then...Orhan. His lips moved as his frantic yet worried eyes stared down at Kamal. Kamal realized then that he was going to die because there was no way Orhan would have that look on his face if he was just mad at Kamal for lying down instead of running; no, Kamal was sure he was as good as dead.

Orhan bent over him and brushed his lips across Kamal's just as sound slammed back into being. "Don't die on me, Kamal, I love you, if you die so will I," Orhan pleaded with him. "I love you, Kamal. Kamal, can you hear me? Kamal... Kamal... my Kamal..."

Kamal started awake and almost fell off the edge of the narrow couch. He looked around, almost expecting to be back there in those woods that had always been home until they were quite literally turned into a mine field. The dim interior of the cabin assured him he had not traveled back in time and the soft mewling noises coming from the corner almost made him wish he had. Sitting up, he lit a smoke before he turned his head to look at the kid; no, he reminded himself, not a kid, not anymore. His eyes swept over the naked body of the young man who was tethered to the wall, lingering first on the limp dick that laid in a nest of golden pubic hair, then moving on to take in the slim but muscled plane of his abdomen and chest. He was well-formed and with the sensory deprivation hood over his face, Kamal could almost pretend that it was some stranger lying there – almost.

It was still early, but Kamal knew he wasn't going to get any more sleep so he used the bathroom, dropping the butt from his hand into the toilet before he flushed. He washed his face and brushed his teeth as he remembered the things he'd read on the type of torture Julien and Koslov's expert had intended to use on the young man in the other room. Sighing, he stared into his dark-rimmed eyes in the mirror and told himself that Orhan had ceased to mean anything to him years ago and his child had never meant much to him in the first place. Though he still felt he owed Orhan for saving his life that night so long ago, he also harbored enough anger and resentment at his later betrayal to make having someone who looked so similar to him at his mercy either the greatest or worst thing he'd had happen to him. Of course, it depended on which side a person was looking at it from, he supposed.

He went out to check on the generator which had proven to be easy to operate and, with the door to its little shed closed, almost silent. Once he was sure it had enough fuel to last through the day, he went back into the cabin. He wasn't stalling, he was just making sure everything was as it should be. In the kitchen, he grabbed a can of *pašteta* and spread some on a piece of bread he'd cut from one of the loaves he'd bought the day before. It was time to feed his guest. Then they'd make the first of many videos which would torment the only man they had in common when he watched them.

Kamal grabbed a bottle of juice to go along with the food. He sat on the edge of the thin, rubber-encased mattress and listened to the soft sobbing coming from beneath the hood. His captive couldn't see or hear anything and the fabric of the mask even held a little pouch with scented beads so his sense of smell would be of no use to him for some time even when it was removed. Kamal's little game of good cop, bad cop would depend on keeping his captive literally in the dark at all times. He set the food and drink down next to him and reached out to pull the hood up. It was designed so the mouth, nose, and ears could be exposed easily without having to remove it completely, which kept the padded blindfold in place.

The kid jerked at Kamal's touch, but being that he was chained to the wall with both arms stretched almost to the point of being uncomfortable, he had little room to escape his fate and only managed to knock his head against the hard wall. He whimpered, but Kamal ignored it as he arranged the mask so he could feed and water the boy. Once the fabric was lifted from the lower face, Kamal removed the ear muffs so he could be heard.

"I've brought you something to eat and drink," Kamal said in his softest, *I'm a nice guy* voice. The kid shook his head and pursed his lips. "Mali, you have to eat and you have to be quick about it because if he gets here before we're finished he'll get mad and you don't want him to be mad."

"Please," Zijad begged, "Please just let me go, I haven't done anything." His breathing was coming fast and hard as he worked himself up.

Kamal placed a hand on the rapidly moving chest, giving Zijad the first of many touches that would get him to trust and, over time, maybe even like Kamal, but he was still too terrified and tried to pull away from it because Kamal was still the bad guy. Kamal kept the contact until Zijad settled. "I know you haven't done anything, Mali, and that is why I will make sure that you're taken good care of but you have to do as I say," Kamal said, planting little seeds that would grow slowly without Zijad even knowing they were there in his brain taking root.

Kamal uncapped the juice and held the bottle to the kid's trembling lips. "Drink, I'm sure you're thirsty," Kamal urged. He knew the drugs he'd given Zijad would leave him with a slight headache and cotton mouth, but again Zijad refused by clamping his lips closed. "Mali, we have little time and if he sees I've failed at my job we will both pay the price for it," he said, trying to build up the other by not naming him, giving the boy's already terrified mind one more thing to fear.

Zijad opened his mouth and took a small sip of the juice, but when Kamal replaced the bottle with the slice of bread he once again refused. "I can't, please, I can't," Zijad pleaded.

"Just one small bite, try it," Kamal said, talking to Zihad as if he were a small child refusing to eat his vegetables.

Zihad opened his mouth just wide enough so Kamal could push the corner of the bread inside. Kamal watched as the perfect white teeth nipped off a small chunk and then the jaw worked as he chewed. It took far longer than it should have for Zijad to attempt to swallow and when he did he choked. He coughed so hard his face turned red, but he managed to clear the obstruction without Kamal's interference. He drank greedily from the juice when Kamal offered it once again, almost draining the bottle.

"Try another bit of food." Kamal once again pressed the bread at the kid's lips.

"No," Zijad refused, turning his head.

"He won't be happy." Kamal put the food back on the plate.

"I don't care," Zijad said, sounding like a grumpy teenager.

"Fine, that's your choice, but don't expect me to take pity on you when he also punishes me for failing to make you eat." Kamal quickly replaced the mask parts he'd removed to show his displeasure at Zijad's refusal to obey.

"Why are you doing this?" Zijad asked the question Kamal had been waiting for and was surprised it had taken him that long to ask.

"Because I once loved the man you call Father," Kamal said. Speaking the truth to the boy who he'd been prepared to love as his own, even though he was the embodiment of his lover's betrayal, felt right even if the ear muffs meant his confession had gone unheard. Kamal sighed and gathered the uneaten food and almost empty bottle before he stood. He needed to prepare for the next step in the plan and it wasn't going to be fun for either of them.

Kamal roughly pulled the mask completely from Zijad's head, leaving him stunned and blinking against the bright light shining in his eyes. Kamal made sure the microphone for the voice modulator was right in front of his lips and that his own mask wasn't blocking his mouth before he spoke. "It's time to send a message to your father, runt," he said, as his voice transformed into something even deeper than his own rich baritone by the small box clipped to the front of his shirt. His disguised voice sounded menacing to even his own ears. The kid let out a shrill scream and pulled his legs to his chest as he tried to melt into the wall. Kamal observed the act with a sense of satisfaction, his plan was working.

Kamal had set up the video recorder he'd found in with Julien's stash of electronics and had set it to recording before he'd started his little act. He made sure to keep the light at his back as he stepped into the shot. "Look at the camera so your *babo* can see those pretty blue eyes of yours," Kamal said as he grabbed one of the kid's skinny ankles and yanked his leg straight, making him scream again. He pulled both legs so Zijad was exposed to the eye of the camera. "Look at the camera and tell your *babo* you love him and that he needs to save you." Kamal let a hint of amusement color his voice.

Zijad refused to look at the camera, keeping his face turned to the side and down. Kamal pinned the boy's feet with his knee so he couldn't try to cover up again as he reached out and took hold of one of the fingers on the hand nearest him. It took very little force to dislocate the second knuckle of the pinky finger on Zijad's right hand but the resulting scream was just as satisfying as if Kamal had broken it. The kid looked at his hand, the smallest of his fingers now bent at an almost perfect right angle in the wrong direction, and started to sob.

"Now, look at the camera and do as I said," Kamal commanded over the wailing of his captive. Again Zijad refused so Kamal moved down the line but instead of just one finger, he dislocated two hoping Zijad would catch on and he'd not have to move to the other set of fingers to complete his next round of disfigurements. "You are your father's son," Kamal said when the kid stopped shrieking in agony but still refused to obey.

After a moment Zijad calmed and finally turned his tear-streaked face toward Kamal and the camera since it was right over his left shoulder. "You don't know anything," the boy said, staring right into Kamal's eyes. It unnerved Kamal since there was no way the kid could find them to make eye contact in the deep shadows the light created over his face, but he could feel them burning into him just before the kid shifted them to the camera. "He would disagree, wouldn't you, *Babo*?" Zijad asked before he lowered his shiny blue eyes. "You should just kill me and get it over with."

Kamal had not been expecting that. He took a brief moment to wonder about what the kid's words meant before he put the hood back over Zijad's head, leaving the ear muffs off so he could still be heard. He got up and switched on the overhead light before turning off both the camera and the spotlight. Sitting on the couch, he pulled his own mask off but replaced the little headset of the voice modulator, and just observed Zijad for a moment. The kid had curled his legs up, once again making himself as small as he could in the corner of the mattress.

"Your *babo* know that you're a faggot?" Kamal used his tone to broadcast disgust. No answer from Zijad but then Kamal hadn't really expected one. "I see," he said as if the boy had answered, "So he either knows or suspects that you like getting fucked up the ass like a cheap whore whose pussy is no longer tight enough to do the job." Kamal knew his words were being heard but Zijad didn't even twitch. "You're a worthless little cocksucker and your *babo* probably

C.L. Mustafic

knows it. Maybe he won't do what's necessary to rescue you and I will get to keep you. Just think of all the games we could play and since you like getting fucked, well, you'd be better than a woman nagging all the time and I could still get my rocks off if I dressed you up pretty, bet you'd make one pretty little girl — "

"Fuck you!" Zijad screamed from beneath the mask, finally giving Kamal the reaction he'd been hoping for.

Kamal moved so fast that he was sure the kid didn't know what hit him, but he'd probably figure it out since they were the only ones in the cabin. He knelt in front of the kid, one hand around the scrawny neck, the other around the kid's cock and balls. Zijad whimpered as Kamal put pressure on both, squeezing with enough strength that the kid lost the ability to draw a breath.

"You watch your mouth, kid, or I'll make sure that you're not able to talk one way or the other, you understand me?" Zijad nodded the best he could while still in Kamal's clutches. Kamal softened his hold on the neck but kept up the tight grip he had on the boy's genitals.

"I'm s-s-s-sorry," Zijad stuttered after he'd taken a large gulp of air.

"As you should be." Satisfied, Kamal finally released Zijad's dick. He pulled back and pushed at one of the unnaturally bent fingers, making Zijad cry out again. "I'll let your wet nurse take care of that when he gets back, just hope he doesn't take too long or they'll never heal properly." Kamal chuckled as he stood. After making some noise while he went about the cabin so the kid would know he was still in the room, he made sure he had his cigarettes and lighter before he went out the door, slamming it so Zijad would know he was alone.

He stepped out onto the covered porch, squinting at the bright light of the noon sun. The little valley would only get about four hours of direct sunlight because of the mountains that surrounded it. This kept the cabin much cooler than Kamal had figured it would be in the sweltering heat of summer. He walked out onto the grass as he lit up. He had to kill a couple of hours before he could go back inside and pretend to be the nice guy again; being two people might get to be exhausting if he had to keep it up for too long. Good thing bad Kamal would only make an occasional appearance since a big part of psychological torture depended on the victim's own mind inventing scenarios in which to torment themselves with. Finding a nice sunny spot, Kamal laid himself out on the grass. He had time to ponder what kind of relationship Orhan had with his son that would make the kid think his sexual orientation would be a problem for him. Orhan had, himself, once loved another man.

Sometimes Kamal wondered if he still did.

Chapter 7:
Hard Lessons

"Okay, that's the last one, just hold still while I tape them up," Kamal said after he'd popped the last of Zijad's knuckles back into place. He grabbed the roll of white medical tape and oddly enough there were tongue depressors in the kit so he used them to brace the fingers before taping them together. "They're going to hurt for a few days, maybe you should think about just doing as he says the next time." Kamal fastened the bandaged hand back into the lined cuff he'd loosened from the wall enough that the kid had just a little bit of play to make him more comfortable so it would be that much worse when Kamal tightened them once again.

Using the crumpled sheet that had been halfheartedly thrown on the mattress, he wiped up the piss Zijad hadn't been able to hold back when Kamal had straightened the first of his fingers. He was only thankful he hadn't gotten soaked when the kid let loose. He dabbed at Zijad's thighs and saw the slight bruising around the base of his penis before the kid tried to draw his legs up to cover his crotch. Kamal pulled the legs back down and continued his clean-up as he swiped away the wetness from the golden curls between Zijad's legs.

Zijad shifted away from his touch. "Don't, please, don't," he whined as he tried to evade the cloth in Kamal's hand.

"I'm just cleaning you up. You don't want to stink, do you?" Kamal asked gently. Zijad shook his hooded head but moaned a little in protest as Kamal ran the sheet down the length of his penis, then over his balls and down under into the crease of his ass. He felt his own cock twitch in response.. Licking his lips, Kamal concentrated on keeping his breathing steady as he finished cleaning Zijad. He pulled the damp sheet away and bundled it into a ball. "See, that wasn't so bad." He stood to dispose of the sheet in the laundry hamper in the bathroom, then returned to gather up the medical kit.

"My hand really hurts," Zijad said, turning his blind eyes to the sound of Kamal's movements.

"I know it does. He's always good about making sure you remember what's been done to you even after you've been fixed back up. Like I said, do what he asks next time and, just so you know, it's much more difficult and painful to fix a dislocated knee, elbow, or shoulder joint." Kamal left the kid a nice bit of information to chew over in his head before he replaced the ear muffs, plunging him back into his own small, isolated world.

Kamal knew that being in the hood would make time hard to track for the kid and part of his job would be to keep Zijad off balance so he wouldn't be able to guess what came next by his routine. He only waited an hour before he prepared a very bland supper of unsalted mashed potatoes and unseasoned chicken breast cut up and mixed in the potatoes for his captive's meal. Selecting a bottle of water, he dosed it with a fast-acting, liquid laxative. Few things were more humiliating than being forced to shit yourself and then having to sit in it until someone decided to clean you. Not that Kamal was looking forward to doing the cleanup, but he still needed to break the kid's spirit enough so he'd submit to whatever Kamal wanted without having to resort to physical pain to persuade him. There were only so many injuries Kamal could inflict on his prisoner that he could also be reasonably sure he could patch back up without causing permanent damage.

Placing everything on the floor next to the mattress, he sat down and reached for the mask. The kid flinched once again from his touch, but when he gently lifted the fabric away, Zijad actually leaned in to his hand. Kamal didn't know if the kid even realized he'd done it, but he let one finger softly brush the kid's jaw as a reward for coming around so quickly before he took off the ear pieces. "Time to eat."

"I'm not hungry."

"You have to eat and drink to stay healthy."

"Why should I stay healthy? So he can hurt me longer?" Zijad asked with a trembling lower lip.

"Your *babo* will get you out of here, he'll do the right thing," Kamal said, sure his words were the truth.

"You don't know him."

"You're right, I don't." Kamal resisted the urge to add *anymore* on to his sentence. "But a father would do anything to save his child and I'm sure yours will do the same no matter the differences between you."

Zijad had nothing to say to that and when Kamal put the spoon to his lips he opened obediently. He ate over half the food without complaint. "Can I have a drink?" he asked, refusing the spoon for the first time to voice his question. Kamal put the water bottle up to Zijad's lips and let him have only a sip before taking it away. He wanted to get all the food into him before he drank because the laxative would begin to work quickly once he'd ingested all of it, which Kamal would ensure he did. A full belly would make the cramping feel all that much more unpleasant. Zijad licked his lips before asking, "Can I have more?"

"Eat a little more first and then I promise you can have the whole bottle." Zijad ate the rest of the food slowly and time seemed to drag as Kamal watched nothing but those lips as they opened to admit the spoon, then closed over it and released it free of food after a gentle suck. Then the swallowing that made the kid's slight Adam's apple bob; it was highly erotic, a fact that did not escape Kamal's attention. His pants were getting a little more than uncomfortable as his hardness bent at an odd angle within them. Once the food was gone, he let Zijad drain the water bottle before he replaced the parts of the hood he'd removed.

"Please, do you have to cover my ears?" Zijad asked after Kamal had already done so.

Kamal stood and walked away with the tray, not answering the enquiry because yes, he did absolutely need to. He put the tray on the counter and unbuttoned his jeans, actually groaning when the pressure against his hard flesh was released. He didn't want to have to jerk himself off, but he saw no other option as his hard-on showed no signs of receding. He sat on the couch and let his eyes wander over all the tanned skin that was exposed to his hungry gaze. He'd always been attracted to younger men; he supposed that was the way of the world because almost every man, he knew, desired youth and beauty. It definitely had nothing to do with the fact that he still pictured Orhan as the young man he was when they'd been in love, never allowing the man to age in his memory even when he saw evidence to the contrary on the television so often. No, that was not the reason at all.

The memory of Orhan's lips and how they'd felt on his body, combined with the physical presence of the man's doppelganger, worked a sort of magic over Kamal's cock which had him shooting over his hand and splattering the coffee table in front of him within minutes. A strange thing happened then, for some reason the memory of the last time he'd found release swam to the surface. Kamal just barely made it to the bathroom to throw up the sandwich he'd eaten earlier. The whole while he was bent over the toilet, Julien's dull gray eyes swam through his mind making him retch even harder.

Kamal stood and rinsed his mouth in the sink. It wasn't the first time in his life he cursed the fact that he was forced by some internal pressure to admit that something he'd done actually bothered him. Even if it was only on a subconscious level most of the time, it was still there making him feel weak. He despised the feeling. He glared at himself in the mirror before leaving the bathroom, swallowing his traitorous memories once again just like he swallowed the sour taste that lingered in his mouth.

There had been a development in the living room in his absence. Zijad was moaning and had pulled his legs up against his belly. "It hurts, please..." he said, as his body contorted once again as if he was trying to find a comfortable position. "Ohhh..." he groaned. Kamal sat on the couch and watched the kid squirm. It didn't take long before Kamal heard the first passing of wind from the boy which made him groan louder and then beg, "Please, I need the bathroom, please, if you're there, Šef, let me use the bathroom, please..."

Kamal braced himself as the kid clenched his one good hand into a fist and curled his legs once more, fighting his need to evacuate his bowels. The helpless boy let out a sob as he lost the fight and soiled himself. The smell hit Kamal in a wave of foulness that almost made him gag as he watched more of the runny glop pour from the kid's asshole, spreading out onto the mattress beneath him in a pool of sludge. Kamal looked at his watch and decided an hour in his own shit should make the kid more pliable, plus it would feel like longer in the dark, silent prison of the hood. It would also be reaching the limits of how long Kamal would be able to sit there with the fetor assaulting his nose and the pitiful sobs tearing at his ears.

Kamal pulled Julian's computer out for the first time since he'd gotten to the cabin. He hooked it up to his mobile hotspot , but in his remote and closed-in location he had very little signal so was prepared to do only what he needed to. He loaded the memory stick from the camera into the port and transferred the video to the computer's hard drive, then began the slow upload of the short clip to Julien's contact within Koslov's organization. It was proof the deed had been done and that the plan was going ahead on schedule.

Kamal couldn't resist checking the headlines on the Avaz newspaper's website to see if there was anything of interest concerning his little venture. The biggest banner was about the disappearance of Orhan Ferhatović's son. There were pictures of Zijad and an article where Orhan pleaded for his wayward son to come home if he was able or for the safe return if he was being held against his will. Orhan had taken no time in sending up the alarm, even SIPA was involved in the search already, showing just how powerful Orhan had become. Kamal was surprised Orhan hadn't decided to run for president. He powered the machine down and stowed it away before getting up and going out to the porch for fresh air and a smoke.

Okay, he told himself after five more of the cancerous little sticks had been burned down to the filter and flicked into the tin can next to the porch, it was time. He'd procrastinated long enough and left the kid sitting for a half hour longer than he'd intended as he chain-smoked on the porch. He opened the door and was sure the malodor had gotten even worse in his absence, but faced with no alternative, he stepped into the cabin. The boy was silent with his head hanging so that his chin rested on his chest. Kamal stood before the kid and watched the even rise and fall of the narrow chest. The kid had fallen asleep while wallowing in his own feces.

Kamal resisted the urge to use his boot to wake the young man and instead rolled his eyes.

Reaching up, Kamal grabbed the handcuffs that were hanging from the ceiling and were attached to a rope and pulley system so the height could be adjusted. He buckled one of the stiff leather cuffs to the boy's wrist after removing the one already there and then the other just as the kid started to rouse, realized what was happening, and began to struggle. Kamal stepped back as Zijad lashed out with his newfound mobility. He grabbed the rope and pulled, jerking the kid up off the bed as he screamed at the abrupt painful jolt to his shoulders. Kamal pulled until Zijad was forced to stand on the balls of his feet on the mattress before tying off the rope to the anchor set in the wall and walking over to remove the ear muffs.

"That wasn't very smart of you, Mali. What have I done to you to deserve you trying to punch me?" Kamal asked, the irony of his question not lost on himself.

"I d-didn't know it was you. I'm s-sorry." Zijad trembled and tried not to hang from his arms.

"You made a mess, like an animal, for the second time. Haven't you learned to control your bodily functions yet? It smells like the inside of a pig pen in here."

"I asked to use the — "

"You should have held it," Kamal said, interrupting irritably. "Now I have to clean up your mess and that will put me in a bad mood."

Kamal rolled up the thin mattress, pulling it from underneath Zijad's feet so he was forced first to dance to keep his balance and then to stand on his toes. Kamal carried it out of the cabin and dragged it to the creek, not wanting to make a big mess in the cabin's small bathroom. He put it in the creek and weighted it down with heavy stones, letting the fast running water do the job of freeing the sealed rubber casing of the noxious waste. Walking slowly back to the front door, he considered for a moment dragging the kid out into the cold water of the little stream. No, he decided, he was supposed to be playing nice with the boy, he'd wash him in the tub…this time.

Kamal reached above Zijad and used the little clasp to hook the cuffs together and then detached them from the rope. He had to steady the boy as he stumbled when his hands were lowered and he no longer needed to balance on his toes. Kamal pulled on the cuffs, dragging the kid behind him to the bathroom where he turned on the water in the tub and waited until it was lukewarm before he said anything to his captive.

"I need you to step up into the tub so I can wash the filth off of you." Kamal put one hand on the kid's waist to help guide him while holding the short chain between the cuffs with the other. Once Zijad was in, Kamal pushed him to his knees and attached the cuffs to a small clip that had been installed in the wall. He pulled the showerhead out of its cradle and switched the water so it flowed through it instead of the tap.

"I'm sorry," Zijad said miserably after a long moment of silence while Kamal tended to him.

"I know, Mali, just don't do it again." Kamal reassured him that he would suffer no further retribution for his lack of control. He used soap and his hand to wash away the mess and was thankful the smell was abating with every swirl of dirty water that disappeared down the drain. Everything was going fine until he ran his soapy hand down the crease of the kid's ass.

Zijad twisted as much as he could manage within the confines of the tub. "Please don't hurt me," he begged when he realized what he'd done and tried to bury his head between his arms.

"I'm just cleaning you. I promise I have no intention of harming you in that way," Kamal lied smoothly while intentionally misunderstanding the boy's plea. He took advantage of the fact the kid had presented him with his front side, rubbing the smooth skin of the kid's thighs as if he was just going back to cleaning even though there was really nothing left there to remove.

Zijad's reaction was less pronounced when Kamal finally made contact with his balls. Though he did flinch and try to close his legs, he quickly remembered himself and let Kamal's hand do what it would. Kamal used a gentle touch as he held the tender bits in his big hand and rolled them lightly, drawing a sharp intake of breath from behind the hood. "Please..." the boy begged.

Kamal was sure it hadn't been an invitation to touch the kid more, but he did so anyway to see if he could provoke any sort of reaction out of his hostage beyond the slight trembling of his goose-fleshed body. Kamal caressed the soft flesh behind Zijad's sac before going further. Once again delving in-between the boy's cheeks and running a finger lightly over his entrance a couple of times, but pulling his hand back before Zijad could take the action as more than a gentle cleansing. Kamal took hold of Zijad's dick, letting the weight rest in his hand as the flesh firmed a little more. Still under the guise of washing him, Kamal gave the stiffening digit a few strokes before releasing it.

"I'm sorry. I didn't mean..." Zijad said, his voice catching on a sob as he tried to hide his budding erection.

"Nothing I haven't seen before, kid," Kamal said gruffly, glad the blindfold hid his smirk from the boy's eyes. Nothing more distressing than getting hard when you're terrified, except for having to try to explain it to the guy who put you in the predicament. One more thing Kamal's study of Julien's notes had taught him. Who knew fear, anger, and sexual arousal all sparked in the same area of the brain and were easily confused in young males? Kamal had been delighted at the prospects when he'd learned that little tidbit. Talk about conflicting messages, and when the kid started to confuse the feelings for more than they were, well that would be even more interesting.

"Okay I think you're clean," Kamal pronounced, leaning over and unhooking the kid's hands. "Stand up and let's get you dried off." Helping Zijad stand and step down from the tub, he toweled him off, not rushing but not being overly attentive to any particular area of the boy's anatomy either. When he was finished he asked, "Do you need to use the toilet?" Zijad shook his head but Kamal stood him in front of the porcelain bowl anyway. "Try, maybe you can squeeze a little more out." Zijad shook his head again this time with more force. "Fine, but I'm not cleaning up any more messes today so if you piss yourself you're going to sit in it until tomorrow."

Kamal led Zijad out into the main room and hooked him back up to the ropes in the ceiling, but left it long enough so the kid could stand flat-footed. He replaced the pieces of the hood, leaving Zijad to stand there while Kamal went about cleaning the bit of mess that had spilled onto the floor. In the waning light of early evening, he went to retrieve the mattress and used a towel while still on the porch to wipe it dry. He sat on the stairs and smoked, contemplating the days ahead. There was a plan to stick to, but he wondered how much leeway he had when it came to Julien's goal of getting Zijad to fall in love with the man who had held and tortured him. He wasn't sure he wanted the responsibility of crushing the kid's heart and fucking up his mind in that way.

Chapter 8:
Going Over the Limit

Two days of mind-numbing boredom was starting to wear on Kamal. He was relieved to have the monotony broken by setting up for the next phase in the twisted little head game he was playing with his hostage. The kid, whom he'd knocked out with an oral sedative, was in position; darkness had fallen and now Kamal was waiting anxiously for him to wake up so they could get on with the night's activities. Restless as he waited, Kamal took the camera off the stand and moved behind the kid as he adjusted the light to make sure it highlighted the sweet curve of the boy's naked backside. The glint of silver that hinted to something hidden within the kid's ass was a tantalizing sight as Kamal trained the camera on it. He rounded the boy, coming back to focus on his face, zooming in on his soft full lips.

Kamal had spent the last two days practically fixated on those lips. The way Zijad used them as his only means of communication, not only verbally, but to show his fear, anger, and helplessness through a mere twist or a nibble to his bottom one, reminded Kamal so much of Orhan. The hood only let Kamal imagine it was him under the fabric and not his progeny. The thought of doing unspeakable things to the boy as his father's proxy was admittedly an attractive proposition and had only grown more alluring as Kamal's arousal mounted over hours of seeing to the boy's every need.

Putting the camera back on its stand, he checked once more to make sure the light was positioned so it would blind the kid when he came around. He pulled the mask over his own face and put the voice modulator on so he would be ready when the time came. Kamal's attention was drawn to his captive's uncovered face as the first groan issued forth from that enticing mouth. It took only a moment for Zijad to come around enough to realize he wasn't in his normal binds and start to struggle. It did him no good since Kamal had tied him down tightly to the padded bench that was just wide enough to accommodate the kid's slender frame. Zijad couldn't do more than move his head and clench his one good hand that was fastened to one of the front legs of the bench.

"About time you came around, fag," Kamal growled as Zijad's bright blue eyes frantically searched the shadows for him. "I thought I was going to have to get your babysitter in here to dump a pail of water over you." Kamal stepped closer so the kid would be able to see the outline of his body. "Did you miss me?"

Zijad shook his head as his eyes welled with tears and once again darted around the shadowy interior of the cabin as if looking for someone to help him. When he found no one there besides Kamal, his eyes finally focused on his tormentor as he started to beg, "No, no, please, leave me alone, don't hurt me again, please..."

Kamal reached in his pocket and hit the button on the slim remote. The boy jolted and let out a scream as the small vibrating butt plug in his ass came to life. Kamal smiled behind his mask. "I thought you'd enjoy that." He switched the setting to random.

"Please, make it stop," Zijad moaned in protest.

"Oh, I don't think I will." Kamal stepped in after taking one more look at those oh-so-familiar eyes before he replaced the blindfold. He'd left it off long enough for whomever would be watching the video later to know who the captive was without mistake while he made sure he never faced the camera. Even with the mesh covering the eye holes of the mask, Kamal worried Orhan would somehow see beyond it and recognize him by his eyes. He also would need to keep himself fully clothed because revealing any identifying marks, such as the gunshot wounds and the shrapnel scars that dotted his torso, would not be in his best interest when the intended target knew most of them by heart.

"Please...oh god...please, no," Zijad begged on an endless loop that grated on Kamal's nerves while also firming up his cock.

Kamal grabbed a fist full of hair and jerked the kid's head up. He ran a finger over the lips he had been obsessing about while Zijad tried to pull out of his grasp, only succeeding in causing himself more pain as Kamal held tightly to his hair. "I don't mind if you struggle a bit, but we will have to do something about that mouth of yours," Kamal said. Letting the boy's head drop, he reached down to grab the gag he'd found amongst Julien's equipment. Zijad tried to evade the device as Kamal placed the leather strap around his head.

"Open that cock-sucking mouth for me, boy," Kamal commanded. He let out a snort of amusement as the kid pursed his lips against the metal ring pressing against them. Kamal plugged Zijad's nose and waited. He hooked a finger over the boy's bottom teeth and let it dig painfully into the soft tissue under his tongue when Zijad was forced to open his mouth to breathe, using his other hand to place the ring in the kid's mouth, just behind his teeth. Once he had the metal bit in place he tightened the harness around Zijad's head, making sure it wouldn't move. Kamal sat back and admired his handiwork. The ring held the kid's mouth stretched open wide, ready to be used whenever Kamal wanted.

A moan issued from the boy's mouth as the sound of the little vibrator alerted Kamal to what was the likely cause of the kid's sudden vocalization. He moved around to the side of the boy and tapped the base of the butt plug, pulling more sounds from Zijad's stretched lips. "You like that, do you?" Zijad shook his head but couldn't stop another groan from leaving his mouth. "I knew you would, you little cock slut," Kamal taunted.

He got up and walked away from the little set-up after another harder pat to the toy embedded in the boy's tight channel. He'd leave the kid like he was for a bit and let the vibrator, and thoughts of what was to come, do the tormenting for him. Sitting on the couch in the shadows, Kamal watched the boy writhe in his bindings. Feeling just a tad on the sadistic side, he played with the settings on the vibrator, finding out which ones made his little captive squeal the loudest. Kamal felt his own arousal swelling as the moans and groans grew louder and the drool drizzled down Zijad's chin to pool beneath him on the floor.

After torturing the kid for over a half hour, Kamal was finally ready to move on to the next stage. He got off the couch and stood behind the camera a moment so he could adjust the frame. Tightening in on the boy's face so when he fucked that pretty mouth, Orhan would feel as though he was right there viewing from

C.L. Mustafic

a front row seat. After adjusting the lights once more, Kamal stood in front of the boy. He knelt down before unbuckling his pants so the camera would catch all the action. He pulled his stiff cock and then his balls out of the opening, not revealing any more of his body than need be as the boy lifted his head at the sound, unknowingly presenting the camera with what looked like his own willingness to take the offered appendage in front of him.

Kamal grabbed the kid by the hair and held him still. "Going to show your *babo* what you're good at now," he growled. Zijad howled as Kamal steadied his dick and fed it through the metal that had been heated to the temperature of the kid's mouth, making it feel like just another part of the moist warm cavity he was invading. The sound cut off abruptly as Kamal's length entered the kid's throat, cutting off his air supply. The muscles squeezed as the boy gagged, trying to expel the intruder, only making it better for Kamal as they massaged the head of his cock. Kamal let his head drop back for a second as he relished the feeling with a growling moan of his own.

He gathered his wits enough to pull back so the kid could breathe. "Fuck, *sine*, your mouth feels just as good as *pićka*," Kamal taunted. The resulting groan from the kid tickled as it vibrated through the flesh of his dick and made his balls tingle. He thrust back in hard and held for a few beats before repeating the process again and then again until the snot from the kid's nose had run down to join the copious amounts of saliva the boy was producing. Without the ability to swallow, it made for a sloppy wet mess that slid over Kamal's balls, giving him another idea.

He pulled his cock free from the kid, letting him whimper and sob, free from the muffling effect of the meat gag which, Kamal knew, would play well for the camera. Kamal lifted one of his hairy balls and stuffed it through the ring into the kid's mouth, but, as if even in his broken state the kid was trying to be obstinate, he stilled and quieted. "Use your tongue like a good little ball washer." The kid moaned, but his tongue didn't do as it had been ordered so Kamal slapped him. "Do it." Still nothing.

Kamal removed his nut from the kid's mouth and cuffed Zijad again and again until the boy was screaming and blood had replaced the snot. Kamal was sure he'd made the kid's ears ring, but the boy needed to learn to do as he was told. Deciding it wasn't

70

worth the hassle to try to make the kid do what he wanted, he thrust his dick back into boy's mouth and mindlessly rutted into the kid's throat until he came. Kamal could feel the hitching of Zijad's body, and wasn't surprised that upon pulling his spent cock from the kid's mouth, a spray of liquid vomit hit the front of his jeans.

"Fucking disgusting fag," Kamal sneered. He turned the kid's messy face to the camera. "Look at your boy, Orhan. Today I only used his mouth, but soon," Kamal paused for dramatic effect, "soon I'm going to fuck that tight little ass of his until he screams for his mama." His words hadn't been lost on the kid, if his mindless scream was anything to go by. Kamal had made his point clear. Releasing the grip he had on the boy's hair caused Zijad's head to drop like his neck couldn't support its weight but the shrieking continued. He left the camera on so Orhan would get a little time alone with his son.

Kamal got up and went into the bathroom to clean himself up. Instead of putting on another pair of jeans, he pulled on a pair of loose athletic shorts that let his junk swing free. He walked out to find the kid's screams had died down to pathetic sobs that racked his body, so he shut the camera off, then grabbed his smokes and left the kid to weep to his heart's content. Kamal wasn't done with him yet. Now that he had what he needed for the video, he was going to take the blindfold off the kid so he could watch his blue eyes, Orhan's eyes, as he used him once again. The prospect of watching those eyes darken in pain and humiliation, feelings Kamal would inspire, got his blood pumping. He hummed a little as he smoked his cigarette.

"Isn't he beautiful, Kamal?" Orhan asked as he held the tiny infant out to his lover to take.

Kamal accepted the little bundle and looked down into the murky blue eyes of the week old boy Orhan had fathered. They'd argued and even come to blows over this child on more than one occasion, but looking down at something that was a part of the man he loved, he couldn't help but smile. "I still think it was a bad idea to bring another person into this mess. What chance does he have to survive, and if he does, what kind of life will he have?" Kamal asked, alluding to the war that was still going full-force around them.

"I will make sure he survives, just like I always make sure that you do," Orhan said as he slung an arm around Kamal's shoulder. "Bring us some of that *rakia*, Selma."

"There's not much left," Selma, Orhan's young wife, said, but she still stood to do as her husband bid.

"I don't care, this is a special occasion. It calls for a toast to the future of our son." Orhan watched as the woman left the room and then turned his head to Kamal. "You know that you will always be a part of my life, an important part, and that no woman will ever replace you in my heart," Orhan said, the words he'd been repeating to Kamal since that day in the hospital after Kamal had been blown up.

Kamal had been shocked, and only the high dose of morphine they had him on had stopped him from killing his best friend and lover when Orhan had told him Selma was pregnant with his child. Kamal had known Orhan was dating Selma, just as Kamal had been dating a few girls from the village; it was for show until they figured out a way to escape their small town full of even smaller-minded people. He had not known that Orhan had been sleeping with the girl and the announcement of the pregnancy had to mean she was well on her way. People kept secrets, especially ones that would cause more strain on the already thin rations the people were given. Adding another mouth to feed was generally frowned upon, but something that still happened with surprising frequency.

"Orhan, you can't mean that," Kamal said as he looked at the babe in his arms. "You married her, you stood up and told her family that the child was yours when you just as easily could have denied it." They were the same words Kamal had kept telling Orhan in response.

"That is my son," Orhan said, looking at the tiny boy Kamal held. "Quite likely to be the only one I'll ever have. Selma was going to abort it if I didn't take her home with me." Kamal could see the pain in Orhan's eyes over the decision he'd had to make and it pulled at his heart.

"This means even if we survive this hell, we'll be stuck here for the rest of our lives so you can keep playing house while I slowly die inside watching you." Kamal tried to hold back the tears he felt pricking at the back of his eyes. The baby's mouth puckered up into an O and he squirmed in Kamal's arms before a rude noise left his bottom.

Orhan chuckled as he took his son and handed him to his mother who had just walked through the door with a bottle and two small glasses on a tray. "He's messed himself." She took the baby and left the room as Orhan poured them each a glass of alcohol, emptying the bottle as he did so. He handed one glass to Kamal and held his own out. Kamal clinked his glass against the one Orhan held. "To the future," Orhan said before slamming the fiery liquid back.

"The future," Kamal repeated, doing the same.

"It will all work out. I promise you, Kamal, you just need to believe me. Have I ever lied to you before?"

"You didn't tell me you were fucking her." Kamal brought up the one point that still nagged at him every waking moment of his life.

"Come on, you can't hold that against me forever. She begged me. What kind of man would they think me if I refused and she told everyone?"

Kamal held his tongue because after all was said and done, he still loved Orhan and believed it when he said things would work out. Orhan had always been the man with a plan. Kamal was sure he had one that would get them out of this mess and keep them together.

"Okay, I believe you," Kamal said just as the sound of the baby's crying cut through the air.

"That's my boy, got a good set of lungs on him, right?" Orhan asked, sounding like a proud papa.

Kamal furrowed his brow because the crying didn't sound right. Its tone had changed, it no longer held the high pitch of a newborn's wail. Kamal opened his mouth to ask Orhan what was going on when…

A scream pulled Kamal out of his drunken slumber to remind him that baby he'd once held in his arms was still bound to the bench where Kamal had left him after he'd used the kid's mouth until he could no longer get hard no matter how he tried. He'd drunk himself into a stupor after he'd removed the gag from the boy's mouth. The split and swollen lips smeared with a mix of spit, blood and come, as well as the blooming bruises around them, had made a warning bell go off in Kamal's head. He'd crossed the line. Kamal was a professional, he prided himself on knowing just how far he had to push to get what he needed. Minimal harm for maximum gain had always been a code he'd lived by, but the kid had suffered so beautifully as Kamal had debased him and he'd lost control. Using him over and over until Kamal's body had given out as his mind pushed him to continue taking what he wanted even if he knew he was taking it from the wrong person.

Kamal sat up slowly. It had been a long time since he'd gotten drunk and had to deal with the resulting hangover. He rubbed his head as the scream pierced into his already aching head, wanting to growl at the brat to shut the hell up, but he bit his tongue and got up instead. He needed to switch into caregiver mode which meant he'd have to speak softly and tend to the kid's wounds, both the physical and mental this time. He stumbled to the bathroom where he rummaged through the contents of the medicine cabinet and finally found something that might help his head. Kamal stood there trying to slip into his other role, but the constant throbbing was keeping that nice guy buried. Sitting on the toilet, he grabbed the pack of smokes he'd left on the counter, thinking maybe the nicotine would help.

The kid's screams had died down to hoarse attempts that hurt Kamal's ears even more than the screaming had. He cleared his throat as he walked across the floor slowly, thankful he'd put the hood back on the kid before he'd gotten shit-faced, so at least he'd not totally fucked himself. Kneeling down, Kamal took off everything except the blindfold which brought on another round of those gravelly attempts at screaming.

Kamal soothed his hand through the boy's hair, it was sweaty and crusty from the time in the hood and Kamal's come. "Shh, quiet now, Mali, I'm not going to hurt you. You know I'm here to take care of you," he said before letting his hand slide down to caress the boy's stubbly cheek. The noises coming from Zijad changed into relieved sobs as he pressed his face into Kamal's palm.

"Please..." Zijad said barely above a whisper.

"It's okay, I'm here." Kamal took his hand away from the kid's face, but Zijad tried to follow it to keep the connection. Kamal gave him one more gentle touch before he removed his hand for real. "I need to get you off this thing, but I won't leave you." Kamal moved around the bench to start undoing the bindings that held the boy to it. That familiar flash of silver reminded him that though he'd shut the vibrator off, he had neglected to remove it.

The kid let out a cry of protest and clenched his cheeks as Kamal's fingers found the device and tugged to remove it. He'd had to pull harder than he thought he should have and the trickle of blood that flowed from the boy's anus was unexpected. He reminded himself to use more lube the next time or even re-lube if the need arose. He laid it aside as he gently caressed the boy's flank to reassure him that his ordeal was over – for the time being at least.

He didn't bother to restrain the kid in any way as he undid the buckles on the manacles, knowing it would be too much for the boy after what he'd been through, but he wasn't prepared for Zijad to throw his arms around his neck and cling to him for dear life once he'd helped him sit up. The blindfold was wet through with the kid's tears, something Kamal couldn't help but notice when he pressed his face into Kamal's neck.

"Thank you, thank you, thank you..." Zijad repeated over and over, refusing to unlock his arms from Kamal when he tried to separate them.

"Mali, please, let go. I need to check you to see if you need any patching up," Kamal said when he started to get a little frustrated at the boy's insistent grip.

"Please, don't leave me alone. He'll come back," Zijad whimpered. His naked body shuddered against Kamal's.

"I'm here for now and I'm not leaving for a bit." Kamal sighed and gathered the kid up into his arms, prepared to carry him to the bathroom if necessary. Zijad had, at some point, both come and pissed on the bench, and Kamal couldn't bring himself to chastise the boy for losing control of his bladder, but he'd be damned if he was going to sit around while it started to stink of old urine. The kid sniveled and burrowed his face deeper into Kamal as he stood and took the boy into the bathroom. "You have to let go so that I can run the bath," he said, leaning down to set the kid in the tub.

"You won't leave?" Zijad asked, sounding so pathetic Kamal almost felt the urge to reassure him again.

"Let go, Mali, I can get mad and if you push me past my limits I will grow upset enough to make you let go." Kamal let a little of the

C.L. Mustafic

anger he was just barely holding back creep into his tone. Zijad finally let his arms drop, but only after he'd expressed his displeasure with a watery little sob. "That's a good boy. Now I will leave your arms free on one condition and it's an important one so listen. You don't touch that blindfold, don't even lift your hands from where they are unless I move them, you understand?"

"Yeah, okay." Zijad nodded.

"Good." Kamal bent over to start the taps and let the water fill as he turned the kid's head toward him, running his fingers lightly over the bruises from the gag and his own rough treatment. The feelings he was having were definitely conflicting. The discolored skin reminded him of what he'd done, making him feel both regret for losing control but also making his blood pump a little faster at the thought that he could do it again – that he wanted to do it again.

Chapter 9:
Frustration and Punishment

Day 10, Day 5 in Captivity

For the next twenty-four hours Kamal let the boy rest, feeding him and taking care of his needs with nothing but the bindings to make Zijad uncomfortable. It was his way of making up for crossing the line and taking his torture of the poor boy further than necessary to obtain his goal. He'd always been a fair man and had always admitted when he was in the wrong. He sighed as he looked at Zijad lying on the thin mattress because now it was time for the next phase of Julien's plan to break the kid, and, by extension, his father. Kamal had to admit he was highly intrigued by the things he'd read. It was a well laid-out plan of psychological and sexual torture. It wasn't his style, he was more for the *hurt them quick*, make it painful enough to convince the parents to roll and be done with it. This long drawn-out torture made little sense to him when he thought removing a few fingernails or maybe even the tip of a finger would have gotten the job accomplished much quicker. His eyes lingered on the naked kid. Who was he to question it?

Digging through the trunk to find the necessary tools, he pulled out a butt plug. It was thinner than the one he'd used on the previous occasion but bent at an angle that would massage the boy's prostate. It also had a double vibrator on it so just the head, pressed to that small knob of nerves, would vibrate or the base and bottom inch would buzz, leaving the kid's entrance almost numb after a couple of hours. He found the cock cage and then the lube, he'd need lots of lube, and finally the ring gag that also had a penis-

77

shaped attachment that could be fitted through the ring and into the kid's mouth. It wasn't huge, just enough to fill the boy's mouth if Kamal felt the need. Last, but not least, was the reusable enema kit; Kamal had a feeling he might need that gag sooner rather than later.

He put his supplies in the bathroom before grabbing a bottle of water and detaching the handcuffs from the ceiling pulley system so he'd have something to restrain the kid with while he worked in the bathroom. He set the handcuffs on the floor before sitting on the edge of the mattress next to Zijad. He touched the boy's chest because he'd found if he touched the boy in certain ways, his reactions were quite different. The response a small touch to the kid's upper body got was a slow turning of the boy's head toward where he thought Kamal was sitting. A touch anywhere on Zijad's lower body got a soft sob and legs drawn up to cover himself, but the biggest reaction came any time Kamal touched the hood first. The boy would scream and try to get out of Kamal's reach no matter how hopeless that struggle was, pleading to not be hurt again. It was interesting to say the least; being able to provoke such different reactions with so little as a touch was sort of a trip.

Kamal took the ear muffs off once he was sure the kid wasn't going to freak out on him. "I have a bottle of water for you." Uncapping it, he held it to Zijad's lips, which were still a little cracked and the bruises stood out starkly even against the boy's tanned skin. Zijad drank deeply from the bottle. When Kamal pulled it back, a small trickle spilled down the boy's chin stirring feelings in Kamal he'd convinced himself he'd worked past during that one brutal night. "Enough or do you want more?" he asked through his thickening saliva.

Zijad shook his head which didn't actually answer the question, but Kamal took it to mean he'd had enough. He reached over the kid's body, almost coming chest to chest with him as he removed the cuff on the first hand. Kamal was sure it wasn't his imagination that had the boy leaning in as if he wished to press his body against Kamal's. Kamal drew back quickly to put space between them but his brow furrowed at the unexpected move on the kid's part. He locked the freed wrist into the cuff and set to work on the other.

"What's going to happen now?" Zijad asked in a tremulous voice once his hands were bound in front of him.

Kamal didn't answer, instead he hauled the kid to his feet and started pulling him to the small bathroom. Zijad dragged his feet, but didn't put up much of a fight, resigned to his fate it seemed. Kamal urged the boy into the tub and locked his bound hands to the clasp higher up on the wall, allowing the kid to stand comfortably with his legs spread wide enough for Kamal to do his job.

Kamal started the taps and read the instructions on the enema kit as he filled the rubber pouch that held the water. Grabbing the lube, he slathered some on the head of the little wand attached to the tube; he saw no need to cause the kid more discomfort than necessary at that point. The enema kit was designed to be used by someone lying on their back, but Kamal didn't have that luxury if he didn't want to clean up a mess. He put the bag on the edge of the tub where it balanced fairly well and guided the kid to turn around to face the wall which Zijad did without complaint.

"Mali, this isn't going to be pleasant for either of us, but if you struggle it will only hurt you more," Kamal warned. He'd considered just shoving the wand up the kid's ass with no warning, but decided on trying to get the boy's cooperation instead.

"W-w-what?" Zijad started to tremble and turn towards Kamal, but a firm hand on his shoulder stopped him.

Kamal's heartbeat picked up with the sudden fear he could feel coming off the kid; maybe he should have just forced it on the boy.

"I'm going to give you an enema," Kamal said, not mincing words.

"Please don't," Zijad whined. Kamal pushed the kid's legs open wider. "Please, Šef, I'll do anything, please don't hurt me again."

"Calm down, Mali, I will try not to hurt you but I must do this." Kamal spread the boy's ass open so his tight pucker was exposed to Kamal's eyes. He suddenly wondered just how tight the kid would be. He already knew the boy would make the most wonderful sounds when Kamal finally got around to finding out. He rubbed a lubed finger over the kid's entrance and watched it quiver before bringing the head of the wand to it. "Just breathe, Mali, and relax."

"Noooo…" Zijad wailed as he was impaled with the slightly bulbous head of the enema wand. Of course he hadn't relaxed at all as he'd been told but instead clenched and fought the intrusion, making it that much more unpleasant when Kamal finished pushing another six centimeters of the cold plastic into him.

Kamal moved the little clamp holding the water at bay and pressed the bag with his knee to help the liquid flow upwards and into the kid's rectum, making sure to do as the directions explained and kept the stream steady and not too fast. The boy's moan was not of pure pain nor exactly like pleasure, and the sound of it shot to Kamal's groin. He watched the kid's body as the muscles lost their rigidness and the boy almost hung limp by his wrists. Kamal's dark eyes didn't miss the rise to half-mast the kid's well-proportioned cock took as he slowly ran out of water, meaning the boy was full to a level that would be uncomfortable, bordering on painful.

"Okay, I'm going to remove the tube now, you need to try to hold the water in for a few minutes." Kamal used a tone that made it clear it wasn't a suggestion. The kid whimpered but the minute the unwanted invasion was over, he clenched his ass tightly to do as he'd been told. "Good, that's very good, Mali. Just a few minutes and you can let it go." Kamal ran a hand down the boy's back, making the kid arch into it like an affection-starved cat.

Kamal made some noise as he moved around the room so Zijad would know he was not left on his own. Cleaning the enema kit first before moving on to inspect the toys he'd use for torture, familiarizing himself with how the cock cage worked and studying the vibrator as he waited for the kid to disobey his order and let go of the water. It took longer than Kamal expected for the boy to start begging for relief.

"Please, Šef, it hurts," Zijad moaned. Kamal stepped closer to the tub and turned the boy around in his chains. "Please?"

The boy's cock was hard and bobbing which brought a smile to Kamal's face. For reasons Kamal didn't quite grasp, the kid seemed to enjoy the enema even as he claimed to be in pain. "You're enjoying yourself?" Kamal asked, bringing attention to the situation for the benefit of humiliating the boy.

"No." Zijad violently shook his head to deny it.

Kamal tapped the head of the kid's erection. "I think you're lying because I have proof right here that says you are."

Zijad continued to shake his head. "No, I just…I…please." The boy's last word came out on a breathy whisper punctuated by a low moan.

Kamal's mind was going a mile a minute, there were so many possibilities being presented by this unforeseen development. When he finally decided on one, he couldn't keep the evil smirk off his face. "Tell you what, Mali, since you seem to like this so much." Kamal took the stiff flesh in his big calloused hand, drawing a groan from the kid. "You can let go as soon as you come." The boy stilled and his mouth fell open as Kamal started to slowly stroke his dick. After only a few of those catching caresses – Kamal looked longingly at the lube but was loathe to let off the kid's erection long enough to grab it – Zijad seemed to get his wits back.

"Please, don't, I can't. Please, Šef, anything but — " Zijad's words came to an abrupt end. The kid's hips snapped forward, pressing his cock through Kamal's hand as he whimpered. He wasn't even jerking the boy off anymore, it was more like the kid was fucking his hand and the action brought a pleased look to Kamal's face. He couldn't help but watch Zijad's lips as he let out helpless little sounds that echoed off the tiles in the small bathroom.

"That's it, you can do it." Kamal urged the boy on while staring at him with hungry eyes.

"No…" Zijad wailed. Kamal didn't know which action the kid was lamenting as he came and released the water at the same time. He was forced to let go of the kid's flagging erection when the deluge of fluid left the boy and splattered the wall and tub. The expelling of fouled water went on for some minutes as the boy hung limply, only clenching the muscles of his stomach to aid in the evacuation as he sobbed quietly. Kamal watched it all, the sight before him both arousing and revolting.

When it seemed that the kid was empty, Kamal turned the water on and used the shower head to hose the boy off. Zijad had no reaction to the tepid water being used on him, not even raising his hooded head. Kamal left him there while he moved his remaining supplies out next to the mattress, deciding the bathroom wasn't the best place to finish his work after all. The boy was still limp, but the weeping had stopped when Kamal reached up to unhook his bound wrists. Zijad slumped into Kamal's arms as soon as there was nothing holding him up and after several attempts to get the kid on his feet, Kamal growled and lifted him into his arms.

Grumbling as he carried the boy through the cabin, Kamal dropped him roughly on the mattress. The kid cried out when he landed hard on the thin cushion. "*Boli me kurac,*" Kamal said irritably in response to the boy's cry. He pulled the rope down and roughly attached the handcuffs to it before putting the ear muffs back on the boy so he could work in peace, not having to answer the kid's inevitable questions and pleas for him to stop.

He eyed the gag but that was the last piece of equipment he'd wanted to put on the kid, knowing it would be the most traumatic after his last run-in with it. He picked up the cock cage and opened it before reaching for the boy's dick. Zijad tried to pull his legs up but Kamal had been ready for that move and he easily kept the kid flat by slinging a leg across his knees, pinning him to the mattress. The cage was easy to snap in place as he ignored the boy's cries and muttered begging that offered Kamal something to think about as he rolled the kid to his stomach. Lubing his fingers, he breached the kid with little ceremony. Only the exquisite feeling of heat and tight clinging muscles slowed Kamal down from his initial frenzied pace to get it done quickly, as he let himself take a bit of pleasure from the act of violating the boy's ass. He was forced to speed up his ministrations when the urge to bury his own hard cock in the kid became almost too much for him to bear.

The butt plug replaced his fingers, making the kid cry out once more. Kamal found the little remote that would let him control the sensations the boy would feel and gave Zijad a brief taste of what was to come. He used the lowest setting that started the head of the vibrator. "Ohh nooo, please nooo, godddd," Zijad moaned as the toy assaulted his sensitive bundle of nerves. The kid writhed and moaned, making Kamal wonder if the boy knew just how inviting he looked when he made those little noises. Kamal switched the setting to off once he was satisfied it would do a proper job of tormenting the boy who would find no release with his cock locked away in the cage.

With the majority of the preparations done, Kamal finally removed the ear muffs and the rest of the hood, leaving only the blindfold in place, so he could speak softly to the panting kid, hoping to get him to accept the gag without too much of a struggle. He rolled the boy back over and bent down so his lips were almost touching the kid's ear. "I know this is hard on you, Mali, and I'm sorry I have to put you through this, but I have to put the gag on you now. Don't fight me and I will leave your mouth free from the plug. That will be much more comfortable for you, I think."

"Please, you don't have to. I'll do anything you want, just not the gag," the boy offered once again, but this time Kamal was prepared to see just how much he meant it.

Kamal pressed two fingers to the kid's lips and bit back a gasp when Zijad didn't hesitate to open and suck the digits into his moist mouth. Kamal let the boy suckle his fingertips for a moment before pushing them in past the second knuckle. He expected the boy to fight back, maybe even bite him now that he had Kamal in a position to cause him some amount of pain, but instead the kid moaned obscenely and sucked harder. Zijad worked Kamal's fingers with his tongue as Kamal fucked them in and out.

"Would you suck my cock like you're sucking my fingers?" Kamal asked, keeping his own need from tingeing his words. The kid could only moan around the objects in his mouth but his nod was an unmistakable affirmative that indeed he *would* suck Kamal's cock if that was what was asked of him to keep him out of the gag which represented the abuse he'd taken only a day before. Kamal pulled his fingers from the boy's sucking heat and jammed his hand against the underside of the kid's jaw so he could put pressure on the joints with his thumb and middle finger. Reaching back, he grabbed the gag and before the boy knew what was happening, Kamal had the ring positioned in his mouth. Kamal rolled to straddle the kid so he could tighten the headband to hold it in place. Just so Zijad would understand he was being punished for offering to do something like suck Kamal's cock for leniency, Kamal also shoved the penis-shaped gag into the boy's open mouth.

"*Jebena kurva*, that's what you are," Kamal spat as he stood up. "Offering your mouth to anyone who would be nice to you. How do you think that makes me feel, that you'd think I'd want your mouth on me?" Unhooking the boy's wrists, Kamal dragged him over to the bench which he'd adjusted so it stood at a height that came to just below his own waist. He made Zijad kneel on the side in the center of the bench before he fastened the kid's arms to the manacles at the ends of the padded bench so his shoulders and upper chest rested on it. Zijad bawled as he struggled against the new position. Kamal used one of the leather belts attached to the side of the bench to buckle the boy's waist to it to keep him on his knees.

After securing the kid, Kamal took a step back to calm down. Getting riled at the kid's response reminded him he needed to keep it together to avoid a repeat of the last time he'd fucked the kid's mouth. He'd been stupid asking the boy that question. Of course he'd do whatever he needed to stop Kamal from hurting him further so why had it pissed him off so much to know it would be that easy to get the kid to suck his cock?

Kamal grabbed his cigarettes and stomped out of the cabin. Once out in the fresh air and sunshine he felt marginally better, he took a walk up the hillside and then around the little valley. He was sweating and uncomfortable by the time he got back to the front door but the exercise had done his mood a world of good. He went straight for the kid, undoing his pants as he crossed the room. His movements were fluid even though his mind was jerking ahead to what he planned to do and the sweet relief he'd find.

Zijad appeared to be sleeping with his head laid sideways on the bench, so Kamal used his hair to pull him up. The sounds of the chains holding the leather cuffs to the bench rattling as the kid pulled and tried to free himself of their hold sent little jolts of adrenaline through Kamal. He removed the little rubber cock and replaced it with his own large musky-smelling one. It took him only minutes to silently spill into the kid's throat. He pulled back to watch his come run out of the boy's mouth and make a little puddle under his chin, then dropped the kid's head and walked back out of the cabin. He waited a few minutes, smoked a cigarette and then entered the cabin again, going straight into the bathroom without a glance in the boy's direction. Kamal showered and shaved and slipped on a pair of athletic shorts but nothing else, it was hot and he didn't need to be uncomfortable as he sat around the little house.

Zijad once again had his head down as he keened softly. Kamal knew he couldn't keep the boy on his knees forever, but he felt no urgent need to move him just yet. He started to prepare a meal they both could eat. He needed to get the kid on a short schedule to convince him more time had passed than actually had, making him lose hope of rescue and slip even further into despair.

Kamal watched the boy stir and lift his head, creepily following Kamal's movements with his sightless eyes, his breath coming in little hiccups that sounded loud in the silence of the cabin. What was left of his anger at the kid dissipated at the innocent sounds coming from his obscenely stretched mouth and Kamal finally started to slip back into the caregiver role which would allow him to give the boy a little consideration. Grabbing a wet rag, he wiped the side of the kid's head where he'd lain in the pool of come. Zijad startled at the touch, but once he figured out Kamal wasn't going to hurt him he whimpered and leaned in to the cloth.

"Let me finish fixing your food and then we'll move you somewhere more comfortable," Kamal said gently. Again the kid's face turned up to Kamal as if he could see him and the boy's tongue moved but the sounds he made were unintelligible. "Just be a bit longer." Kamal patted the kid's cheek before going back to his cooking.

Chapter 10:
Head Games

Day 16, Day 11 in Captivity

Kamal lay lounging on the couch, wearing only a pair of athletic shorts and the ear muffs he'd taken off the kid. He was staring at the ceiling, watching as a spider spun its web between the light fixture and the ceiling above it. The weather had been so hot and humid in the last week that he'd taken to barely dressing. His eyes flicked to the boy on the mattress, not like the kid minded at all. Kamal had removed the bottom half of the mask and the ear muffs, and they were well into the twelfth hour of listening to random noises coming from the speakers Kamal had set up two days prior. Well, the kid was listening; Kamal had grown weary of the noise and had donned the muffs to protect his own sanity. It was almost time for the boy's one hour nap before Kamal would begin the whole process over again; letting the sounds drive the hostage insane while Kamal slept.

With only Julien's tablet – that held mostly books in French – the slower-than-fuck-internet, and a deck of playing cards as his only entertainment, Kamal had grown bored. The busy work of the first few days, that set a routine to condition the kid in ways Kamal couldn't figure out would benefit anyone, began with Kamal waking the kid by turning on the vibrator in his ass. He'd sit and watch as the boy cried out time and again when his trapped penis tried and failed to rise in response to the stimulation. Half an hour after starting that he'd use the boy's mouth to get off. Then Kamal would remove all the torture devices, toilet and bathe the boy, feed him, put him on his knees for an hour in the full hood before feeding him again over protests of him not being hungry. Then more time in the hood, followed by another meal and lastly the routine of putting him back in his 'outfit' as Kamal had come to think of the toys the boy wore throughout his night. Zijad's days had been reduced to a mere six hours of wakefulness and four hours of sleep, which meant by the time Kamal started the noise torture, the kid probably figured he'd been in Kamal's care for over twice as long as he actually had – that was if the kid could figure anything at all at that point.

The line between good cop and bad cop had blurred for both Kamal and his captive as the sexual torture continued. The further the kid sank into his depression, the less he fought against Kamal's use of his mouth. The last time Kamal had shoved his dick in the boy's mouth, he'd barely even gagged and actually swallowed Kamal's load instead of puking it back out. But those days had been replaced by starving the kid and driving him mad through sleep deprivation. He sometimes wondered if all of this was going a bit overboard since the boy already seemed to be broken. He was full of abject hopelessness over his situation, and sobbed and begged Kamal to just kill him whenever he had the chance.

Kamal got up to get the bottle of juice he'd give the kid once he turned the sound off and told him to go to sleep for the night. He took the ear muffs off his own head just in time to listen to the sounds of a woman being raped by a gang of men. He shuddered, remembering that wasn't even the worst of the things on the soundtrack. It was a relief when he pushed the button that silenced it. The kid's head didn't even turn toward him as he approached, a sign of just how downtrodden the boy was. Kamal sat on the mattress next to his captive and let his hand settle onto the slowly rising and falling chest but the touch got no reaction.

"I've brought you something to drink, Mali." Zijad made no move to turn his head toward Kamal to take the offered drink, so Kamal touched his chin, using just the tip of his fingers to turn the blinded boy to him. "Come on, take a drink," he urged, pressing the bottle to the kid's lips.

"I think you drug my drinks sometimes," Zijad said quietly before he took a small sip. He nodded his head as if Kamal had admitted he'd slipped the kid drugs through his drink. "Why not just give me too much and help me out of this?" He made it sound so simple.

"Because I have to do what I'm told, just like you." The boy took another drink out of the bottle when Kamal tipped it.

"It's been too long," Zijad whispered more to himself than to his captor.

"What's been too long?" The kid didn't answer Kamal right away, and he was just getting ready to ask him again when the boy sighed.

"If my father was going to do whatever it is you want him to do to get me back, he'd have done it by now. You know that you'll have to kill me eventually, why not now? I know you aren't a bad man, you've been kind to me, do me one last kindness and kill me." Zijad said more words to Kamal during that one little monologue than he'd uttered in the last few days and it had been a plea for his own death.

"I won't kill you, Mali, no matter what you *will* leave here alive," Kamal said before he could think better of it. First contact wouldn't even have been made yet, there were still three days left until the two weeks would be up. Only then would Orhan receive the first video Kamal had sent Koslov, but the boy didn't know that.

Zijad cocked his head and considered Kamal's words. "You sound sure of your words, but I don't think you're the one that gets to make that decision, are you?"

His quiet and calm demeanor threw Kamal off, it was as though the boy had come to accept his own mortality, and instead of tears and begging, he was going to meet it with serenity. Kamal didn't think this was how things were supposed to go.

"I may not make the decisions but I know the plan and it doesn't call for killing you." Kamal tried to put the issue to rest but he was sure the kid knew that sometimes plans changed.

"I need the bucket, please," Zijad said after a minute of silence where he'd hung his head and Kamal thought he'd fallen asleep.

Kamal undid the cuff holding Zijad's still taped-up fingers. He found if he did it in the right order, injured hand first, he didn't need to restrain the kid while he took care of his necessary bodily functions. It had only taken one squeeze to those still healing fingers for Zijad to get the picture of what was in store if he tried anything at such times. Kamal still wondered how the boy could think he wasn't a bad guy. He stood and bent to help Zijad get to his feet.

Usually the kid let Kamal lead him to the bucket, but this time when he tugged the boy's arm to get him moving Zijad didn't obey.

"Come on, you said you needed the bucket." Kamal flinched when the kid's hand landed in the center of his bare chest. Zijad let out a little gasp when Kamal grabbed his wrist but he curled his fingers, letting them tangle in the chest hair he found under his palm. The boy didn't tug or try to cause any pain but he didn't let go either when Kamal tried to move his hand.

"Mali," Kamal growled deep in his throat.

"Why are you naked?" Zijad tilted his head back as if he meant to look at Kamal's eyes.

"I'm not," Kamal said, once again trying to remove the hand but not yet annoyed enough to hurt the kid to do it.

Zijad relaxed his fist and let his hand lie flat against Kamal's chest. "I can feel your heart," he whispered.

"You sound surprised." Kamal said, taken aback by the kid's weird actions. He forgot he was supposed to be removing the hand, not liking the way it felt against his skin.

"I lied when I said you weren't a bad man. I know you are. You have to be to let him do the things he does to me and I wasn't sure you had one, but now I have proof that you do," Zijad said quietly, letting his lips turn down in a frown. "What's this from?"

Kamal took his eyes off the lips that still fascinated him to look down at his chest where the kid was fingering one of the many scars dotting Kamal's flesh. "Old war wound," Kamal answered. It was as though he was in some sort of trance, answering questions about himself was something he usually avoided at all costs.

"This one too?" Zijad's fingers found another.

"Yes, but that was a bullet, not shrapnel like the first."

"You were shot?" the kid asked with wonder in his voice.

"More than once, yes."

"You must be really strong to survive all that," the boy said softly.

"Luck had more to do with it," Kamal said, finally getting a grip on himself and pulling the kid's wandering hand off his chest. "You need the bucket or not?"

Zijad bit his lip and nodded as he let Kamal lead him to it. Kamal stood nearby while the kid did his business but had to get involved when he indicated he was finished. Kamal used a bottle of water along with paper towels to make sure the kid's ass was wiped thoroughly. It would have been easier to take the boy into the bathroom and have him take a shit, but making him feel less than human by being forced to use a bucket was on the list of pre-approved torture techniques, a list Kamal was thinking less and less of as time wore on. There were a few things on the list that didn't make sense to him, like shitting in a goddamn bucket for one. With his captive being as easily broken as he'd been, it was all a bit much, but Kamal found no alternate plan in Julien's notes allowing for any deviation from the original. It was something Kamal had been considering, knowing he only had to do the things Koslov wanted videos of. Who would know if he didn't do the others and did the things he wanted instead?

He put the kid back in his handcuffs, and just as he finished a sound broke the silence. Kamal nearly jumped out of his skin as his phone rang for the first time since he'd started the job. The kid tensed at the sound and opened his mouth as Kamal jammed the earmuffs on his head. Zijad started screaming just as Kamal got to the phone. He noted the number and let it go to voicemail. Kamal glared at the kid, but didn't do anything to stop him from hollering his fool head off. Did he really think Kamal was stupid enough to answer his phone in the same room with his victim?

Grabbing his phone, cigarettes, and a beer, he looked longingly at the *rakia*, then prepared to go out on the porch to make his call. Hopefully the boy would wear himself down by the time he was done. He made himself comfortable, opening his beer and lighting a smoke, before he hit the callback button.

"Kamal," Demetri answered, "I had an interesting discussion about a mutual friend of ours."

"Oh yeah?" Kamal asked, surprised Demetri cut straight to the point. He leaned back against the railing and took a long pull off his beer.

"I was having a meal at Brajlović when one of Orhan's men approached my table."

"What was one of his men doing at Brajlović?" The restaurant was a known mob hangout; there'd been a shooting there only the year before so no respectable politician or anyone associated with one would be caught dead in there.

"Well it seems he was looking for me," Demetri said, his tone indicating he was delighting in the information he was about to tell Kamal, but no words tumbled out to fill him in.

Kamal released a long stream of smoke out of his nose in annoyance at the fat man and his fucking games. Why did he think he needed to draw it out, couldn't he just fucking say what he wanted to say and get it the fuck over? Kamal waited.

"He wanted to know if I could get his boss your number," Demetri finally said.

"What? Why?" Kamal sat up straight, almost dropping his beer.

"I told him I couldn't give that information out to just anyone. He gave me a card and told me to tell you to call your old friend, it seems he may be interested in employing your services." Kamal could hear the man's smirk through the phone line.

Kamal thought on it for a moment. "Give him my number." Kamal hung up before Demetri could ask any more questions. Shit, what had he just done?

Kamal was antsy as he waited for his old lover to call, pacing the floor of the small cabin, smoking and muttering to himself. He'd let the kid fall asleep with the hood on and hadn't even woken him after his hour was up. Kamal was the one who should have been sleeping like a baby, not the boy. He just couldn't bring himself to return to the senseless noise torture because he didn't really understand what it was supposed to accomplish since the boy was already listless and depressed. He stopped mid-step when the kid started thrashing and calling out in his sleep. It was nothing new, the boy's nightmares had grown increasingly violent, even more so since he'd been forced to listen to the tapes. Kamal suddenly wished he had a second set of the noise canceling headphones.

Once again he sought refuge in the outdoors. The evening air was still hot and heavy, but it was better than being cooped up in the small space with the kid's tormented dreams. He sat on the steps, phone in one hand, his ever present smokes in the other, and just felt the weight on his shoulders settle a bit more. What could Orhan want? Was he looking to retaliate against Koslov? Kamal hoped the other man wasn't stupid enough to rush head first into something he could never understand. The underworld of politics was something Kamal was sure Orhan was aware of, but Kamal wasn't sure if he knew just how deep and dark things could get.

Orhan had always kept himself aboveboard, he played by a whole different set of rules than the ones that governed Kamal's life.

As if his thoughts of the man had summoned the call, his phone rang, startling him once more. He stared at the screen, but all it showed was an unknown number. He debated answering it or letting it go to his generic voicemail, but then he straightened his spine and got ready to talk to his former lover – a man he'd not spoken to in almost eighteen years. "*Molim?*"

"Kamal?" The voice was one he recognized – it was Orhan's – but age had changed it so it was not the one he remembered. Kamal felt a lump form in his throat that made it impossible to answer. "Kamal, please, if that's you, answer me."

Kamal swallowed the bitterness that had formed the obstruction and coughed to clear his throat. "I'm listening, say what you have to say."

He heard the audible sigh come over the phone, and took it to mean Orhan was relieved he'd gotten the right number. "Kamal, I'm sorry, I know that I promised never to seek you out after — "

"Just tell me what you want, I don't need your apologies."

"Kamal…"

Kamal could hear the wariness in his voice but it only pissed him off. "God fucking damn it, just tell me what the hell you want," Kamal growled, ready to hang up. Orhan could find someone else to do what it was he thought he needed Kamal to do to help him get his kid back. That was surely the only reason the other man had called and broken the promise he'd made Kamal all those years ago.

"I need your help," Orhan blurted.

"I figured that." He paused to light a cigarette, and when Orhan didn't start talking he asked, "Just what do you think I can do to help you?"

"I'm sure you've heard by now that Zijad is missing."

"I have."

"I've heard that you work for a certain man. Kamal, how secure is the phone you are on now?" Orhan asked, as if he'd just realized he was about to implicate Kamal in all sorts of crimes if he said Koslov's name.

"It's probably more secure than the one you're on."

"Okay, well as I was saying, I've heard that you sometimes do some work for Koslov," Orhan said. Kamal wasn't going to admit or deny he worked for the Russian mobster no matter how secure the line was. "I was wondering if you'd heard anything. Zijad's been gone for almost two weeks and I haven't gotten anything to indicate that he's being held for ransom."

"Maybe the boy ran away," Kamal offered.

"What does he have to run away from?" Orhan asked, but didn't wait for Kamal to answer before adding, "He's only here for the summer and then he heads back to London for another term at university, there's nothing for him to run from. Someone's taken my boy, Kamal, and I need your help to find out who."

"I haven't heard anything." The lie came easily from Kamal's lips.

"Please, Kamal, if you can help me, please, for my son, whom you once loved as your own. He's an innocent in all this, he doesn't deserve to be…" Orhan stopped and took a deep breath. "Please just agree to meet me and talk about this. Can't we let the past go for a moment for Zijad's sake?"

"I can't help you. I'm not even in Sarajevo right now." Kamal tried to ignore the warm feeling that rose in his chest as he told Orhan no, but he had to admit it felt damn good to deny the begging man his one request.

"What if they hurt him or even kill him?" Kamal cocked his head because something in Orhan's tone was off. He sounded worried, but not the sort of worried a man whose only son had been missing for eleven days should sound, not the teary-eyed anguish sort of worried.

"Maybe you deserve for him to die. Maybe you should have just done what they asked of you because you knew that your son and wife could be potential targets. It was your choice to put him in harm's way. What could be so important that it would make you chance your family's safety?" Kamal asked.

"That's harsh, even coming from someone like you."

"It may be harsh but it's the truth. Just make sure that if they do have him, you do whatever they tell you to do to get him back," Kamal said with more intensity than he'd ever said anything. Thoughts of having to kill the kid in the cabin floated to the surface of his mind and for some reason he rejected them just as quickly as they popped up.

"You know I will, but please, if you hear anything, or if you can help him, please, remember, he is not me, he's just a child."

"He's not a child and I know he's not you, no one could ever be you." Kamal hung up, then pulled his hand back, cocking his arm to throw the stupid device as far away from him as he could. Instead he let it drop into his lap in defeat. Why had he taken the call and allowed his past to make its way into his present? What had he expected when he'd gotten himself into this mess? Really, he deserved whatever came his way for sticking his nose where it didn't belong. It was true, he owed the man for saving his life, but he also owed him for making it what it was at that moment and, for that, someone needed to pay.

Chapter 11:
Unexpected Acceptance

Day 17, Day 12 in Captivity

Kamal was relieved to see the kid had calmed down and seemed to be sleeping peacefully by the time he headed back into the cabin. He glared at the speakers that had been blaring for the last two days and in a fit of resentment at having to follow someone else's idea of how the job should be done, he grabbed them and carried them to the front door. Walking back out on the porch, he chucked them as far as he could, the sound of breaking plastic satisfying to his ears as they hit the paved path. He went back in and lay on the couch. He knew he had to make another video soon but other than that, under Kamal's control, the boy would suffer whatever Kamal saw fit to do to him. With that decision made, Kamal drifted off.

"They say that the war will end soon, they're going to sign the peace treaty," Orhan said confidently as he let his hand trail down Kamal's chest. He was careful with his caresses, making sure not to disturb the dirty bandages that covered the couple of three-week-old bullet wounds.

They were relaxing on a dirty old mattress they'd covered with a somewhat clean blanket in a blown-out house just outside the village. Their coupling had been quick and intense, it had been over a week since they'd had a chance to lie together so they'd both been eager. Now that they were satiated Kamal knew Orhan would tell him what was on his mind. What had his clear blue eyes twinkling? It was always something that portended a plan.

Kamal covered Orhan's hand with his own to stop its wandering. "I don't believe that any more than you do so why are you trying to sound as if you do?"

"One of Selma's cousin's is in Beč," Orhan said.

"So what does that have to do with the war ending?" Orhan knew he hated it when people tried to dance around what they were trying to say instead of just saying it.

Orhan shrugged, telling Kamal that it didn't have anything to do with anything, it had just been a segue into the conversation he wanted to have. "He sent word that he could send papers for family members to join them there. If we could get to Tuzla where they have the UNICOR camp, they could process us and — "

"And you'd leave?" Kamal asked, the thought pushing him quickly toward panic.

"Well if we were there, they're much more progressive in Austria than here and I'm sure I could make an agreement with Selma so that we could — "

"You do realize that I'm not a part of her family, or yours for that matter? I have no one who could send me papers. If you go, you go without me." Kamal knew it was selfish. He should want his lover and family to go where they would be safe even if it meant that they would be separated for however long it took; either for Kamal to find a way to go to him, or for the war to end and the country to stabilize so they could return. He just couldn't imagine his life without Orhan in it even if he had to share him.

Orhan picked his head up off Kamal's chest to look him in the eyes. The hurt and sadness was evident as his blue eyes filled with tears. "I didn't think of that. I'm sorry, Kamal, I just always assume that it's me and you together. It didn't even cross my mind that if he sent the papers..." Orhan's breath hitched and a tear slid down his cheek to catch in the scruff of his scraggly beard.

Kamal pulled him into his arms and comforted him. "I know, I'm sorry. I know you'd never consciously make a plan that didn't include me." Kamal knew in his heart that it was true.

Orhan kissed him with renewed passion. "I love you and if I have to stay in this hell for the rest of my life to be with you like this, I will." Orhan's words rushed out before his tongue plunged into Kamal's mouth again.

More fervent kisses and Orhan moved so that his leaner body was atop Kamal's. They rocked together as their flesh once again firmed to hardness. Orhan didn't even break the seal of their lips as he lifted just enough to let Kamal position his cock at the right angle for Orhan to settle on it. The remnants of Kamal's first release eased his passage and once Kamal was fully seated within Orhan, neither of them moved. Both men were content just to feel the deep connection while they kissed as if it was the last time they'd have the chance.

The sweet dream, not the usual type Kamal had when they involved Orhan, left him to wake with an achingly hard problem lying on his abdomen. Kamal groaned and rolled over so his cock was trapped between his body and the couch which only made it worse. Pushing up on his arms, he looked over at the kid. Too bad he hadn't put the gag in the boy's mouth the night before, he could have used it at the moment. Just as the thought crossed his mind, the kid turned his hooded head in Kamal's direction and Kamal would swear that the boy used his tongue to wet his lips just to mock him.

"Šef, are you there?" Zijad asked quietly. Kamal didn't bother to answer since the kid's ears were covered but he waited to see if the kid would call out again. "Please, I need the bucket if you're there." The boy's voice trembled a bit, making Kamal wonder just how badly he needed to go to the bathroom. He could just let him mess himself, and then he'd have a reason to punish him, but he'd have to deal with the cleanup, which was enough of a deterrent to get Kamal off the couch.

Touching the kid's chest briefly to let him know not to panic, he then removed all but the blindfold from the boy's head. Zijad whimpered, but let Kamal get him out of the cuffs and to his feet. The kid turned instinctively toward where the bucket had been sitting, but Kamal redirected him to the bathroom. The boy walked placidly along behind Kamal as he used one arm to guide him across the cabin. Kamal put him on the toilet where he sat with his hands on his thighs. Kamal waited as the boy urinated and then startled when the sound of the wind he passed was magnified by the porcelain bowl.

"*Oprosti*," Zijad said as his cheeks beneath the blindfold turned pink.

Kamal almost laughed, but held back. "Really, Mali, after all we've been through, you're embarrassed by me hearing you fart?" He enjoyed watching the kid turn even redder at his words, there was a resurgence of the erection in his shorts. He took the few small steps needed to cross the distance between where he was leaning on the door jamb and where the kid was still seated on the toilet. He grabbed the boy's hair, making him flinch back.

"I'm sorry." Zijad's hands remained on his legs and he made no move to fight back against Kamal's hold. Kamal watched his full lips tremble for a moment as he held the boy still.

"What are you sorry for, Mali?" Using his other hand, he ran a rough fingertip over the boy's bottom lip. Zijad's lips parted and his warm moist breath washed over Kamal's hand when the kid sighed. Before Kamal could even think about forcing anything on him, Zijad tentatively touched the tip of his tongue to Kamal's finger as if asking for permission. When Kamal didn't reprimand him for it, the kid went a step further and sucked the tip into his mouth even as he let out a little sob.

Kamal let him suck the finger for a minute before he offered another. The boy's soft groan as he accepted the second digit filled Kamal with wonder. His cock bobbed, unhindered by underwear in his loose shorts as he stepped just a bit closer so the tip of the cloth-covered appendage could settle in right under the kid's jaw. Kamal smiled at the position, it was much like holding a loaded gun on the boy. Oh, it's loaded, Kamal thought as he stifled a groan of his own, loaded and almost ready to go off, though the payload wouldn't hurt nearly as much as a bullet.

"Mali." Kamal fisted the hair in his hand a little harder to get the kid's attention. The boy's tongue and lips stopped working Kamal's fingers as he silently waited for what came next. To Kamal's surprise and delight the kid moved his jaw in what looked like a deliberate attempt to rub against Kamal, the slight stubble poking at the head of Kamal's cock through the nylon of his shorts. Kamal pulled on his fingers and Zijad quickly released them. The elastic waistband was easy to maneuver with one hand, Kamal hooked his thumb in it and eased it over the raging hardness within, flicking the shorts to the side when they pooled at his feet. Smooth, sensitive skin brushed against rough bristle making both Kamal and the kid gasp.

Kamal knew it was risky, sticking his dick in the boy's mouth with all those sharp teeth and nothing to stop them from biting down, but he was going to take that risk because he needed to take the boy more than anything at that moment. He moved back enough so the tip of his dick rubbed the kid's lips instead of the underside of his jaw, and waited.

"*Šef?*" Zijad questioned in a tremulous voice. His lips caressed the head of Kamal's cock with their movement, only making Kamal all the more eager to have them wrapped around his dick.

"Open up, Mali, and thank me for letting you use the facilities like a normal human being."

Zijad licked his lips and in doing so caught the small bead of precome glistening in the slit of Kamal's cock. The sight sent a shiver of lust up Kamal's spine, but he held his ground, waiting for the boy to willingly take him in. He didn't have to wait long. The kid engulfed half the engorged length in one go, only pulling back when he started to gag, but Kamal's hold on his hair stopped the retreat. Kamal waited; if the boy thought to take some modicum of revenge on him with his sharp teeth it would be the time for it. The kid only struggled a bit but didn't clamp down on the vulnerable flesh in his mouth as he took frantic breaths through his nose, making his distress apparent.

Kamal let go and smoothed the sweaty hair off the kid's brow before cupping the back of his neck. Zijad seemed to like the gesture and relaxed his jaw enough that Kamal could easily fuck in and out without fear of getting scraped and he did just that. He kept his thrusts shallow at first, letting the kid's saliva build up to ease his way. He didn't have to use any force to hold the boy who actually used his tongue to aid the slicking of Kamal's cock.

Kamal couldn't tear his eyes away from those lips, he was in a trance and only the kid's hands wrapping around his thighs brought him out of it. "Hands on your legs, now," Kamal growled as he pushed his cock in deeper making the kid gag. He couldn't believe he'd gotten so caught up in his own pleasure that he'd forgotten to watch the boy's hands. He should have handcuffed the kid but then the hands left his body and returned to the boy's slim thighs, drawing Kamal's attention to Zijad's own erection, and he had a better idea.

"Jerk yourself off," Kamal commanded. The kid made a pitiful sound around Kamal's cock and made no move to do as ordered. "Do it now." Zijad's trembling hand went to his own hard member but he just gripped it tightly. Kamal plunged into the kid's mouth until his cock head was buried in the tight heat that reflexively squeezed in an attempt to expel the obstruction so the boy could breathe. "I'm not going to move until your hand does," Kamal threatened. The kid's hand started pumping rapidly and Kamal shifted back so the boy could heave in a breath before going right back in.

"That's good, Mali, I want you to stay hard to show me how grateful you are." Kamal's eyes bounced back and forth from the lips stretched around his cock to the hand moving steadily up and down the kid's. He took his time fucking the boy's mouth, enjoying the little sounds issuing from the kid's stuffed throat. Kamal reached down and cruelly twisted one of the boy's tiny pink nipples. The pained noise the kid made traveled from Kamal's cock to his balls like a fuse to a bomb. Kamal jerked the kid's head, making him take the entirety of his cock until his nose was nestled in Kamal's pubic hair and the boy struggled against being smothered.

Kamal wasn't prepared for the wet warmth when it hit first his thighs and then dribbled on his bare feet. His first thought was that the boy had pissed on him and his anger surfaced, making his hips jerk back so he could spear the kid over and over with thrusts that would probably have broken the boy's neck had Kamal not had it held in his steely grip. He rushed to climax through the kid's stifled cries, dumping what felt like an enormous amount of come down the boy's throat. He was buried so deep in the kid that Zijad didn't even have to swallow to keep from drowning in it.

Kamal pulled roughly out of the boy's mouth and raised his hand to strike the kid for his accident but before he could land the blow he realized it wasn't urine running down his leg, it was come. The kid had hunched over on himself and was rocking as he keened quietly. Kamal wished he could take the blindfold off so he could see the tears streak down the boy's flushed cheeks and the beauty of the pain and humiliation in his expressive blue eyes. His hand reached out as if it had a mind of its own but stopped short as the kid spoke.

"I'm sorry, *Šef*, please, I didn't mean to," Zijad sobbed, reminding Kamal he'd ordered the kid to stay hard. He was sure there was no way the boy could have remained so after coming which meant Kamal had to think fast because a punishment was in order and, for some reason, smacking the kid didn't seem like the appropriate choice.

"You keep saying you're sorry, Mali, but this time you must tell me what you're sorry for." Looking down at the back of the kid's head, Kamal tried to compose himself back into something other than a lust-riddled fool.

Zijad sniffled and took a shaky breath. "I'm sorry because..." The boy stopped as his breath hitched; instead of continuing, he sniveled until Kamal grabbed his hair and pulled him up from his cowering position. The kid's flaccid penis laid limply in the shallow valley of his tightly squeezed thighs.

"You're not very good at following directions I see," Kamal said before flicking the damp head of the boy's dick.

"I'm sorry that I came!" Zijad raised his voice in his hurry to apologize for not obeying, then covered his mouth with his hand when he realized he'd practically shouted.

The kid's response amused Kamal, and replaced the anger he'd felt when the kid failed to follow a simple instruction. He pulled the boy off the toilet by his hair, making him squeal and put his arms out to stop himself as if he thought Kamal was going to throw him to the floor. Kamal made sure the kid landed firmly on his knees at his feet. Looking down at the boy brought a malicious smile to Kamal's face. He liked the way the kid looked in that position, but the boy wasn't going to like what was coming. Kamal pressed the kid's face closer so his lips hovered over the little rivulet of come that was rapidly drying on his leg.

"Clean up your mess," he ordered. The boy lifted his hand and blindly groped for Kamal who knocked the hand away. "With your tongue." Zijad stuck out his tongue and jerked back when it met Kamal's skin, as if surprised to find himself so close to the other man. Kamal held him steady until he dared to dart his little pink tongue out once again and then guided him to the areas where his own come was matted in Kamal's leg hair. The kid worked diligently until even Kamal's feet were cleaned with his spit. Satisfied, Kamal got the kid back onto his knees.

C.L. Mustafic

"Good job, Mali. Maybe you're not as worthless as I thought." Kamal praised the boy at his feet and Zijad's shoulders relaxed. "But you still need to be punished." The kid groaned. "No complaints unless you want to wear the gag." The boy's shoulders shook as he silently sobbed but no sound escaped from his lips. Kamal was starting to realize the kid was surprisingly easy to handle, he hadn't even needed to restrain him. Most victims would have fought if given the chances he'd given the boy, while Zijad had only meekly obeyed. It was something Kamal would think about when he had the time.

Retrieving his shorts, Kamal pulled them on before he picked the kid up by putting his hands under his armpits. The boy wobbled when Kamal set him on his feet but steadied quickly. He walked as if Kamal was leading him to the gallows, but again Kamal noted Zijad's docile acceptance as he buckled the manacles around the kid's slim wrists. He left enough play in them that he could turn the kid around on his knees, bent at the waist with his hands and forehead pressed against the wall. Zijad made his first noise of protest when he realized how Kamal had positioned him, his ass presented to his captor's eyes.

"Shh, Mali, you'll take your punishment silently like a man or I'll have to get that gag you like so much." Kamal patted the kid's ass before he got up and went to the trunk to retrieve one of the toys and a bottle of lube he'd grudgingly put away when he'd been following Julien's plan. He returned to the boy's side and without any preparation other than the slicking of the slim vibrator with plenty of lube, he spread the kid's cheeks and inserted it until the base rested against the boy's ass. Zijad grunted at the sudden violation, but didn't struggle against it.

Kamal flipped him over and turned the toy on. Zijad moaned and squirmed against the sensation. Kamal leaned over the boy, letting his breath tickle his neck as he whispered in his ear. "Since you like to come so much, let's see how many times you can manage it before lunch," he said, relishing the thought of pushing the kid through orgasm after orgasm, until pleasure turned to pain.

Chapter 12:
Rewards and Realizations

Day 17, Day 12 in Captivity

The kid lay on the mattress, wailing as another orgasm ripped through his body. It was his third where no fluid was released. Figuring the boy had learned his lesson, Kamal hit the button and stopped the vibrator from its assault on the kid's overly stimulated prostate. He set the plate he'd been putting food onto on a tray and added a bottle of juice for the boy and a beer for himself, then on second thought added a second beer. The kid would probably need a few minutes to compose himself enough to eat – Kamal would kill the time with a beer and a smoke. He put the tray on the coffee table before he sat on the floor next the boy.

Kamal's eyes roved over the kid's body, the flushed, sweaty skin radiated heat even in the warmth of the cabin. The boy had calmed to a quiet weeping that left the visible part of his face twisted into an unmistakable mask of pain. His stomach and thighs were glistening with more than sweat, his first couple of orgasms had produced enough come to leave evidence of them behind. Kamal studied the filmy white substance with a discerning eye, trying to decide on how it would be put to its best use.

He rubbed the boy's sweaty, heaving chest and Zijad sobbed, but still pressed into the touch. "P-please!" The plaintive plea would have tugged at anyone's heart.

"Shh, Mali, it's over now and you're okay," Kamal said while he kept rubbing the overheated skin under his palm to further calm the kid.

"Please, *Šef*, it hurts."

"What hurts, tell me and I'll fix it for you." Kamal wondered what hurt the boy the most, his abused ass or his balls that had been drained dry.

"My..." Zijad's sob cut him off but Kamal waited to hear what he'd say – if he'd say it. "Please take it out?" the boy finally asked, telling Kamal in his own roundabout way that his ass hurt.

As Kamal rolled the kid onto his side, Zijad twisted his arms – still bound by the chains – to allow the move to go more smoothly. Kamal couldn't help but stare at the boy's ass filled with the flesh-colored toy. Using one hand to spread the pale cheeks of the kid's toned rear end, he grasped the base of the vibrator with his other. Zijad groaned as Kamal jiggled the hard plastic device before he pulled it out quickly. The removal of the toy made a squelching noise, a sound that made Kamal think the boy's ass was protesting its sudden emptiness, and the image of his own hard member filling it again made him shudder. Kamal's cock was hard once again, but this time, as he stared at the swollen, shiny ring of the kid's stretched entrance, he just knew the boy's mouth wouldn't be enough.

"Thank you, *Šef*, thank you, thank you, thank you." Zijad chanted as he made to roll onto his back, but Kamal stopped him by placing a hand on his bony hip.

"Stay still, Mali," Kamal said softly. As if the boy had read what Kamal was thinking in those three small words, he stilled, even his breathing had halted as though he thought the predator wouldn't see him if he didn't make a move. Kamal lifted his own ass and pulled his shorts off. Once his erection was freed, he lay down behind the boy, positioning his body to cradle the smaller frame that tried to draw itself into a ball.

"You did so good, you took your punishment very well," Kamal murmured against the kid's hair. "I think you deserve a reward." Zijad whimpered, but his actions didn't match the sound, he pushed back against Kamal, gasping when he felt the hardness of Kamal's cock positioned perfectly at his entrance.

"No, please, not that," Zijad begged, but his struggle to move away only ended in him being suddenly impaled by the head of Kamal's dick. The boy let out a high-pitched shriek at the sudden penetration.

Kamal gasped as the tight heat engulfed his cock. Still stretched and slick from the toy, it seemed to suck at him, pulling him into that wonderfully convulsing tunnel as the kid struggled against it. Kamal held the boy's hips tightly as he pushed in until he couldn't go any further and then took a moment to revel in the sensation of being buried so deeply in his captive's tight body. Kamal let his hand wander over the boy's skin, up and down his side, over his flat hard abdomen and finally settling on his flaccid member. Zijad blubbered as Kamal handled his cock and then squeezed his recently drained balls in his big rough hand.

"Quiet, Mali, I won't hurt you. This is a reward, you should appreciate it as such." Kamal let go of the boy's tender bits and continued to explore his lithe body as he started slowly moving his cock in and out of the kid's tender ass, careful not to angle for his abused prostate which was likely to cause him extreme pain after the over-stimulation. The boy in his arms cried softly as Kamal took ownership of his body in steady, deep strokes.

Kamal's mind played tricks on him as he stared at the back of the blond head and held a body that was completely foreign to him yet so familiar in its shape and size. He closed his eyes to shut out the memories but that only made them clearer…

Kamal held Orhan in a tight embrace as the man he loved sobbed. "You have to go, I understand," Kamal reassured him as he plunged his cock deeply into Orhan, letting him feel his frustration over their situation.

"I want to stay, but I'm afraid I will never see him again if I don't go," Orhan cried. The tears were running off the side of his face and dripping onto the arm Kamal had under his head to pillow it.

The population of the village was slowly dwindling as the able-bodied trekked through the mountains to the relative safety of Tuzla where the international peace forces had declared a safe zone. Groups left on a daily basis, some people made it, many didn't as the bands of refugees were attacked by the opposing forces with no regard to the women and children among them. Kamal had volunteered to stay behind and guard the people who couldn't leave, the elderly or those, like his own mother, who were too fragile to make the journey.

"I know you do, but I also know that we'll be together again. I have faith in us, it's the only thing I believe in anymore," Kamal said. Orhan turned his head to face his lover. The crying had left his nose reddened and his blue eyes shiny as he lifted his head for a kiss which Kamal gave him, putting his whole heart into it.

The rattling of chains jolted Kamal out of his memory, but as he opened his eyes it seemed that reality had shifted on him because he was sure he was still kissing Orhan just as he'd done all those years ago. A low groan issued from his chest as he plundered the soft lips crushed beneath his. The motion of his tongue mirrored that of his cock as he drilled into the inviting body crushed to his chest. Kamal felt his orgasm blossoming outward like the ripples around a rock thrown in water. As he found his release in the tight channel around him, the greatest pleasure centered over his groin, but the sweet waves radiated out to fill his whole body. He felt like he was floating, until his mouth went slack and his partner started to cry out in protest against his lips. Anger flooded Kamal with the realization that he'd been kissing the kid like he was some sort of lover instead of what he was – his captive, his job, a toy to be used as he saw fit to fill the time.

Pushing the boy roughly away from him, not wanting to feel the warmth of his body any longer, Kamal rolled and got to his knees. The kid pulled his legs to his chest and tried to hide his head behind his stretched arm. He sobbed, but then Kamal caught a hiccupped word that stopped him cold. He yanked the boy back toward him.

"What did you say?" he demanded.

"*Hvala, S-S-Šef, hvala*," Zijad answered quickly, but he flinched back as though he expected to be hit. Kamal was too stunned to hit the boy. Why would Zijad thank him?

"What for?"

The kid's lips twisted into a frown and he thought for a few moments before he answered. "For my reward."

It was the first – and probably the last – time Kamal had ever been thanked for raping someone and it made him feel... he wasn't

106

sure what the feeling was, but he found he liked it. "You're welcome, Mali." His anger forgotten, he caressed the kid's face, delighting in how the boy pressed close for more. "You need a shower and then we'll eat," he said as he got up to unfasten the kid's wrists.

Day 18, Day 13 in Captivity

Kamal was relieved it was the last time he'd have to perform in front of the camera with the kid. He'd taken his time with the set-up for this shoot, following Julien's painfully detailed plan to the letter. After he'd knocked the boy out with a doctored bottle of juice, he'd dressed him in the strange clothing he'd found in the trunk. He questioned why there was a need for the leather leggings – a complete and utter bitch to get on someone who was as limp as a ragdoll – that left both the kid's ass and crotch area exposed. Naked would have done just as well. He put the complicated leather harness on the boy's torso, then completed his task of attaching and inserting the toys to complete the ensemble. After replacing the cuffs on the kid's wrists, he sat down to wait.

Kamal's head cocked to the side when the boy's moans made him aware that Zijad was coming around. Kamal quickly pressed the record button on the camera and used the rope and pulley system to hoist the kid to his feet. Pulling the leather mask over his own head, he made sure everything was in place on his person before the kid could wake fully.

Zijad groaned and his head slowly lifted to take in his surroundings. Kamal delighted in the way his bound captive's eyes changed to a deeper shade of blue, filmed over with the sheen of unshed tears, and his face became a perfect mask of terror when he was finally able to comprehend his predicament. He was totally helpless, chained as he was to the ceiling, arms stretched above his head until the point of pain, legs spread and held apart by a bar buckled between his ankles. He couldn't even express his fright vocally since the gag was in his mouth complete with the small penis-shaped plug. The boy could only moan and make high-pitched noises to let Kamal know he wasn't enjoying the new game.

"About time you joined me. I was getting lonely waiting for you to come around," Kamal said through the voice modulator. Zijad's eyes widened and he shook his head. "Oh, you're not happy to see me?" Kamal chuckled, a sound made even more chilling when filtered through the little machine clipped to his shirt.

Kamal started the vibrator in the kid's ass, making the boy jolt and try to stand on his tiptoes as if he could move away from the sensation. When that didn't work he tried to move his hips forward, but that was when Kamal employed one of the other hidden treasures he'd found within the trunk. The small vibrator that was attached around the base of Zijad's penis, nestled snug between his flaccid length and the top of his ball sac, came to life making the boy voice a series of garbled noises. The toys did their job, though, as the kid's member thickened and started to stand out from his body.

"Oh, you are happy to see me, after all," Kamal said as he walked to the boy and gripped his cock to give it a couple of hard yanks. The boy whimpered, but his hips bucked into the touch as if he wanted more. "Such a *drolja.*" Kamal shook his head as he let go of the kid's dick. Walking behind the boy, he retrieved the stiff riding crop and smacked it against his palm as if to test its mettle, but his sharp eyes didn't miss the way the kid flinched at the sound.

Kamal stood behind the boy and reached around to pull the plug out of the gag before leaning close to whisper in the kid's ear. "Let's see if your cock stays hard through this, Mali."

Zijad's head snapped around and his eyes flew open wide as he tried to articulate something through the gag. "Oooo, esh oooo eeef ease oh." Zijad's garbled speech meant nothing to him, but he wondered what the boy was trying to say as he stared at Kamal with eyes that seemed to shine with a new light of understanding even through his tears.

Kamal took a step back and the kid tried to turn to follow him, but grabbing a handful of his hair, he turned the boy back to face the camera. "You don't want Daddy to miss how pretty you look when you cry, do you?" Kamal asked. It was then that it hit him. The deeper voice from the box reminded him that when he'd whispered in Zijad's ear, there had been no distortion. The boy's wide-eyed look and attempt to talk made sense now. The kid knew it was him, that he was the same man who had fucked him almost tenderly only the day before. The jig, as they say, was up. There was nothing Kamal could do about it right at that moment, he had to carry on.

Kamal raised the crop and, only using a small amount of strength, he let it fall right across the boy's pale backside. The kid squealed. "It didn't hurt that much, don't be a baby," Kamal chided the boy as he let another harder stroke land a bit lower than the first. Once again the boy cried out. "Do you want me to plug your hole again?" Even though the sounds were actually something Kamal enjoyed, he knew the boy trying to stifle his cries would be even better since there was no way he'd manage it.

Zijad moaned and shook his head as Kamal let another and then another blow land on his ass. The skin was turning pink and the sight made Kamal's chest tighten; the only word that came to mind was *beautiful*. Kamal started letting the crop fall on the kid's upper thighs too and soon he was lost in the rhythm of it. The boys sobbing was a nice accompaniment to the sounds of the small leather pad hitting soft flesh. When finally Kamal's arm started to feel the strain of swinging the crop, he stopped to assess the damage he'd wrought to the previously unmarred skin. The kid's ass was striped with bright red slashes that bled into one another and stood out prettily against the light tan skin of his lower back. Kamal took a deep breath as he reverently ran a hand over the heated flesh, making the boy whimper.

"That should do nicely," Kamal said. Letting the crop fall to the floor, he reached up to undo the gag before he removed it from the kid's mouth, letting it too drop to the ground. He rounded the boy and noticed even though the little vibrator was still going, the kid's cock was only at half-mast. "Oh, you didn't enjoy that as much as I thought you would." He took the boy's cock in his hand and stroked it gently until it plumped back up. "But I don't think you hated it as much as *you* thought you would either."

"Please, *Šef*," Zijad pleaded, using his usual moniker for Kamal as if he wanted to let him know that he knew.

"Please what, *sine*?" Watching the kid's blue eyes search his masked face as if he could see beyond the leather, Kamal kept stroking the boy's cock as he waited for his answer.

"Please, d-d-don't hurt m-m-me, *Šef*." Zijad finally choked out as he lowered his eyes.

"I still can't hear you, boy. It seems as if you like this so much you don't want it to end." Kamal shoved another finger in to join the two already rooting around in the boy's slick tunnel. Zijad could no longer control his movements and he swayed with the rough thrusts of Kamal's hand. It seemed to take him a few minutes to remember he'd been told to do something, so Kamal prodded him by trying to add a fourth finger into the mix.

"Please, *Šef*, fuck my ass with your cock!" he screamed.

Kamal smiled as he pulled his fingers out of the boy's ass. "Since you asked so nicely." Kamal turned the kid to the side so the camera would capture the big moment. Pulling the zipper on his leather pants, he slowly freed his cock which was eager for what was on offer. He lined himself up and didn't hesitate to bury his dick fully in the boy's ass. The sound that came from the kid combined with the feeling of possessing him so completely went right to Kamal's head, he felt so powerful in that moment he didn't want it to end.

He didn't give the boy any consideration as he drove into him. It was the way Kamal preferred to do his fucking, but was hard to find a willing partner so he was going to take what he could while he could get it. Zijad cried out over and over as Kamal slammed into him, his hips bruising the already sensitive flesh of the boy's ass and adding another layer to the pain. Kamal had to remind himself what the goal of the whole production was before he lost it inside the kid. Regaining control over his errant hips, he slowed his thrusts and grabbed the leather harness to pull the boy up against his chest while he turned to face the camera.

"You're going to come for me now," he whispered into the boy's ear, letting him hear his normal voice.

Zijad allowed his body to rest against Kamal, making it easier for him to hook the boy's cuffed wrists back over his neck, leaving Zijad completely exposed to the lens. He popped the snap on the vibrator around the kid's cock and let it drop before taking him in hand. The flesh was hard and smooth in his hand as he worked the boy in time with his own well-aimed thrusts. Zijad moaned, this time it was unmistakably one of pleasure. He ground back against Kamal and then forward into his fist, making Kamal take what was offered with renewed zest. When he felt his climax approaching, he sped up his pumping fist.

"Come, Mali, come for me now," he urged the boy in his arms.

The warmth over his fist surprised him at first but then his own orgasm hit him hard. His vision blurred around the edges as he came inside the clamping heat of the boy's ass. As he stroked Zijad's softening member, the kid's soft mewling sounds made Kamal shudder at the thoughts they provoked. He could get used to having the boy soft and malleable like this, and that was not something Kamal was prepared to even think about.

Chapter 13:
Misdirected Anger

The boy lay quietly in the tub as Kamal used a soft cloth to clean him. His ass was tender and it had been a struggle to get him in the bath, he'd only sat after Kamal had put a towel down for a cushion. Now it was a whole different story as the kid was relaxed and almost purring under Kamal's tender touches. Kamal on the other hand was on edge as he waited for the boy to ask the inevitable question of why? Why would he pretend to be two different people? What had he hoped to gain from his little ruse? Kamal wondered how things would change now that the kid knew. Would he fight Kamal even when there was nothing to fear from him? He was sure that had to be the case, but for the moment the kid seemed to be content to just lie there and let Kamal wash him.

"You have to lean forward now, Mali," Kamal said when he was finished with the boy's body. He reached for the shower head as the kid obeyed without question, starting the water and letting it warm before he wet the boy's hair. Zijad moaned as Kamal shampooed the blond locks and a small smile touched Kamal's lips. It probably felt nice being it was only the second time he'd attended the boy with such care, his poor scalp probably itched from the buildup of sweat. The smile faltered when Kamal noticed the blindfold had started to mat into the back of the kid's hair. He pulled at it, making the boy whimper which was a sound Kamal had to admit fit him much better than the moan had.

113

"I need to take this off for a moment, it's tangled in your hair." Kamal tried to work out the hair knots around the band. The kid turned his face toward Kamal and opened his mouth but Kamal cut him off. "Close your eyes and keep your head down," he commanded. He waited to see if he'd have to use the hair still in his soapy hands to make the boy obey, but Zijad quickly did as he was told.

Kamal pulled the blindfold off the kid's face so he'd have more play in the band as he worked to free it. His eyes darted between his work and the boy's face, nerves making him work hastily; it would only take one glimpse of his face for the kid to be able to give them a description that could lead to Kamal's downfall. It was risky and Kamal's hands stilled just as the mask came free. What the hell was he doing? He roughly pushed the blindfold back down and grabbed the shower head to finish his task.

The boy sputtered and struggled when the deluge of sudsy water took him off-guard, but Kamal held him still as he rinsed out the soap. After that was done he yanked the kid to his feet, toweled him off, and marched him back to his corner. The anger Kamal felt at himself bled into his actions toward the boy – a fitting target since he was the true source of the feeling. Kamal swatted the purpling flesh of the kid's ass when he tried to protest against sitting on his mattress, making the boy cry out which only inflamed Kamal more.

"Fine, you don't want to be comfortable? I have a solution for that," Kamal growled. He took the kid to the bench and forced him to his knees.

"Please, Šef, I'm sorry. I'm so sorry, I'll sit, I promise, I'll be good. Please!"

"You had your chance," Kamal snarled as he buckled the cuffs around Zijad's wrists and then his waist. He put the full hood over the kid's head hoping it would shut him up, but the boy only sobbed louder. Kamal left him to lament his fate as he cleaned up the mess of discarded tools he'd used for the video.

When everything in the small cabin was once again in its place, he removed the card from the camera and turned on Julien's PC. He downloaded the video and watched it to make sure he hadn't done anything to give himself away in the moments where he'd lost himself. After he was certain there was no way he could be identified he started uploading the video and the one he'd recorded previously to his contact per the contract arrangement. This time instead of erasing the card, he left it intact and secreted it away in his computer bag.

Out on the porch, he had a beer and a couple of smokes before going back in to put the boy to bed. The moment he released the kid from the belts holding him, Zijad turned on Kamal so fast Kamal almost punched him, but when the boy's hands went to the waistband of his shorts, he pulled his fist up short. The kid had an uncanny way of knowing just where things were in relation to his body, he held the material in his trembling hands before leaning his head forward against Kamal. Staring down in fascination as the boy nuzzled his hooded face against his groin, the sudden need to feel the kid's skin against him made him reach down and pull the hood off.

"I'm sorry, *Šef.*" Zijad tilted his head up and Kamal could only imagine the pleading look in the boy's blue eyes still hidden behind the blindfold.

"Go ahead, Mali, show me," Kamal encouraged.

Zijad gently pulled the shorts down, exposing Kamal's groin before pressing back in, this time taking the whole of Kamal's semi-hard cock into his mouth. Kamal sighed and let his hand rest on the top of the boy's head as he was suckled to hardness. He let the kid clutch at his hips as he drove Kamal toward his orgasm. Zijad pulled off after he'd swallowed all that Kamal had given him and leaned his forehead against Kamal's hip.

"What do you say, Mali?"

"Thank you, *Šef,*" he mumbled quietly.

Kamal ran his hand through the boy's sweaty hair, slightly amused by the kid's actions after he'd been punished. "Good boy, I bet you're tired, let's get you to bed. Stay," he commanded before stepping out of the kid's grasp. Retrieving the handcuffs, he returned to the boy to cuff his wrists and when Zijad made to stand he pushed him back to his knees. "No, on your knees, it's not far to your cushion." He pulled on the short chain and Zijad immediately obeyed by shuffling along on his knees to his mattress. He compliantly sat down with only a hiss to relay his discomfort. Kamal laid him flat and hooked him up.

The boy rolled onto his side and sighed. "Goodnight, *Šef.*"

Kamal grunted, but left the boy to sleep without the hood for this one night.

Day 19, Day 14 in Captivity

Kamal's hand pushed the kid's head down in his lap, making the boy take more of his cock into his throat. The kid relaxed and let him fuck up into his willing mouth until he felt his release rising and then spilling over into the boy who swallowed around him. Zijad licked his softening shaft until Kamal stopped him when it was a little too much. He let the blond head go and the kid straightened his back so he was kneeling rim rod straight at Kamal's feet.

"Now, thank me for letting you make it up to me."

The boy bowed his head as if in shame over his refusal to eat the meal Kamal had fixed for him. "Thank you, *Šef*, for letting me make it up to you," he repeated, giving Kamal's words back to him.

"You're welcome, Mali, you did good." Kamal petted the boy's cheek just to see the reaction it caused. As always he leaned into the touch, but the small uptick of his lips surprised Kamal, it was the first time he'd seen the kid almost smile.

Kamal's phone made a noise alerting him to an incoming message. The boy's head turned toward the sound, but Kamal stopped the movement and brought his attention back to him. "Give me your hands." The kid lifted his unbound hands in front of him and made no move to struggle against the cuffs Kamal placed around them. He made the boy shuffle on his knees across the rug to his mattress where the kid sat on his still tender ass and raised his shackled hands for Kamal to hook them in place.

"Be good and I'll leave the hood off."

"Yes, *Šef*, thank you, *Šef*," the boy said as he nodded enthusiastically.

Getting up, Kamal grabbed his phone before settling back on the couch. *You might want to check out the headlines*, the message said from Demetri. Kamal had a bad feeling in the pit of his stomach, there was no way it could be good news.

He set up the computer on the table in front of him, leg bouncing with nervous energy as he waited for it to connect to the internet.

After punching in the keys to pull up the newspaper's website, it was another agonizing wait until the site popped up on the screen. Kamal had to bite his tongue to stop the stream of expletives perched on its tip. He couldn't believe what he was reading, but he finished the article anyway.

Orhan Ferhatović Declared the Presidential Nominee for the SDP, read the main headline. The article went on to say how even in his grief over his missing son, he had to accept the nomination on behalf of the party because it was what the people wanted.

Kamal slammed the laptop shut. *"Jebi ga!"* he shouted, making the kid yip in fright. He ignored the boy and grabbed his phone and cigarettes before stomping out the door. He so badly wanted to hit something, but instead he found the unknown number in his call log and dialed it. He was going to rip Orhan a new one, there was no way he was going to get his son back in one piece with this latest stunt.

The phone rang once and then went to the prerecorded message telling Kamal the number he'd dialed was no longer in service. He crushed the phone in his fist and rounded on the cabin. The pain went all the way to his shoulder when his fist connected with the side of the small house. Of course Orhan would have used a disposable number to call him. What had he expected?

"Jebem ti mater. Jebat ću ti oca, svog psa i tvog boga!" Kamal screamed into the silent night.

With nowhere else to direct his anger, he entered the cabin in a huff. The boy was whimpering on the mattress and those soft sounds just drove Kamal over the edge. He opened the trunk and grabbed a few things before making his way to where the kid lay mewling. With no soothing touches, Kamal grabbed the boy's legs and secured them to the spreader bar he'd placed between the boy's knees.

"Please, *Šef*, what did I do?" Zijad cried out as Kamal hooked the metal ring around his neck. The ring supported the arm bar and left the kid looking like he was locked in stocks from the medieval times. "Please, no, please, please…"

Kamal ignored the repeated pleas from the boy as he locked in his arms and then shoved the kid's upper body down on the mattress. Grabbing the boy's slim hips, he pulled him to his knees; his captive was totally helpless before him. Kamal had the presence of mind to at least slick his throbbing cock with lube before he drove it savagely into the kid's ass. Zijad screamed as he was speared over and over.

Kamal closed his eyes and pretended the body beneath him was not the boy but his father. He wanted to kill Orhan, but the man was out of his reach. Maybe if he fucked his son hard enough the father would feel it through some parental bond – wishful thinking he knew, but it didn't keep him from brutalizing the poor boy with that thought in mind.

Kamal let loose and spilled into the kid. "Orhan, you bastard," he muttered as he slumped over the boy's body, completely spent.

"Please, Šef, I can't breathe," Zijad hiccupped out through his sobs.

Kamal rolled off the boy and lay on his side on the thin mattress. He didn't feel any better for having taken his anger out on the kid, he didn't feel any worse either. He wanted to sleep, but no matter how much he wanted to punish someone, the metal around the boy's neck wouldn't do for an entire night. Flicking the latches on the wrists and then the neck ring, he pulled it off and tossed it to the side before slumping back on the bed next to the kid.

Zijad curled himself into a ball next to the wall and wept for all he was worth. Kamal touched the boy's back, but quickly pulled his hand away when the boy shrieked at the contact. He'd broken the kid, and for that he was sorry enough to fight the kid's weak protests against further handling to remove the bar between his knees too. Kamal knew it left him completely capable of trying to escape but he was a light sleeper and with his big body blocking the boy's exit, he was fairly confident in his decision. The kid's pained sobs accompanied Kamal into sleep like a sad lullaby.

The sound of suffering was all around him as he and Meho carried the last of the villagers into the shelled-out factory where they were instructed to gather. The peace accord had been signed and their little enclave was being emptied out by the opposing forces. The foreign peacekeepers ignored the pleas for water and help as they stood silent guard over the operation. It was stifling hot in the July heat and there were thousands of people crowded together. Some of them had been kept inside the building for a full day and a half and were showing signs of heat exhaustion.

"Women, children, and elderly in this building. Men are to report to the east building for their bussing assignments." The announcement was made by one of the Četniks that were walking through the crowd, separating men from their families and pushing them toward the door that would lead to a short path and then into another building.

Kamal watched as some of the mothers fought for their teenage sons to stay with them, but in the end it was futile, the young men were dragged away, crying like the children they were. Meho grabbed Kamal's arm and he stopped to listen. There was screaming coming from somewhere in the back of the building that could only be heard if he blocked out the wailing around him. The screams were blood-curdling in their terror. Meho threaded his way through the crowd, crouching down to avoid being spotted by the men charged with culling the herd. Kamal followed in his steps.

He wasn't prepared for what he saw and knew the images of that day would forever haunt him. It wasn't the women being repeatedly raped that bothered him; it did, but it wasn't something he hadn't seen before; it was the pregnant woman screaming as her baby slid out onto the floor in a gush of bloody fluid that made him gag. If that wasn't bad enough, one of the Četniks standing over her stepped on the newborn infant's head, producing a sound Kamal immediately wished he could forget. If there had been anything in his stomach, he was sure he'd have thrown up.

"Let's go," Kamal whispered as he tugged on Meho's arm. The other man's sickened look of horror mirrored that of Kamal's as he nodded.

The two men snuck around to a busted-out window that wasn't being guarded. They climbed up and through it. The fenced-in yard in the back of the factory wasn't being watched as closely as the front, there were no peacekeepers watching, and Kamal crouched down in one of the small recesses on the exterior of the building. Meho squished himself in beside him and they waited.

Kamal was trying to form a plan to get them out and away from what he was increasingly sure was going to be a very bad situation. As if his worried thoughts brought it about, a door opened in the east building and a group of men armed with machine guns walked out. They started walking and then a line of men followed them out. They were obviously Bosniaks, Kamal could tell by the rags they wore and the way their emaciated bodies swayed as they limped along behind the armed men. The line went through a gate in the fence and out into the field behind the factory. They disappeared from sight shortly after they left the factory grounds.

"Where are they going?" he asked Meho. There was no way the busses were parked back where they were being led.

"I don't know," Meho said as the first shots rang out in the distance. There were more and they had come from the direction in which the men had been taken.

Kamal started shaking uncontrollably, but told himself that what he thought had just happened couldn't be. They couldn't do that with the peacekeepers watching, it was impossible! The soldiers came back alone and entered the building. Kamal tried to keep track of time in his mind but he wasn't sure how long it took before another group was led out and away. He knew then he wouldn't go into that building. If he was going to die, it wouldn't be like a sheep led to slaughter. He would die fighting to survive.

"We'll wait until dark, then we'll leave," Kamal whispered to Meho.

"Where will we go?" Meho asked. "And what about our mothers?"

"I don't know, maybe back to the village," Kamal said, pausing to think of what they'd do about their elderly relatives still inside before coming to a decision. "I'm sure they'll leave the old people alone and if not, there's nothing we can do to save them." It was harsh but true, they were only two unarmed men, it would be suicide to attempt anything resembling a rescue. He didn't even have a plan to save himself and Meho, except to escape the fate he foresaw if they joined their brothers. He needed time to think and at least the village would provide them with shelter and time to make a plan.

The two men waited and watched as more and more men were taken away. When full dark finally fell, Kamal had counted over three thousand men being led out to die. They made their way from the factory easily since there were no lights outside the building. The village was about four kilometers away and the men jogged the entire way up the hillside, avoiding the main road and hiding whenever either of them heard a noise. They collapsed sweaty and out of breath in the first farmhouse they came to on the outskirts of the small town. After a few moments to catch their breath and find water, they barricaded themselves in one of the small rooms at the back of the house.

"What will we do, Kamal?" Meho asked as they lay side by side on a bare mattress.

"We'll wait and try to make our way through the forest when things calm down." The woods were a mine field, literally and figuratively. The way to safety had been blocked by troops who were rounding up stragglers so Kamal was in no hurry to try his luck. He hoped that soon the troops would grow bored when there were no more people to be found, then they would make their escape.

"I'm hungry. What will we eat?" Meho asked. They both knew there was little-to-no food to be found and Kamal wondered if Meho expected him to pull a hunk of lamb out of his ass like magic.

"We'll find something. Go to sleep," Kamal said irritably. It felt a little strange telling the older man what to do and for a moment Kamal wished he was alone instead of now apparently responsible for another. Meho rolled over and was soon sleeping. Kamal's mind wouldn't let him rest though. He was hungry too, and scared. Kamal was more afraid than he'd ever been and with the life he'd lived so far, that was saying something.

Chapter 14:
Waiting is the Hardest Part

Day 20, Day 15 in Captivity

Kamal rolled in his sleep, trapping the boy to the mattress with his arm and half his body, making the boy cry out and try to get free which woke him up. "Mali, calm down and be good," Kamal growled. The kid whimpered as Kamal tightened his arm around the boy's chest and his other snaked under his head to hold him in a restrictive embrace. "Be still, you're okay, you're safe, go back to sleep," he murmured, as sleep tried to pull him back under. The boy trembled a little but stilled before he burrowed his face into the crook of Kamal's elbow and soon he was relaxed and silent in his slumber. Kamal drifted off only to awaken a short time later with the kid wrapped around him. He sighed but let the boy take his comfort where he could get it, even if it was just in his dreams.

Kamal awoke like he normally did – one second he was asleep and the next he was fully aware. Only alcohol made him fuzzy upon waking and he'd been stone cold sober when he'd fallen asleep. The weight on his shoulder shifted a bit but Kamal gave no indication he was awake when a hand tentatively made its way across his chest. The slim fingers traced the road map of scars that told the tale of Kamal's life. He let the kid work his way down over his puckered skin, let him pet the soft hair trailing from his belly button to his groin, and even put up with the boy twirling his fingers through the mess of curly pubic hair without a word. The kid's knuckles brushed the underside of Kamal's morning hardness and he was certain it wasn't an accident when it happened a second and then third time.

"Šef, I know you're awake," Zijad whispered, like maybe he was mistaken and didn't dare wake Kamal if he was sleeping.

Kamal thought he detected a hint of amusement in the kid's voice. When he opened his eyes, he fully expected the boy to have pulled his blindfold off, but when he looked down at the back of the kid's head where it laid on his chest, the dark band securing the mask was still there. The boy shifted so Kamal could feel the warmth of his breath flowing across his nipple. The hand that had been tangling its fingers in his hair moved and cradled his balls before the kid ran his finger up the shaft to circle the crown.

"I could hear your breathing change and your heartbeat pick up," Zijad said with a little sigh that tickled Kamal's nipple to hardness.

Kamal remained silent in the face of the boy's observations, but his body's arousal grew at the kid's gentle exploration. The boy grew bolder and grasped Kamal's cock lightly in his hand, the caress was soft but firm enough it made Kamal want more. He covered the boy's hand with his own and squeezed, then pumped a couple of times so the kid would get the idea. Zijad pumped him with a strength that surprised Kamal when he released his own grip. Closing his eyes, he let the feeling take him over until he felt the kid's own hardness pressed into his hip.

"Don't you come on me, Mali. I'll need you hard for the punishment you'll get for touching without permission," Kamal warned, startling the boy into losing his rhythm and then stilling altogether. Kamal reached down and resumed the movement for him. "You didn't think you could get away with taking liberties with a sleeping man, did you?"

"No, Šef, I'm sorry," Zijad said breathily. He regained his timing with his hand, but his hips stopped grinding against Kamal in an effort to stave off his own release.

Kamal held out as long as he could, waiting to see if the boy would lose control, garnering even greater punishment for his disobedience. In the end he came over the kid's hand onto his own stomach; the kid let out a strained whimper as he bucked his hips in response, but he held on. Kamal was just about to command the boy to clean him when Zijad lifted his hand to his mouth and licked Kamal's come off it. He watched with hungry eyes as the kid's tongue lapped at his stomach and then dipped lower to clean his dick.

"You are a good little come bucket, Mali," Kamal praised the boy.

"Thank you, *Šef.*" Zijad ran his hands over Kamal's skin to make sure he hadn't missed anything.

Grabbing the boy's shoulders, Kamal pulled him up and stared for a moment at the full red lips, shiny with a mixture of his come and the kid's spit. He leaned forward and for the first time in a very long time, Kamal kissed someone because he wanted to, only wanting to taste himself inside the kid. He pressed his tongue against the boy's lips until he finally gave way and let Kamal in. The taste was bitter and salty, he didn't know what he'd expected and started to pull away. Zijad moaned into his mouth and pressed his tongue to Kamal's, pulling him back while giving him a stronger taste of his own essence mixed with that of the boy. That was when he knew he'd found what he'd been looking for. The taste of his own come overpowered the kid's natural flavor but it was still there, thriving faintly under his, much like the boy himself.

Kamal ended the kiss before the kid could get any ideas about tender sessions of lovemaking that Kamal wanted no part of. He pushed the boy roughly onto his back, making Zijad squeak when he hit the mattress, but then a lascivious moan left his puffy lips as Kamal took hold of his cock. Squeezing it in one hand, he grabbed the kid's balls in his other.

"Please, *Šef.*"

"Please what?" Kamal asked.

"Please, don't…" Kamal tightened his grip on the kid's nuts while stroking his cock, making him grunt.

"Don't what? Make you come?" Kamal taunted. Zijad cried out as Kamal increased the pressure on his balls but only lightly stroked his cock.

"Please…" The boy groaned and tried to push up into Kamal's hand, but that only pulled at his trapped nuts causing him more pain. "Oh god, please make me come!"

"Oh, you're going to come for me," Kamal said, making it sound more like a threat than a promise. The boy nodded and then hissed as Kamal started stroking him harder but didn't let up on the grip he had on the boy's testicles. "Don't make me wait, if my arm gets tired I'll stop and you won't get to come at all today. Maybe the cage and vibrator would be a fitting punishment if you fail me." The kid moved his hips even though it had to hurt, helping Kamal jack him off. "I'm already feeling a bit — " The warm spurts into his hand cut off his words as the boy let go with a throaty groan. Kamal smiled at the flushed look of the boy in the throes of his orgasm as he finally released his hold on the kid's nuts. He offered his soiled hand to the boy, nudging his lips, and Zijad lapped up his own ejaculate quickly, even cleaning in between his fingers.

"I knew you liked it with a little pain, you're a slut for it." Kamal watched the pink tongue lap at him like a starving kitten. "Make sure you thank me for giving you what you needed to get off."

Zijad lay back when Kamal moved his hand. "Thank you, *Šef*," he mumbled, sounding sleepy.

Kamal needed to pee but looking at the relaxed boy next to him, he weighed whether it was worth the hassle of chaining him up before making a quick trip to the bathroom. Instead he got up and pulled the boy to his knees. "Bathroom time, then maybe we can nap," Kamal said, giving in to the kid's wide yawn with one of his own.

They were lying on the mattress sometime later after their physical needs had been taken care of and Kamal was growing uneasy with the way the boy wanted to touch him. They were just casual touches, but still it unnerved him in a way that made him fidget, yet he was too lethargic to get up to put some space between them. He'd lain down with the thought that the kid would fall asleep quickly, leaving him to get up and roam the cabin while making plans of how he'd kill Orhan, especially now that he was sure to be heavily guarded. The boy rolled onto his side and put his hand on Kamal's chest, seeking out one of the old bullet wounds. Just when Kamal thought he'd have to crush the kid's hand to send the message that he didn't like to be touched, the kid asked a question.

"My father didn't pay the ransom, did he?"

"Why would you ask that?" Kamal countered, instead of answering a question.

"I'm not stupid, *Šef.*" There was a slight tremble in the boy's voice.

"I haven't heard for sure." Kamal had read the headlines, but that wasn't proof Orhan hadn't agreed to the terms, though it did make things look less favorable for the boy. Kamal realized he should check Julien's emails to see if there were any further instructions.

"Will you kill me?"

"You mean if they tell me to?"

"You never answer a question, just ask one back. Of course that's what I meant," Zijad said, showing a little more spirit than Kamal thought he had in him.

Kamal thought about it. Though killing the kid didn't sound like something he'd enjoy, he couldn't say for sure if it was off the table if it was what was expected. "I don't know."

Zijad's lip trembled, but he didn't cry. "Will you do one thing for me if you have to?" he asked in a small voice.

"Depends on what it is, Mali."

"Will you let me see your face just once before you do it?" he asked and at the same time he reached out and touched Kamal's cheek.

Kamal was uncomfortable; the touch, the soft reverent way the boy had asked the question, and the thought of looking into those clear blue eyes as he pulled the trigger did strange things to him. Pulling the kid's hand away from his face, he reminded his body that he was over forty, his dick should not get hard that quickly at the thought of taking the only thing the boy had left to give – his life.

"I'll think about it, but you shouldn't lose hope so quickly, there is always a chance that Orhan will do what needs to be done," Kamal said.

The boy lifted his head and tried to look at Kamal through the blindfold once again. "My father is ashamed of me. He sent me away to boarding school when I was ten because he knew there was something different about me. I have never spent a holiday at home with him, my mother always came to me. He hates me. I would be better off dead and I'm sure he thinks so too," Zijad said, his words dripping with resentment but still holding a tinge of sadness. "You

126

made a mistake in taking me; you should have kidnapped his dog. He loves her."

"Give me your hands, Mali." Kamal sat up suddenly. The boy opened his mouth as if to protest, but then his narrow shoulders slumped and his lips turned down into a frown as he presented his wrists for the cuffs. Locking the kid up before he got off the mattress to retrieve the hood, he put it and the ear muffs on the boy, plunging him into silence with only his own tortured thoughts for company.

"I'm sorry, Šef, I'm so, so sorry," Zijad mumbled as he started to softly cry.

Kamal looked at his captive and shook his head at the pathetic creature he saw. Orhan had not only fucked up Kamal's life, he'd fucked up his own kid for exactly the same reason. He should have felt pity for the boy, some sort of kinship for their shared suffering at the other man's hands. Instead he pretended indifference when he saw how the boy suffered, but Kamal wasn't indifferent. It was just what he told himself to keep the budding attraction to the kid's pain buried so he wouldn't embrace it – that would only end badly for both of them.

Day 21, Day 16 in Captivity

There had been no word from Koslov in Julien's emails. No further instructions on how to proceed now that Kamal was almost certain Orhan hadn't acquiesced to Koslov's demands. Kamal's job turned into one of waiting with nothing to tell him how long it would last or if the outcome would be one of success or utter failure. The unknown was what caused Kamal to all but ignore his captive, only doing what was necessary to keep the kid alive throughout the day. Kamal sat and chain-smoked as he turned a deaf ear to the boy's repeated pleas to remove the hood. He hadn't even given in to smacking the kid when he tried to reach for him on a trip to the bathroom; instead, Kamal had turned the kid back, making him wait another hour to use the toilet, and then he'd kept his hands to himself.

Kamal lay down on the couch for the night, exhausted though he'd done almost nothing, but sleep eluded him. The kid had napped on and off during the day, leaving him awake and quietly snuffling behind the hood. He mumbled words Kamal couldn't make out in between his sobs. Putting his pillow over his head only made him feel like he was suffocating, so once again he was forced to listen to the boy's caterwauling.

Kamal threw the pillow across the room and sat up. In the kitchenette he found the *rakia* and downed a couple of shots, then lit a smoke and sat down with the bottle. "*Šuti!*" Kamal hollered at the boy before taking another shot. Already he could feel the buzz of the potent alcohol as it ran through his veins, but another shot would be even better. Kamal turned his dark eyes on the boy, who just wouldn't shut the fuck up. He got off the couch and without thinking about it grabbed the small gun he'd used when he'd abducted the kid.

Straddling the boy's legs, Kamal yanked the hood off, the muffs flew up and then clattered to the floor. Kamal shoved the muzzle of the gun up under the kid's chin before leaning in close to his face. "Are you praying?" The boy's lips were moving, forming soundless words Kamal figured was a last ditch effort at begging Allah for help. "There is no god to help you here," Kamal sneered. He dug the gun harder into the soft flesh under the boy's chin. "I could kill you right now and bury your body so that no one would ever know what happened to you except me. I own you right now. *I'm* your god, *I'm* the one you should be begging."

"Please, *Šef*," Zijad pleaded.

"Please what? Are you begging me to kill you or to save you?" Kamal pressed closer.

"I-I d-don't know," Zijad cried out. He pushed up against Kamal, making his arousal at the situation evident. "Save me, *Šef*, please... save me."

Looking down at the kid for the first time, Kamal saw him. He was not Orhan. He was not a substitute for his father, he was a whole and complete separate person. A broken mess , but still a person. He was Zijad. Kamal couldn't save him, he knew that, but maybe during their time together, what remained of it, he could at least acknowledge that he existed outside of the mess he'd been dragged into.

Kamal dropped the gun and unhooked Zijad's wrists from the wall but left them cuffed together. "On your knees, *kurva*," he commanded. Zijad hesitated a moment, earning himself a swat to the outside of his thigh. "I will punish you for disobedience." That statement got Zijad moving, he rolled quickly and rose to his knees and elbows. Kamal made good on his word and let his hand land on the boy's backside. "What do you say?"

"T-thank you, *Šef*," Zijad answered. Kamal landed blow after punishing blow and though Zijad sobbed, he thanked him for each one.

Kamal's hand was stinging by the time he felt some of the tension of the day seep out of him. He stopped spanking the boy to reach for the lube that had been tossed off to the side the day before. Slicking his fingers, he shoved two into the boy's ass, pumping them and then crooking them to find that small spongy bundle buried within. Zijad cried out in pleasure as Kamal massaged him.

"Don't come, Mali, this is not for your pleasure, it's for mine and you coming would not please me," Kamal growled.

"Yes, *Šef*, thank you, *Šef*," Zijad mumbled and then whimpered as Kamal continued his assault on the boy's prostate. He added another finger, stretching the boy's asshole wide before his eyes. He wondered how much the boy could take, if he could get his whole fist in there, but that was something for another time. This time he wanted to fuck the boy and make him cry and beg him to stop. Just the thought of the noises the boy made when hurt spurred Kamal to pull his fingers from the boy and get to his knees.

"Going to fuck that sweet tight ass of yours now, you slut. Tell me how much you want it." Kamal rubbed the head of his cock against the boy's ass, running it up and down the crease then over his slick and ready entrance.

"Please, *Šef*, I want it." Zijad pushed back against Kamal, but Kamal grabbed his hips to stop him.

"That wasn't very convincing. Make me believe that you want me to fuck you, Mali. Beg for it," Kamal urged.

"Please, *Šef*, fuck me, please, I want you to fuck me, please!" Zijad cried, again trying to push back to make Kamal take him. Holding him still, Kamal waited through his sobs which grew in intensity, until he started thrashing his head about and then, "Please, *Šef*, I need it, fuck me please!"

Yes, that was it, that was what he wanted to hear. He pulled the boy's hips back and thrust forward at the same time, burying his dick all the way in. Zijad screamed and the sound almost pushed Kamal over the edge, it was perfect. Kamal drove into him, over and over, letting his body have complete control to take what it wanted just how it wanted it with no thought to the vessel underneath.

Kamal howled as he came but he managed not to fall forward on the boy. Reaching under to give the boy his reward after he caught his breath, Kamal found there had been an unwanted discharge. Kamal pulled his hand back and stared at the slimy residue on his fingers. Zijad was wailing and blubbering at the same time so Kamal had to concentrate to make out what he was saying.

"I'm sorry, I couldn't stop it, please, I'm sorry, forgive me, *Šef…*" Zijad repeated the words on an endless loop.

Kamal flipped the boy over, but even the swift action didn't stop the words falling from his lips. He grabbed the boy's hair and pulled him up so that his face was level with Kamal's groin. "Clean up the mess," Kamal demanded. The boy balked at the task he'd been given, and Kamal couldn't fault him for it, but he held his head there regardless.

"Please, no, *Šef.*"

Kamal tightened his hold and rubbed his soiled dick in the boy's face. "You came. I told you not to. This is your punishment. You shouldn't have come if you couldn't handle the consequences. Now do it or — " Kamal couldn't even finish his thoughts as the boy's soft mouth closed over his limp dick and sucked it clean, mewling in protest the whole while. The boy continued to lick until Kamal pulled him back, satisfied that he'd had enough. "What do you say, Mali?" Kamal prodded.

"Thank you, *Šef.*"

"I shouldn't have to keep reminding you. I think I'll punish you each time you forget." Kamal let the boy's head drop. He'd let the kid brush his teeth for the first time since he'd taken him and then maybe he could finally sleep.

Chapter 15:
Marching Orders

Day 22, Day 17 in Captivity

"Watch where you're going, Mali," Kamal said with a grin as the boy very nearly brained himself on the edge of the coffee table. He watched as Zijad gave up trying to cross to the bathroom on his knees and opted to crawl on all fours instead. It was amusing, which was why Kamal had set the boy free and let him wander blindly about the cabin with the only caveat being he had to do so on his knees. The boy had caught on quickly that Kamal found his antics funny and had tried very hard not to do the things that got a chuckle from him. He was not at all successful because Kamal had started ordering him to do things and placing obstacles in his path to trip him up. Kamal finally had some entertainment.

Kamal got off the couch to follow him into the bathroom. The boy's flush of embarrassment ran all the way down his chest when he turned to Kamal. "Please, *Šef*, can I stand?"

"No, Mali, you have to sit to pee. I don't think your aim is very good and I don't feel like cleaning up after you, unless…" Kamal let his statement trail off so the boy could imagine what sort of humiliating punishment he might endure if he peed on the toilet seat or floor. Zijad pulled himself up to sit on the toilet without another word. "Wise choice," Kamal said.

"Thank you, *Šef*." Zijad relieved himself under Kamal's watchful eye.

He let the boy follow him out into the living room when he finished. Instead of letting him crawl back to his mattress, Kamal said, "Follow behind me, Mali. Stay at my heel unless I tell you different."

"Yes, *Šef.*" Zijad acknowledged he heard the command and followed Kamal into the kitchen area to kneel at his feet while Kamal prepared their afternoon meal.

When he was finished, Kamal carried the tray over to the coffee table and sat on the couch. "Come kneel over here by me," Kamal ordered. The boy crawled slowly over to him and then knelt stiffly at his feet. Though the boy's hands were free, Kamal still hand fed him. He ate a few bites of his own supper, canned goulash and instant mashed potatoes, before picking a piece of meat out of the bowl with a chunk of bread and offering it to the boy. Zijad took the offered morsel, cleaning the gravy from Kamal's fingers with a gentle sucking motion.

"Good, Mali," Kamal praised him before going back to his own food. They ate like that, Kamal feeding Zijad bites of food and lifting a bottle of water to his lips until the food was gone. "Do you want more?" The boy's lips twisted and he swallowed hard. "Answer me, Mali, it's not a hard question."

"I want more if you want me to want more, *Šef,*" Zijad finally answered.

Kamal considered the boy's answer before he shook his head at its meaning. "So, if I were to make you eat until you threw up, you'd want that because it's what I wanted?" Kamal asked, giving the boy something to think about as he picked up the tray and carried it to the kitchen. The boy had followed him and knelt at his feet again as he washed the few dishes they'd dirtied.

"Yes, *Šef,* if it was what you wanted," Zijad said quietly after some thought.

Kamal patted the boy's head. "You're something else, you know that? Don't worry, I have no intention of making you eat until you puke." It would give him no pleasure so it wasn't something he'd subject the boy to. He led the boy back to the couch and, finding there was nothing else to do, used his mouth to get off.

Day 24, Day 19 in Captivity

The boy was bent over the bench, he wasn't secured to it but his fingers clutched at the leather cushion as Kamal landed another blow with the slim crop.

"Twenty, thank you, *Šef!*" Zijad cried out, counting and thanking his tormentor after each stroke. He gulped for air through his sobs.

"Do you think that's enough to make you obey next time?"

"Yes, *Šef*, please, I promise I won't do it again."

"I doubt that, but I think I may have a way to help you at least try to keep that promise." Kamal put the crop down and picked up the leather strap he'd found in the trunk before stepping closer to study his handiwork. The striped skin of the boy's ass and upper thighs only made him harder in anticipation of fucking him, but he made the boy stand and turn to face him. The boy's own erection bobbed proudly in front of him. It never failed to amaze Kamal that Zijad got hard no matter what the punishment Kamal meted out to him – as if he enjoyed it.

Kamal grasped the boy's cock in his hand and gave it a caress that drew a loud, needy moan from Zijad which made Kamal's lips twist into a wry grin. He wound the leather strap around the base of the boy's cock and balls and fastened it.

"Wha-"

"Shh, Mali, just a little something to help you so I don't have to punish you again so soon. This will keep you from coming," Kamal explained, interrupting the boy's question. The strap wouldn't prevent the boy from climaxing, but it would slow him down a little and hopefully along with his need to please, he'd be able to hold off until Kamal gave him permission. He turned him back toward the bench. "Now show me."

Zijad shuddered, but he bent over the bench, laying his chest on the top, before reaching back to spread his tender ass cheeks wide enough for Kamal to see his pucker. It was still greasy from their earlier activities, the ones that had brought about the boy's punishment.

"What do you want, boy?" Kamal stepped closer and ran a finger along one of the welts he'd left on the boy's flesh.

"I want you to fuck me, *Šef*, please." When Kamal made no move to do so, the boy begged in earnest. "Please, I need it, please fuck me, fuck me, please..."

"You are so slutty, Mali. You'd think you would have had enough already today," Kamal chided, which only brought on more impassioned pleas from the boy. "I think...you'd be happy to have a cock shoved up your ass all day. Would you like that, my little whore?" Zijad groaned but didn't respond, which to Kamal was answer enough. Kamal bent over to get closer to the boy's ear. "You'd like it if I brought a bunch of men here and let them use you like the come dumpster you are," Kamal jeered.

"Please, no," Zijad whimpered as if Kamal saying it would make it happen at that moment.

"No? Why no?"

"Only you, Šef, I just want you," Zijad murmured.

Kamal stroked the boy's back as he stood up. "You are perfect, you know that?" Kamal whispered, too quietly for the boy to pick up. He slid his shorts off, slicked up and slid home. Grabbing the kid's hands, he pulled them up onto the bench and braced himself on top of them as he began to move. The sound of his flesh smacking against the boy's and the knowledge that he was hurting Zijad with every thrust drove him insane with lust.

"Don't you come, Mali, don't you dare," Kamal hissed as he hit the boy's prostate repeatedly, tempting him with the pleasure of it. Zijad made beautiful sounds as he absorbed the pain and denied himself pleasure. Leaning down over the boy's smaller body, Kamal nibbled at his neck. The action produced a new sound Kamal liked even more, a vulnerable, needy sound that told him the boy was completely his in the moment. When he released one of the boy's hands to reach around and feel his hardness, it seemed the strap was doing its job.

"Please, Šef," Zijad said as he pushed into Kamal's hand.

"If you make it through, I'll give you a special gift, Mali, just a while longer." Kamal let go of the boy's dick so he could grab his hip and drive into him harder. The boy squeezed down on him and Kamal groaned. He almost slapped the boy's ass for trying to make him come, but then he was coming and he forgot what he was upset about. He collapsed onto the boy's back, face pressed against the sweaty skin.

"Thank you, Šef," Zijad said quietly, reminding Kamal he still had something to attend to.

He stood up and his softening cock slipped from the boy's body. "Stand up and turn around, Mali." Hesitant, the boy did as he was told, revealing his dick which was an angry red from the trapped blood it held. Zijad cried out when Kamal released the strap. Lifting the boy, Kamal sat him on the bench, earning a pained sound as his butt connected with the leather on the bench. "Shh, you're okay, Mali," Kamal hushed the boy. "You did so well, you're a good boy." Kamal petted the narrow shoulders and let his hands caress the skin of his arms, making Zijad shudder under his touch.

"Thank you, Šef. Please." Zijad tried to press closer but Kamal held him back. Placing the boy's hands on the bench behind him so he could support his weight, Kamal pushed him to lean back on them.

"Keep your hands where they are or no reward, understand?"

"Yes, Šef, I understand."

Kamal leaned forward and let his breath tickle the moist skin of the boy's neck just before his lips landed. He ran his tongue along the column of his neck to his ear. "I'm going to show you what you can have if you're a good boy and obey me at all times. What's possible if only you can manage to hold yourself back," Kamal whispered into the shell of the boy's ear. Zijad nodded as Kamal began his assault on the boy's body.

It wasn't easy to remember how to be gentle and Kamal had to remind himself he was supposed to be showing the boy what could be, even if it wasn't something he'd ever get again. He worked his lips and teeth over the boy's chest, sucking his small nipples into stiff peaks before moving down. Dipping his tongue into the boy's navel when he reached the small indent produced a shudder as Zijad shook under the simple touch. Kamal blew cool air over the skin he'd licked and watched as gooseflesh popped out before continuing his journey down.

He skipped over the boy's groin, even though Zijad tried to push up into him as he did. Kamal used his hands to hold the boy's hips down and continued his slow torture by kissing up the inside of Zijad's thigh until his nose was buried in his scrotum. The musky smell of his own release leaking from the boy's entrance encouraged the low hum in his chest that vibrated through the boy's balls as he took them into his mouth.

"Please, *Šef*, I can't..." Zijad's breath was coming in fast pants that heralded his imminent release.

Kamal let off the boy's balls and used the flat of his tongue to run the length of his hardness before taking the head between his lips. Zijad cried out in anguish as he held his orgasm for a moment longer. Kamal gave the crown one quick suck before lifting his head and taking the boy in hand. "Now, Mali, come for me now." The command was clear even though Kamal used a hushed voice to issue it.

Zijad came with a helpless shout. Kamal caught the boy's seed in his hand, giving Zijad a moment to gather his wits before offering him the hand. The boy opened his mouth, but instead of cleaning Kamal's hand he said in a trembling voice, "Thank you, Šef, thank you."

"Clean your mess, boy." Zijad's tongue made quick work of the come on Kamal's hand.

"Thank you, *Šef*," Zijad repeated once his job was done. Kamal smiled, but the blinded boy couldn't see just how pleased he was with what he'd wrought.

Day 26, Day 21 in Captivity

Kamal sat back and watched as the boy lay on the bank of the small creek, soaking in the first rays of sunlight he'd been allowed since he'd been abducted. The sun shone through the trees and cast dancing shadows over his bare flesh, making Kamal want to touch, but he held himself back. He was quickly becoming addicted to the boy and the reactions he could provoke from him. Kamal hadn't come so many times a day in his life as he had in the past week, like a newlywed on his honeymoon and it was a thought that made him snort in disgust. There was nothing he could do about it since he'd still received no word from Julien's contact even after three weeks.

Standing from where he was sitting, Kamal stepped into the shallow creek. The water was still very cold as it was fed by a spring deep in the mountain. He cupped his hands to scoop up some of the crystal clear water and drank deeply. It was colder than the bottled water in the fridge and the taste was wonderful, so wonderful he decided to share some with his captive. With a mischievous smile on his lips, Kamal splashed the boy and laughed in delight at his startled scream. Zijad sat up and swiveled his head as if looking for the source of his chilly shower.

"Were you sleeping, Mali?" Kamal asked, still chuckling as he made his way to the boy's side.

"Yes, Šef, I think I dozed off. The sun feels so good after being locked inside for so long." A small smile tugged at the corners of his lips as he turned his face to the sun. He looked so young in that moment Kamal almost felt sorry for what he'd done to him.

"Lie back, enjoy your time in the sun, Mali." Kamal pushed the boy so he was laying once again in the position he'd been in when he'd been disturbed.

"Thank you, Šef," Zijad said, letting the smile loose to take over his face.

They passed the day laying on the grass and splashing in the stream when they got too hot. Zijad clung to Kamal at first, unsure of the rocky bottom, but soon even in his blinded state, he ventured off by himself. Kamal watched as he walked perhaps twenty meters down the small stream.

"Zijad, that's far enough. Come back to me now," Kamal called to the boy. Zijad turned so abruptly, he stumbled and landed in the water on his bare ass. Kamal ran to him, not even trying to stifle his laugh at the boy's clumsiness. Picking Zijad up, Kamal set him on his feet. "Mali, there is not enough water to jump in, it's too shallow, you'll break your butt," he said, letting the boy cling to him for balance. Zijad's mouth worked but nothing came out at first. "What is it?" Kamal looked around thinking maybe the boy had heard something he hadn't.

"You said my name, Šef, you know my name," Zijad finally said. The astonishment was clear in his tone, he was surprised Kamal knew his name.

"Of course I know your name, Mali, don't be stupid," Kamal said, preparing to shove the boy away from him. Before he could complete the action, Zijad wrapped his arms around Kamal's waist and pressed his cheek against his chest.

"Thank you, Šef, thank you so much." Zijad started to sob and, not knowing what else to do, Kamal held him as he wept.

"Maybe you've had too much sun, let's go inside and eat something," Kamal suggested when he quickly grew weary of waiting for the boy's crying fit to end.

He led the boy back to his prison.

Day 32, Day 27 in Captivity

"Fuck, you've gotten so good at that, Mali," Kamal growled as the boy licked the come he'd failed to swallow off Kamal's balls.

"Thank you, *Šef*, it's my pleasure to serve you this way." Kamal ran a hand through the boy's hair as he nuzzled against his thigh – petting the boy always got a sweet moan in response.

"Did you come?" Kamal asked. Zijad shook his head. "Sit up and let me see." The boy reluctantly sat back on his knees to reveal his still hard cock. "You can jerk off now." Kamal watched as the boy took himself in hand and came after only a few rough yanks. He caught his own release and licked it from his hand.

"Thank you, *Šef*," he said quietly after he'd completed his task.

"You're welcome, Mali, now go lie down, it's time for you to sleep."

The boy crawled to his mattress and settled down, curled up on his side facing Kamal. "Good night, *Šef*," he said through a yawn.

Kamal waited a few moments until the boy's breathing evened out, then opened the laptop and powered it on. He'd followed the same ritual for the past thirteen days, since he'd sent the last video. He brought up the newspaper first to check the headlines. Orhan was gaining a head of steam with his campaign that settled around building up the economy and family values, returning to the ways of old where family came first. Kamal read the articles with a sneer on his face. He hated the man more and more the longer Kamal held his boy, knowing Orhan's refusal to pay the price kept the boy in his care.

When he finished with the news, he opened Julien's email. The little icon showed there was one new message, Kamal's heart sped up just a little. He was certain that this would be the order for Kamal to kill the boy. Kamal closed his eyes after reading the short message and flopped back on the couch, just sitting still for a moment. When he opened his eyes they went straight to the boy. It was settled then, tomorrow would be their last day together.

Chapter 16:
The Beginning of the End

Day 33, Day 28 in Captivity

Kamal felt the exact moment when the boy came awake. The slick channel his cock was buried in became almost unbearably tight as the boy clenched his muscles against the invasion. Kamal waited a moment and that's all it took for Zijad to relax once again. The boy had become accustomed to being used in his sleep and to waking in the exact position he found himself in, but it didn't stop that one moment of fear when alertness came to him. Kamal started fucking the boy slowly as he ran a hand from the boy's hip to his chest, pressing Zijad's body closer to his own and making the boy sigh.

"Good morning, *Šef*," Zijad mumbled sleepily.

"Mali, it's about time you joined the world of the living." Kamal picked up the speed, to drive faster and harder into the boy's willing flesh. Zijad moaned wantonly as he pushed his hips back to meet every thrust until Kamal's hand stayed him. "This is for me, for my pleasure, Mali, if you come before I tell you to, I'll have to punish you."

"Yes, *Šef*, sorry," Zijad whimpered. He lay still as Kamal fucked him forcefully until his own release threatened.

"Now, Mali, come for me," Kamal ordered.

"*Šef?*" Zijad questioned the command. Kamal understood the confusion. He'd never let the boy come while he fucked him, only after Kamal was satisfied was he allowed to find his own end.

"I said come for me." The words came through gritted teeth as Kamal staved off his own orgasm. Grabbing the boy's hand, he

140

wrapped it around his seeping erection and started pumping him almost brutally hard before letting the boy take over. "Come quickly, Mali, I don't have all day."

"Yes, Šef." Zijad let loose a long moan when Kamal hit his prostate to move things along.

Aiming his thrusts perfectly, the boy soon fell apart in his arms. The tight clenching around his dick felt amazing. He flipped the boy over and Zijad got to his knees without being told so Kamal could drive into him harder and faster as he chased his pleasure. Kamal came with a grunt that was a barely contained shout, then lay, draped over the boy's slender body, for a moment until the spasms inside the boy's ass stopped. Kamal listened to the soft, wet sound of his cock leaving the boy's body. It was the last time he'd ever hear it and he wanted to savor the moment.

He flopped onto his back at the edge of the mattress, and Zijad attended to him with his tongue before lying down next to Kamal.

"Thank you, Šef," Zijad whispered quietly. Kamal knew the boy was thanking him for something other than letting him lick the remnants of his orgasm off his cock, but chose to ignore it.

"I have some things to do today, Mali, I have to put the hood back on you for a few hours." Kamal had no idea why he was telling the boy his plans instead of just forcing it on him, but for some reason it felt right that on this last day the boy should have at least a little peace in his life.

"But why, Šef? Did I do something wrong?" Zijad asked. Kamal watched the boy's lips as they trembled, he knew the boy would start to cry after his announcement. Kamal touched the boy's face, letting him nuzzle at his palm.

"No, Mali, you haven't done anything wrong. It's just my job," Kamal said. The boy's shoulders shook as he cried silently. "You're a good boy, Zijad, a very good boy." A sob broke free at the sound of his name and he reached up to seize Kamal's hand, clinging to it as he wept. Kamal waited silently, locking away the sound of the boy's wailing into his memory.

Zijad finally calmed enough to ask, "It's over, isn't it?" Kamal took his hand back and sat up. "Please, Šef, just tell me," Zijad pleaded, but his cries went unanswered as Kamal locked his wrists up in the cuffs and then put the hood over his head. Kamal stood and strengthened his resolve. This was a job and he would do what was necessary to see it through to its completion.

He moved through the cabin, making a plan on how best to start their evacuation of the place. There was little in the way of consumables left, he had actually been contemplating a trip into the nearest town but now was glad there was so little to get rid of. He packed up the bathroom before wiping it down, then moved on to the kitchen and did the same, only stopping to smoke a cigarette every now and then. The boy had gone silent after he'd worn himself out and appeared to be sleeping as Kamal packed up the trunk of toys while trying to ignore the memories they brought to mind.

After packing the things he'd have to take with him into duffle bags, he piled the things he'd dispose of in the mountains to one side. The day had slipped away as he'd taken care of everything except the boy. Kamal stood over him, letting his eyes drink in the body he'd enjoyed abusing for the past four weeks. He would miss the boy's easy submission, but there was no way out of their situation . He'd known he couldn't keep the boy prisoner forever.

Kamal gathered what he'd need to finish things. In the end there was no gun, just a needle.

Kamal drove slowly through the streets of Sarajevo, looking for the designated parking lot where he'd transfer his package over to someone else to deliver to Orhan's doorstep. He found the spot and pulled in beside the *kombi* waiting there. The men in the front seat got out and stood between the two vehicles. Kamal shut off the engine and got out to join them.

"You the one with the package for Ferhatović?" one of the burly men asked.

He looked around, nothing seemed off but he waited just the same.

"Koslov sends his regards and thanks for a job well done," the other man said.

"I guess I'm the man with the package then." Kamal turned to open the back door of his car. "Open the door so I can transfer it.." The men opened the side door of the *kombi* and stepped back to allow Kamal room to maneuver. He pulled the blanket-wrapped body of the boy out of the back seat and turned to deposit it on the floor inside the other vehicle. He patted the boy's chest, saying a silent goodbye to his captive.

One of the two men raised an eyebrow at Kamal when he stepped back away from the door, but Kamal ignored him. He got into his car and slammed the door. He wanted to stomp his foot down on the gas pedal and peel out in a rain of gravel, but he took a deep breath to calm himself and gave the two men a nod before driving away. It was done and he was free.

Kamal let himself into his apartment. It was the same as always, only the layer of dust had gotten thicker in his absence. Going straight to his bedroom, he dropped his bag on the desk. He didn't bother turning the television on, instead he got out his computer and logged into his accounts. He needed a job, the sooner the better. Scrolling through his emails, he noticed he'd missed plenty from Koslov's contacts but there were a few more recent ones that he opened. He read through until he found something that would take him away from Sarajevo for at least a week and accepted the job. He'd pack his gear and leave in the morning.

While putting his computer back in its bag, the small memory card fell from the pocket. He picked it up and slumped back in his chair. Kamal fingered the little piece of plastic, then rubbed it between his fingers as he contemplated whether it would do more harm than good to watch it. Retrieving a bottle of *rakia* from his little-used kitchen and a dusty glass that he rinsed in the sink, he returned to his room and drank himself into oblivion, while repeatedly watching the video of him and his boy.

It was harder to cross into Slovenia since they'd gotten into the European Union, but Kamal's papers were all in order so they couldn't deny him entry to their godforsaken country. He'd been driving for over seven hours by the time he finally crossed the border and had another hour and a half to go to Maribor. He wasn't tired, but his head still throbbed from the evening before. Chain smoking and listening to Bosnian folk music on CD as the kilometers ticked away, he actively avoided the news that broke in between the music on the radio. He was finished with Orhan and his family, he didn't need to know how the events of the previous night had played out.

The hotel room he'd rented was on the edge of the city and came complete with a kitchenette he wouldn't use. He took a quick shower and dropped into bed even though it was only just after eight pm. His mind was restless as he waited for sleep to take him, but he refused to give in to its insistence that he watch the video again. He closed his eyes tightly and eventually sleep took him.

Kamal lay on the dirty mattress next to Meho. He didn't have the energy to move much after hiding out in the village for over two weeks. He looked down at his body, his ribs stuck out in sharp peaks that threatened to poke through the skin that contained them. They needed food. They needed more than just the scraps and crumbs they'd found in the abandoned houses if they were going to survive.

Kamal nudged Meho with his elbow getting only a weak groan in return. "We have to get up. We need to find food, there's nothing left here and we're going to die if we don't eat soon," Kamal said as he sat up.

"I'm too tired to go," Meho whined.

"I'm going and if you don't come, I might not come back," Kamal threatened, to get his friend moving.

"Fine, but I don't know what you hope to find, there's nothing out there," Meho grumbled, even as he sat up.

"We're leaving the village. There has to be food we can find somewhere." Kamal stood and held out a hand to help Meho up. Meho was even more unsteady on his feet than Kamal which worried him, but they needed to move.

Kamal held up his hand to halt Meho's stumbling through the underbrush. He cocked his head and listened, sure he'd heard other people somewhere up ahead. He heard the sound again, but wasn't able to make out if it was friend or foe that awaited them. He readied his gun; knowing he only had five shells for the old hunting rifle made him twitchy.

"What is it?" Meho whispered next to his ear.

"I hear voices on the trail up ahead. We need to tread lightly." Kamal started slowly picking his way through the thorns as the voices became more distinct. He caught some of the words and just before he and Meho came to the fork in the path he saw three men standing in a huddle. Kamal was sure his eyes were deceiving him because he recognized at least one of them.

"*Salam alaikum*, brothers," Meho greeted in a way too loud voice. Kamal grabbed his arm but Meho shrugged him off and rushed toward the other men who stared at them with startled, fearful eyes. Kamal stayed back until recognition dawned on their faces and they broke into smiles. Meho hugged the man Kamal had thought he knew and the resemblance was clear, he was Meho's cousin from the village further up the road.

Kamal finally stepped out to join them. "*Salam alaikum*," he said and shook hands with the dirty band of men.

"*Alaikum salam*. Where have you two been?" Emir asked Meho.

"We were in the village. We had to hide in the water container for an entire day when the Četniks searched every house and barn in town," Meho said. "Where have you been hiding?"

"We've been at the hunting shed up over the hill but we roam around a bit since, every once in a while, people come by there," Emir said.

"Do you have food?" Kamal asked when he grew impatient with the chit chat.

"We were just going to look in the village over there." Emir pointed behind him in the direction Meho and himself had been heading. "We ate the last of what we found yesterday. Do you want to come with us?"

"Let's go with them, Kamal, it's safer with more of us," Meho said.

Kamal wasn't sure that was the case but he didn't really want to end up alone and he knew Meho would leave with his cousin if given the chance. "Okay, we'll go with you."

The group of five trudged up the hill in silence. The village they entered looked like all the others, it was a ghost town. There had been mostly Bosniaks who had lived there so it wasn't surprising to any of them. They split up and started searching the houses. Kamal found a couple of small hardened *pogače* that he stuffed into his bag. He entered his third house when the smell of something long dead hit him. He gagged, but after pulling his shirt up to cover his nose and mouth, went back in. The smell was coming from the kitchen in the back of the house and Kamal followed it. There was nothing in the room that could give off that sort of a stink, but then he noticed a small door he figured must lead outside.

With some hesitation in his steps, Kamal walked over and pulled the door open. It wasn't the outdoors he found, it was a small cold storage area where the family had most likely kept potatoes and onions, maybe smoked meat. He stepped in, but with no light he couldn't make anything out. He searched his pockets and came up with a box of matches. Lighting one, Kamal prepared himself for the worst. It wasn't a dead body that he found; not a human one at least. There in that small root cellar Kamal found more meat than he'd seen in the last four years. It was rotting there in the small, too warm, room. Kamal's stomach both turned with nausea and rumbled with hunger at the same time.

He searched the kitchen and found a couple of burlap bags, and shoved the stinking rotted flesh into them before turning to leave. Kamal found Meho and the other men standing in the center of the village pooling together the small bits of food they'd found. Their eyes widened when they saw the size of the bag he had slung over his shoulder.

"Kamal, what did you find?" Meho asked excitedly. His excitement waned a bit when the smell hit him. "Do you have a dead body in there?"

"It's meat, it's spoiled but I think if we cook it good enough we could eat it," Kamal said. The other men cringed at the thought, but Kamal wouldn't back down. "I'm going to eat it and if I die then so what? I'm probably going to die of starvation soon anyway, a grown man can't live off what we've been eating for long." He turned on his heel and started walking away. If they didn't want what he was offering then they could just fuck the hell off. It only took moments for them to start following him.

They reached the hunting shack just as night fell. Kamal sat his load down and collapsed on one of the hard wooden benches in the lean-to. He was exhausted. Meho sat next to him and worried his lip with his teeth. "What?" Kamal snapped.

"If we build a fire to fix the meat..." Meho let his thought die when Kamal's eyes hardened.

"I don't care anymore. I will cook that meat because I need the energy it will provide. I've decided that I'm leaving tomorrow. I'm going over the mountain," Kamal said. He'd either make it to safety or they'd catch him and he'd die, he couldn't be bothered to care which it was. He was done with it all. Not even the thought of being reunited with Orhan could make him care about his fate.

Kamal awoke with a start, the taste of slightly charred rotten meat on his tongue, but he knew he wasn't back there in those woods waiting for daylight to come so he could make his escape from hell. He was still disoriented while his eyes tried to adjust to the darkness and he turned to look in the corner where the boy should be. His surroundings became clearer and he remembered he was in a small hotel in Maribor and he had a job to do.

Killing was easy when you were prepared and your plans worked out the way you hoped they would. Kamal took no satisfaction in ending the man's life, it was just a job. The grief he'd bring to the man's family never entered his mind as he pulled the trigger and watched as it entered and then exited the man's head. He was right where he'd left off as if there had been no interruptions to his normally scheduled life. Kamal was a killer and he was good at it.

The drive back to Sarajevo was long enough for Kamal to come down from the adrenaline high that finishing a job always gave him. He would visit Demetri when he returned and maybe Hamza would be there. He smiled at the thought of the young man on his knees in the dirty alley. Kamal was going to be just fine.

Chapter 17:
Revelations

Kamal walked into Demetri's café, not expecting the welcoming smile he got from Hamza. He nodded at the young man and raised an eyebrow to let Hamza know they were on for later. He found Demetri at his regular table, smoking while he read the newspaper and watched the football match on the television at the same time. Demetri looked up, there was no surprise on his face when he took in his newest visitor. Sitting down opposite the fat man, Kamal dropped his pack of smokes on the table between them. Hamza brought a bottle of *rakia* and coffee for Kamal before either of them spoke a word.

"So, you're back," Demetri said.

"I'm back," Kamal confirmed. He lit a cigarette and fixed his coffee while Demetri poured the shots.

"What do you think about the latest scandal then?" Demetri asked with a smirk. He raised his glass and Kamal clinked his against it before they downed the shots.

"I don't know what you're talking about." Kamal took a long drag from his smoke, "I've been out of town."

Demetri chuckled, but the amusement didn't reach his stony eyes. "I heard you took your first job in over a month. Koslov was about to send the cadaver dogs into the mountains to find your body when you didn't accept anything for so long." Demetri took a drink of his coffee and sat back in his chair. "Julien's gone missing. Koslov had him set to take care of something for him in Norway and he never showed up for the job."

Kamal nodded. "Maybe he should send the cadaver dogs into the mountains, *maybe* they would find something for him."

This time Demetri's eyes shared in his laughter as they twinkled with mirth at Kamal's little joke. "You seem different somehow," he commented.

"I'm the same as always. Nothing has changed since we last saw one another." He filled his shot glass and then Demetri's.

"So it doesn't bother you to have the video of you fucking another man all over the internet?" Demetri asked. He knocked back his shot before adding, "Of course your face is masked so there's no way to identify you, which is fortunate." He smiled, but his eyes narrowed as he took in Kamal's reaction to the news.

Kamal's hand stalled in its path, leaving him holding his glass a few centimeters from his lips as Demetri's words sunk in. The video of him and Zijad was on the internet? That couldn't have been Orhan's doing, surely he wouldn't air his dirty laundry in public like that. Which only left Koslov, but what did he have to gain from releasing it? Kamal swallowed his drink as he tried to puzzle it out in his head. He savored the burn as the alcohol went down. Maybe he should have checked the news after all.

"You really haven't been keeping up with current events, have you?"

"I didn't think there was anything I needed to keep up with." Kamal said, "The job was done."

Demetri laughed out loud. "Oh, Kamal, only your small part in it is done, but the job goes on with the materials you provided to Koslov." Demetri paused and waited for Kamal to grasp what he was saying. "You don't have any idea of Koslov's master plan. He always gets what he wants and your friend rolled like a dog on command after he viewed the first video of his son receiving your tender mercies. You didn't know that Orhan running for the nominee among the Bosniaks was part of Koslov's plan, did you?"

Kamal didn't know what to say. He felt even more betrayed by Orhan now that he knew the other man had actually gone along with Koslov's plan only to have the video he considered private leaked to the public where anyone could see his boy at his most vulnerable. Kamal suddenly needed to leave the stifling atmosphere of the small restaurant. Standing, he took a breath to calm himself.

"There's something I need to attend to," Kamal said curtly. He turned on his heel and walked out, ignoring Demetri's farewell and Hamza's questioning look as he strode through to the door.

Kamal had to search through the archives on the Avaz site to find the news stories from the previous week so that he could follow the story from the beginning, no matter how much he wanted to search for the video to see what the hell Demetri was talking about. He started with the day after he'd made the drop.

Missing Son of Orhan Ferhatović Found

Zijad Ferhatović, son of Orhan Ferhatović, missing for almost a month, was found late last night in a club notorious for its rampant drug culture. The twenty-two year old was rushed to the hitna pomoć *with an apparent overdose when patrons failed to rouse him. As of right now he is in stable condition and expected to recover fully. The authorities are standing by to question Zijad about his disappearance when he is able to give a statement.*

When asked about the sudden reappearance of his son, Gospodin Ferhatović said only that he was happy to have his son back alive.

The story went on but Kamal skipped ahead to the next one his search turned up.

Son of Orhan Ferhatović Found to Have Links to Underground Sex Club

Zijad Ferhatović, son of Orhan Ferhatović, is still unable to communicate with authorities, but there have been others who have come forward to shed some light on the young man's life that may be helpful to those investigating the case of his disappearance. Two men who wish to remain anonymous have come forward to speak to the investigating officers about what they know of the time Zijad was missing. From their statements they place the young man at several clubs in Split the day after his disappearance. They drank with Zijad and followed along as he bar-hopped through the night. The last time they saw Zijad he was leaving a known fetish club with an older gentleman.

Kamal growled under his breath as he hit the link for the next story. He could see where this was leading .

Orhan Ferhatović Denies Rumors of Son's Participation in Drug Fueled Gay Orgies

Gospodin Ferhatović, the nominee for the SDP party, denied rumors that his son's disappearance was due to the young man frequenting sex clubs throughout Europe. More men have stepped up to tell the details of parties fueled by drugs and gay sexual orgies in which Zijad Ferhatović was an eager participant. Ferhatović would not share the details of the statement his son has given police nor would the investigating officers reveal anything pertaining to an ongoing case...

Kamal hit the next link . He picked up the glass he'd left on his desk and threw it across the room. The shattering of glass did little to satisfy his need for destruction when he saw the still photo that accompanied the article. It had been pulled from the second video Kamal had made and anyone could see that the boy, his boy, was naked and tied to a bench.

Video Sex Scandal: Politician's Son's Secret Life Exposed

Kamal couldn't even read the article because he knew it was all lies. He clicked the next link as a plan started to form in his mind.

Orhan Ferhatović Falls in the Polls

Kamal skimmed the article, but didn't really care if his ex-lover's political career was over. The next link provided another picture of

151

Zijad, this time hanging by his hands from the ceiling. Kamal recognized himself, even though he was masked, as the man wielding the crop poised to land on the bare behind of the boy.

Second Video Surfaces of Young Ferhatović

Again Kamal decided not to read the lies they were telling about Zijad. He clicked the next link and this time the picture made him sit up and lean in closer. There was Zijad being led from the hospital by his father, they were surrounded by security but that didn't stop the photographers from getting their pictures. Orhan's face was hard, his mouth set in a grim line. The boy looked lost as he stared into the lens of the camera with blank, hollowed-out eyes. He actually resembled the drugged-up party boy they were portraying him as. Kamal wished he could wring the boy's neck for playing into their hands with that dazed expression of his. The headline made him sound like a criminal.

Zijad Ferhatović Leaves Hospital Under Guard

Zijad Ferhatović was released from the hospital today and into the care of his family. A friend close to the Ferhatović family released a statement on their behalf. "Orhan and Selma are happy to announce that Zijad's health has improved enough for him to finish his recovery in the comfort of his own home surrounded by his family whose love will aid in his healing. They ask for everyone to respect their privacy while Zijad is recuperating."

Sources close to Gospodin Ferhatović say that the popular politician is handling the scandal surrounding his only son with a heavy heart...

Kamal had seen enough. He went to Google and searched up Zijad and the first things that came up were links to the videos where they were being sold – the profits going into Koslov's pockets no doubt. Kamal's anger bubbled over and his computer was the next thing that hit the wall with a loud crash. Standing abruptly, he flipped the desk over to get to his hiding spot. He ripped the floorboard up and pulled out all of the contents. A plan had formed in his mind, and someone was going to pay.

What Kamal had planned would be an undertaking of some magnitude. It wouldn't be easy to take down a man like Koslov on his own, but he was going to do it or die trying. He'd pooled all his resources and called in every favor ever owed him to get a lock on Koslov's whereabouts and his routine. Only Demetri balked when Kamal called in his chip. The fat man even tried to talk Kamal out of his crazy plan as he'd handed over the names of Koslov's inner circle, but Kamal would not be swayed. Kamal left Demetri sitting in a stupor when he'd detailed what he'd do to the man's young teenage son if he dared breathe a word of his plan to Koslov. He'd only had to point to Zijad as proof that Kamal wouldn't hesitate to hurt someone he knew.

When Kamal had finished with all the preparations he could make in Sarajevo, he loaded his car and left the city behind. He didn't know if he'd ever see it again, but it had never really felt like home anyway so it was no great loss, except for one thing he'd hopefully be back to claim as his own.

Kamal drove a rental car, he'd used a false name and paid cash that required leaving a hefty deposit but it was worth it not to leave a paper trail, three hours northeast to Bratunac. He made his way through the city and then parked in one of the public parking areas along the banks of the Drina. Kamal got out of the car and, under the cover of darkness, he finished dressing in all black. Shouldering his backpack, he grabbed his duffle bag out of the trunk, then made his way down to the wide but shallow river that served as the border between Bosnia and Serbia. Kamal was taking no chances, not even daring to use one of his false documents to cross the border into the country where Koslov had eyes everywhere.

He waded out into the knee deep water and took it slowly over the slippery rocks until he reached the far bank, stepping out of the river and into Serbia. He made his way down the bank toward Ljubovija where he'd meet an old friend and get a car that would take him to one of the smaller cities outside of Belgrade. He walked to the parking lot of the *stočna pijaca* on the outskirts of the small city. There was only one car parked, as the place was closed for the night. Kamal walked over as the door opened and the occupant got out.

"Kamal, *rodak*, it's been too long," the man said as he took Kamal's duffle bag from his hand. Kamal let the man give him a one-armed hug.

"Emir, it has been a while," Kamal said as he took the backpack off his shoulders.

Emir smiled and nodded. "I thought you'd never call in that favor I owed you. Thought you'd forgotten." Emir pulled out a pack of cigarettes and offered one to Kamal who took one and let the other man light it for him.

"I never forget a debt, either owed or due."

Emir laughed nervously as he lit his own smoke. "You've not changed from the man I followed through the mountains all those years ago," he said. The smile on his face turned sad.

"I've changed, but not in ways you'd understand." Kamal looked at the car his old friend had brought him and shook his head. "A Yugo? Was that the best you could do?"

"You said you didn't want to stand out on the back roads. What better way to blend in than to drive the pride of Yugoslavia?" Emir said with a wry twist to his lips.

Kamal snorted. "I guess you have a point, but will it get me to Obrenovac?" Kamal had another rental car waiting for him there.

"It runs just fine, it's my brother-in-law's car and he swears by the Slavic engineering of its engine."

"If you say so," Kamal replied. He couldn't afford to be choosy and though he hated that Emir had betrayed his country and those that died for it by marrying a Serb, he knew the man would keep his secret as sure as he knew he'd kill Koslov. "How much does he want for it?"

"Would sixty thousand sound too high?" Emir smiled when Kamal snorted at the price.

"This piece of shit is probably worth half that," Kamal said. Sixty thousand dinar wasn't even five hundred euros but he was right, the car's value was less than half that.

"I know, but he's rather fond of it," Emir said.

"I'll give you fifty-five in euros."

"Fine, I'm sure he'll be pleased with that amount."

Kamal pulled a roll of bills out of his pocket and handed over a five hundred euro note to Emir. "A little something extra for you to buy something for your children," Kamal said when Emir just looked at the bill in Kamal's hand.

"For the children, yes." Emir took the money and shoved it in his pocket.

Kamal clapped the man on the shoulder and took his duffle bag back from him. "Thank you, Emir, and you can consider your debt to me paid. Have a good life." Kamal opened the back door of the Yugo and put his bags inside before opening the driver's side to get in.

"*Sretan put*, Kamal," Emir called as Kamal started the car.

Kamal nodded his farewell to a man he figured he'd never see again before driving off. He made good time to Obrenovac, where he ditched the uncomfortable Yugo for an Audi that made the Yugo look like a child's push car. He drove into Belgrade just as the sun crested the horizon. The hotel he'd chosen was close to the banks of the River Danube and was upmarket and discreet enough that no one would question Kamal pulling out a wad of cash to pay for his stay. He took the elevator to his room and slept most of the day away since he couldn't put the first part of his plan into action until night had fallen.

The small house had been no trouble to break into, which was surprising when the man who lived there was the head of security for Koslov's home. Kamal crept silently up the stairs and into the room where the smallest occupant of the house currently slept soundly in a crib. The little girl was less than a year old, her chubby cheeks moved as her lips pursed and made a sucking motion as if there was an invisible bottle poised at her mouth. Kamal looked down at the helpless child for a moment before reaching into the crib and pinching her fat little thigh hard enough to not only wake the baby but to make her first cry a startled wail of pain.

Exiting the small room, Kamal hid in the doorway of another one down the hall. He waited and just as he'd expected, a woman emerged from across the hall and entered the nursery. He listened to her murmur to the infant before he moved stealthily down the corridor and into the room she'd come from. Shutting the door behind him, he crossed to the bed where the man he was looking for lay facing away from him. He turned, maybe to ask why the baby had cried or why his wife had returned so quickly, but his eyes widened when he saw a man standing there instead.

"Be very careful, your lovely family is just across the hall. You wouldn't want them to get involved in this, I'm sure," Kamal said, low enough to keep their conversation just between them. The man's eyes darted to the door and then back to Kamal as he nodded. "I need some information and you're the one that will give it to me. If you do this one simple thing, your family will come to no harm." Kamal rounded the bed and sat next to the man.

"I don't think — "

"You don't need to think," Kamal murmured as he wrapped his hand around the man's neck. "I need to get into Koslov's house and you're going to tell me how to do it."

Kamal pocketed the empty insulin pen and left through the window before the woman returned from soothing her child. He didn't stick around long enough to hear her wail when she found her husband dead in their marital bed in the morning.

Chapter 18:
Retaliation

The house was in one of the wealthiest parts of town. Dedinje was just where he'd expected Koslov to live. The neighborhood had large houses situated on spacious treed lots. Koslov's house was set back from the road and surrounded by an ornate brick and wrought iron fence, with a gate stretched across the drive that was paved with large etched concrete slabs. The place just screamed money. Dirty money was what Kamal heard as he pulled up to the gatehouse and rolled down the window of the delivery truck he'd 'borrowed'.

The guard in the little shed looked at his clipboard before coming out of his shelter. "Where's Damir?" he asked as he approached the vehicle.

"He's off sick, I'm just filling in for him," Kamal said casually.

"Well, you're late, there's no one here to help you get that unloaded, so maybe you should come back tomorrow," the guard said as he checked his watch.

"I can do it myself. Come on, man, the boss will give me shit for getting lost on my way here if I bring this load back."

"That's a lot to do on your own," the guard said, but Kamal could hear him giving in already.

"I'll be quick, I've done more by myself alone before," Kamal wheedled. "I'm only thirty minutes late, I'll be out of here before five." The guard should have turned him away; there were to be no deliveries after four, but Kamal could see the guard's resolve melt away at Kamal's pleas.

"Alright, I'll let it slide this time but next time I'll give your boss a call myself." He went back into the guardhouse and opened the gate. Kamal looked right at the camera as he passed, knowing it was only a live feed and there would be no evidence left behind.

Driving to the back of the house where there was a discreet entrance for deliveries, he backed the truck in and swung out to the ground. After pressing the button beside the door, Kamal waited. Another guard opened the heavy wooden door and furrowed his brow after seeing Kamal standing there.

"Who are you?" he asked.

"I've got your water delivery," Kamal said, gesturing over his shoulder at the truck behind him.

The guard looked to where Kamal was pointing and then back at him. "You're late."

"Yeah, I already had this conversation with the guy out there." Kamal tried to look put upon.

"Hurry up then," the guard said before stepping back into the house.

Kamal went to the truck and grabbed one of the nineteen liter jugs of water from the back. Carrying it over his shoulder into the house, he followed the guard to a small room and put it down when the guard showed him where it went. He went back out and grabbed another, taking his time as the guard watched over his work. Finally the guard stopped him.

"Hold on, buddy, my replacement is here, can you wait out by the truck for a couple of minutes?"

The changing of the guard was just what Kamal had been waiting for so he smiled and nodded at the man. "Sure, mind if I smoke?" Kamal asked, pulling out his pack.

"Nope, but don't drop your butt on the ground, make sure it goes in the can over there." The guard pointed to the ornate outdoor ashtray before leaving Kamal on his own.

Kamal studied the back of the house as he stood there waiting to finish his delivery as the new guard came on duty. He knew they'd be advised of his presence, but that didn't bother him at all. The replacement guard came out to get him ten minutes later. His scowl told Kamal all he needed to know about what he thought of Kamal's late delivery, but he went about unloading a couple more bottles until he heard the gatehouse guard call over the radio that he was opening the front gate to let the first two guards leave.

Setting the bottle he'd been carrying down, Kamal turned on the guard who had been watching him. The sound of the man's neck snapping was loud in the small room but Kamal was sure the occupants of the home didn't hear it from their lofty rooms above. He laid the body out flat on the floor. Grabbing the radio and keychain the dead man had been carrying, Kamal closed the door behind him when he left. He went out the door he'd been using to bring the water into the home. The positions of the cameras left enough gaps that he made it to the guardhouse undetected. He dispatched of the second guard in the same way as the first and propped him in his chair to make it look like he was just dozing on the job.

Walking back to the house, Kamal used the vegetation of the yard to conceal his movements in case anyone happened to look out the window. He wasn't quite ready to show his hand. Kamal shut and locked the door when he got back into the house, but this time he walked up the small set of stairs and entered the main area of the home. It was richly furnished and the plush carpets muffled the sound of his steps as he made his way through the downstairs rooms. His surveillance, along with what the head of security had told him, put the two people he was looking for on the upper level in separate rooms at opposite ends of the hall.

Kamal knew he'd have to subdue the biggest physical threat first, so he took a right when he got to the top of the open staircase. He could hear loud music coming from the room he was heading for which he deemed to be a good thing since his target would not hear him coming. He took a deep breath as he pulled the syringe out of his pocket and turned the door knob.

The lights weren't as bright as the ones he'd used at the cabin with the boy, but they would do to light the scene for the camera just as well. He'd gotten the scene set up perfectly as his victim had slept off her small dose of valium. Kamal just had to wait for her to come to and he was good at waiting.

The woman started to rouse and Kamal trained the camera on her face to catch the first glint of awareness in her eyes. He wasn't disappointed, the bitch's eyes got wider than a five km coin and then the struggling began. Kamal smiled because it wasn't until she glimpsed the body strung up beside her that she tried to scream through the gag. Kamal let her wail through her nose for a good ten minutes, it was the least he could do for the grieving mother. He zoomed out so the camera could capture the grisly scene.

Kamal was pretty proud of his handiwork. Koslov's teenage son hung by his wrists from the same sort of rope and pulley system Kamal had gotten so used to using with his boy. He'd have to remember to thank Koslov for giving him so much time to perfect some of the finer techniques he'd employed as he'd tortured Koslov's son. But the kid wasn't feeling any pain at the moment; no, he'd never feel anything again, not with that gaping neck wound of his. It was a shame, really, Kamal thought, he'd screamed beautifully.

Kamal turned his attention back to the woman who was tied to a chair. Koslov's wife was tied, naked and bent over the back of the heavy wooden arm chair. She'd given up on craning her neck to look at her son and now her head was hanging between her shoulders as the sobs shook her body. Kamal felt no sympathy for the woman. If she'd wanted a normal, long and healthy life she shouldn't have married a man like Koslov.

Kamal stepped out from behind the camera and into the light; this time, unlike the others, his face was bare of any mask. He didn't need to hide from the only man who would view this tape – in fact, he turned and smiled wickedly at the lens. The woman had caught sight of him and renewed her struggles. Kamal wasn't going to take as much time and care with the bitch; he'd done what he needed to get his message across to Koslov when he'd abused and violated the boy. Grabbing the chair, he turned it roughly, making the woman stumble and cry out. He punched her in the face a couple of times, enough to make her lip and nose bleed, then held her by the hair so that her bloodied image would forever be captured on film.

"I bet your husband will be sorry he decided to visit his mistress tonight instead of coming home to watch me fuck you," Kamal said, letting her head drop. He used a condom for two reasons; one, he had no idea where the slut's husband had been before dipping his dick into her, and two, for the small amount of lube it contained. Fucking someone dry didn't only hurt the getter, it could also be hell on the giver, a lesson he'd learned the hard way with a chafed prick. He finished positioning the chair so nothing was blocking the camera when he shoved his cock into the bitch's ass. She squealed through the gag but Kamal ignored it and fucked her as hard as his body would let him.

It took a long time for him to finally come. He pushed away from the cunt and spat on her back. "No wonder he fucks other women, even your ass is so loose it took me forever to come," Kamal sneered at the sniveling woman. He took the condom off and put it in his pocket as he adjusted his pants. He walked around so he stood in front of the woman once again. Kamal grabbed her hair and crouched down to eye level with her. "I just want you to know the reason you and your son are suffering and being put down. My name is Kamal Hodžić, I have done many things in the name of your husband, but only one that I regret, and now he has to pay for making me feel it. You are that payment."

Standing, he pulled the same knife he'd used on the boy from the sheath on his hip. He ran the sharp blade across the thin flesh of the bitch's neck as she weakly struggled against his hold. Kamal watched as the life ran out of her in a steady stream of crimson. His job here was finished, it was time to find the man himself and show him his cinematic masterpiece.

Koslov's high-rise apartment would have been much harder to gain entry to if Koslov hadn't given keys to the guards at his house. Kamal whistled to himself as he walked through the lobby of the building. It was a nice place, it had a restaurant and bar on the main floor to one side and to the other was a gym and pool. He bet Koslov had paid a pretty penny for the penthouse he kept for the express purpose of having a place to fuck his various whores. It was fortunate for Kamal that Koslov was a creature of habit who held to a strict schedule; it was how his head of security knew Koslov was out at the ballet with his favorite mistress that evening. Kamal took the elevator to the top floor and used the key to enter one of the only two apartments that occupied the floor. The apartment was huge and Kamal wandered over to the windows that offered a view of the Danube and the city beyond. At least Koslov's last moments would come with a view, Kamal thought as he grinned into the dark night.

Patiently he waited in the bathroom for either Koslov or his whore to enter, hoping they wouldn't both need to pee at the same time. He could hear them in the other room, talking and laughing, but that would end, and soon enough there would be little in Koslov's life to laugh about. Kamal grew bored as time wore on and eventually he knew he'd run out of patience for waiting. Switching to plan B when he heard Koslov and the whore fucking in the adjoining room, Kamal readied his weapon and grabbed the door knob. With a deep cleansing breath, he stepped out of the small room to face the man he'd come to kill.

They didn't even notice Kamal until he stood, gun against the cunt's head, above Koslov. With no hesitation he pulled the trigger and the muffled sound of a gunshot ended the whore's bouncing movements. She slumped forward onto Koslov who pushed her off and sat up just in time to meet the butt of Kamal's gun as it slammed down into his temple. To Kamal's surprise, Koslov didn't go down with the hit which should have rendered him unconscious.. Koslov managed to land one slightly painful punch to his ribs before Kamal could get the gun pointed at Koslov's face.

"What are you doing here?" Koslov asked. He didn't look scared at all, just pissed off.

"I've come to kill you," Kamal stated simply.

"Really? And you think you can get away with killing me? Do you think there will be no consequences to that?" Koslov asked, and then the bastard smiled because he really thought Kamal cared whether or not he'd pay a price for his actions. But then Koslov didn't know what Kamal knew and it was time for Kamal to enlighten the man a bit.

"I don't think the consequences will be as bad as you think." Kamal smiled back with a grin that was ten times scarier than that of Koslov's because it came from a true psychopath. The man on the bed didn't look quite as confident as he did a moment before. "You see, there has been a contract out on you for quite some time. The thing is, nobody was crazy enough to take it. But guess what?" Kamal asked as he tapped the gun on the side of Koslov's head. Koslov didn't answer as his eyes darted from side to side looking for something he could use to gain an advantage. "I'm probably the craziest motherfucker you'll ever meet, and so not only do I get my revenge for you selling my tapes, I also get paid to do it. Oh, and it's a lot of money, so I thank you for making me a rich man."

"I don't understand. What tapes?" Koslov's brow furrowed in confusion.

"The tapes of Ferhatović's son," Kamal said, wanting the man to know why he was about to die.

"You're crazy. How do you have any claim to those tapes? They were made by the man I paid to do the job and therefore mine to do as I please with," Koslov said arrogantly. Once again his eyes darted around for an escape from a man he thought was completely mad.

Kamal pushed the muzzle of the gun more firmly into the side of Koslov's head. "I killed the man you paid to do that job. That was me in the video with that boy, *my boy!*" Kamal shouted the last two words into his face to make sure Koslov was aware of his ownership of the boy. Koslov's face twisted as he thought about what Kamal said.

"You're fucking crazy," Koslov said defiantly.

"Didn't I just tell you that?" Kamal asked, with a grin.

"So what do you want? You want the money from the sales or what?" This was the bargaining stage, Kamal knew it well, but as with all his other victims there would be no buying back of Koslov's life with money or favors. "You want me to pay you for the contract on top of that? That could be arranged and with that amount of money, you could disappear. Think about it."

"I don't want your money. You took something of mine and I have taken something of yours in return for that, so that debt is paid," Kamal said.

"What do you mean? What have you taken of mine?" Koslov's eyes flicked to the dead whore in his bed.

Kamal laughed. "Oh, I don't think that whore is worth all that much to you. I took something much more precious to you than that." He smiled again at Koslov's angry expression. "Don't worry, soon you'll join your wife and son in whatever hell they're in right now."

Koslov's eyes were no longer angry. Kamal had expected a fight from the man and he was prepared when Koslov made his move. The gun flew from Kamal's hand and landed halfway across the room when Koslov brought his beefy arm up. Kamal stood and let Koslov follow him off the bed. He punched Koslov in the face with a well-aimed jab, causing blood to flow from what was surely a broken nose. Koslov returned with a few jabs of his own, catching Kamal in the ribs. Kamal punched back, knowing Koslov's aim was for the gun he'd knocked away.

Koslov made his move.

With arms wrapped around Kamal's waist, they hit the floor. The air rushed out of Kamal's body as he hit hard with the bigger man on top of him. Kamal struggled, but Koslov came up with the gun. The cold hard metal pressed into the soft flesh of Kamal's chin as Koslov grinned down at him in victory. Kamal closed his eyes for a moment and took a deep breath.

Chapter 19:
Revenge

Kamal opened his eyes and smiled coldly up at the naked man sitting astride him.

"What are you smiling at?" Koslov sneered, "I'm the one holding the gun." He pushed the gun harder into Kamal's chin. Kamal only chuckled at the act. "Don't you fucking laugh, you piece of shit! Did you really think you could get away with this? You think you're smarter than all the others that came before you and tried to take me out? I'm where I am because *I'm* the craziest motherfucker, not you." Kamal stopped smiling and Koslov grinned as if he thought his words had hit the mark, that he'd finally made Kamal understand he would not win this fight.

"I think the title is still up for grabs," Kamal goaded.

"You just want me to shoot you so that I can't give you to my men. They will rip you to pieces."

"No, I don't want you to shoot me," Kamal said honestly. "Not before you watch my video at least." Koslov's eyes narrowed. "That's right, I want you to watch the video of me raping and killing your wife. But what I *really* want to see is your reaction to the sweet screams of your son as I fucked his tight virgin ass."

There was a click and then another.

Koslov stared down at the gun in his hand as if it had betrayed him. Kamal laughed, a full-on belly laugh that shook Koslov with its power. Koslov tried the gun once more before quickly rolling off Kamal and trying to make his way to the nightstand. Kamal let him go, waiting for the disappointment when he realized Kamal had been in the apartment long enough to find Koslov's home security

165

system in the drawer next to the bed. Koslov growled in frustration as Kamal pulled himself off the floor.

"I'll give you a choice," Kamal offered. Koslov stood and readied himself for a fight. "You can sit in that chair over there and watch the video before I kill you with one clean shot through your head or you can fight and I'll tie you to that table and fuck your ass while you watch it. Then I'll still kill you with a clean shot through the head." Kamal grinned at Koslov's expression of horror but thought he was giving the man a very fair offer.

Kamal put his hand in his pocket just before Koslov charged him.

Kamal was getting a little sleepy as he waited for Koslov to shrug off the effects of the drugs. He hadn't even knocked the other man out completely, just administered enough to make him too woozy to fight. It wasn't easy getting Koslov strapped to the table but he'd managed it, and now he sat in the chair Koslov had shunned. Kamal stared at the man's plugged asshole, remembering the way he'd squealed like a stuck pig when Kamal had shoved it in there. He'd fought the ring gag and tried to bite Kamal's fingers as he'd fitted it into the man's mouth. Even with the drugs, Koslov was a feisty one, Kamal would give him that.

When the struggles grew in intensity, Kamal knew it was time. He'd set up a laptop he'd found in the living room on a small tray. On the screen was a frozen image of Koslov's son, tied down over a makeshift bench much like the one Kamal had used with the boy. The look of terror on that young face, and what came after, got Kamal hard enough that he'd have no trouble fucking the hairy ass he'd been staring at.

Kamal walked around the table and bent down to look into Koslov's eyes. They were clear and alert. It was time. "I see that you're ready now to watch this little show I made just for you," Kamal said as he started the video. The sound of the kid's pleading voice filled the air. Koslov turned his head, but Kamal grabbed his hair and made him watch. Koslov moaned around the gag and then closed his eyes. Kamal snorted, he'd been prepared for this. Grabbing a pillow and some duct tape, he used them to prop and immobilize Koslov's head. He pulled out a short surgically sharp knife and showed it to Koslov.

"I was going to cut your eyelids off so you couldn't close them." Kamal watched the way Koslov's eyes darted around like a frightened animal caught in a trap before he put the knife on the tray by the computer. "But then I decided that it would take too much time and I'm eager for you to watch how much your boy liked my cock. So your eyelids will be spared...for now." Kamal used the duct tape instead. Wrapping it around Koslov's head and the pillow, he pulled it up and tight enough across the man's forehead that Koslov couldn't blink. The video playing in the background provided the screams Koslov was unable to voice for himself when he realized he'd have no choice but to watch his family's demise.

Kamal patted Koslov's head when he was through. "There now, that's much better," he said, then turned to restart the video from the beginning. Koslov still struggled but he had to watch and that was what mattered to Kamal.

The kid's pleas must have been heart-wrenching for his father to hear, knowing there was no way he could help his son. Kamal watched for a moment, but then he rounded the trapped man so he stood behind him. Freeing his dick, he let his hand and the images of himself with the kid get him hard. He put on a condom before he pulled the large dildo out of Koslov's ass. A brief thought of having the man suck his own shit from the toy flitted though Kamal's mind, but then he tossed the soiled dick to the side instead.

Kamal watched as the other him took the same position behind Koslov's son on the video. "Watch closely, I think your son liked it when I..." Kamal let his words hang in the air as he showed Koslov just what he'd done to the boy. Kamal slid a little easier into Koslov's ass than he had the kid's. It was still tight, though, and Koslov clenched to avoid the penetration, which only made it that much more difficult for both of them, but eventually Kamal was fully seated.

"Your boy begged me and he promised me that you'd do anything you could if I'd stop hurting him. I wonder if that's true. Would you have taken his place if you could?" Kamal asked as he pulled all the way out and slammed ruthlessly back in. Koslov let out another squeal but his noises did nothing for Kamal, not like the ones coming from the speakers which drove his lust. Kamal fucked

Koslov harder than he'd ever fucked anyone in his life – not even his anger at Orhan had driven him to these heights of cruelty.

"Your son's ass was the second most heavenly thing I've ever felt squeeze around my dick. He bawled like a baby until I fucked the screams out of him," Kamal growled, and thrust harder. He lasted longer than he'd done with the son and was still fucking the father as he ran the blade across the neck of the kid on the video. Kamal came as the boy uttered one last gurgled scream. The scene shifted as Kamal pulled out. He left Koslov with the video of his wife as he made his way to the bathroom for toilet tissue, where he bundled the shit and blood covered condom into his pocket to dispose of later. He used the toilet and then washed off in the sink.

The video was winding down when he joined Koslov again. He let the video come to an end and then removed the memory card, making sure it was safely tucked away in his pocket before he turned to Koslov. The man's face was wet with tears. Kamal didn't fool himself into believing they were emotional tears, Koslov was just as much of a monster as Kamal knew himself to be.

"Well, it seems we are about finished here," Kamal said as Koslov's eyes rolled to follow his movements. "Just one more thing I need to do and then..." Kamal used two fingers to imitate a gun as he pointed them at Koslov's forehead.

Grabbing his knife from the tray, Kamal had one more job to do. He had to kneel down and then get under the table to get to his prize. He grasped Koslov's limp cock and started to cut around the base. Koslov screamed around the gag and struggled, but Kamal had done a very good job restraining him so his body wouldn't budge an inch from where he'd wanted it. Kamal didn't stop cutting, but Koslov eventually stopped moving. Kamal sat back and looked at his handiwork, the man's dick and balls laid in the palm of his hand, free from his body. Kamal crawled back out to find that Koslov had passed out from the shock and pain of his little amputation.

Kamal would wait. He still had time until the sun would rise and the new guards at Koslov's home would discover what he'd done. Then, eventually, someone somewhere would wonder where Koslov was, but Kamal would be long gone by then.

Koslov did recover consciousness long enough for Kamal to take the small penis-shaped plug from its place inside the ring gag and replace it with the real thing. He took a picture to send to his contact as proof that the deed was done. Then he took out his gun and shot Koslov in the head twice, once for him and once for his boy.

Kamal sat at his desk in front of his computer. Almir had tricked out a new one for him and told him not to throw it against the wall as he handed it over. It had been only three days since he'd taken his revenge on Koslov. Kamal was surprised at the upheaval Koslov's death had caused. On the dark web, Kamal was now known only as The Ghost. There was wild speculation about who had finally taken on the contract. The source of the contract was anonymous, which usually meant some government agency in a foreign country, and the suggestions of who carried it out were as farfetched as some of the wildest conspiracy theories on the web. Next thing, they'd be fingering him for the one who killed JFK.

Kamal's phone vibrated and pulled his attention from the screen of his computer. He gave it a glance and upon seeing Demetri's phone number, answered it.

"I see you made it back safely from your latest endeavor," Demetri said in greeting.

"Don't I always?" Kamal grunted.

"Yes, I guess you always have, but this one..." Demetri let his words hang on the line.

"It was a job. I always do the job."

Demetri's laugh rolled down the line. "Always so pragmatic, Kamal. I'm glad you have returned. I need to see you, tonight."

Kamal lit a smoke and let his first drag out of his nose slowly. "I can't make it tonight," Kamal said shortly, thinking of the plans he still needed to make.

"This isn't a request." Kamal heard the change in the other man's tone – gone was the jovial fat man.

"You can't command me to do anything."

"I can't, but if you don't come it could affect your future. Nobody wants a dog that will turn and bite its master at the slightest thing," Demetri said.

"I'll be there in an hour." Kamal hung up. He'd heard the threat in Demetri's words and the last thing Kamal needed was for the one person who knew The Ghost's identity pissed at him. He dressed and took the tram which was an uncomfortable ride. He'd never noticed how people looked at him before, but for some reason now he was acutely aware of the way people tended to give him more space – like sheep huddled together when they sensed a predator.

Hamza avoided eye contact when Kamal entered the dimly lit café, but Kamal shrugged the snub off as he made his way to Demetri's table. Demetri eyed him as he approached and waited until Kamal was seated.

"I know you're not happy about me asking for this meeting," Demetri began, but paused to offer Kamal a cigarette and then light one for himself. "I needed to talk to you in person before I leave."

Kamal raised an eyebrow at the man across the table. "Where are you going?" Hamza showed up at the table bearing their usual coffee and *rakia*, he poured them each a shot before walking off.

"I have a meeting to attend back home. It seems a position has opened up and they are asking me to consider it," Demetri said with a grin.

"You?" Demetri had never struck him as the type of man with such lofty ambitions, but as his grinning face morphed into a shrewd look, things fell into place. The pieces started to come together in Kamal's head and he almost laughed. Demetri had played him like a well-tuned instrument. Kamal had done Demetri's dirty work for him, clearing his way to rise to power, without the fat man even asking him to – or paying him for that matter.

"I see you are starting to get a better picture of the things you set in motion when you went to meet your old friend in Neum." Demetri slammed back his shot. "Of course, poor Julien didn't expect to end up dead but that was an unforeseen event. I guess when dealing with someone as predictable as you, one should never forget that it's always the quiet ones who end up dealing out the most damage in the end."

"So none of this has ever been about Orhan's political career," Kamal said softly. His mind went back to the beginning and, yes, he'd been played. His anger at Demetri swelled with the thought that the fat man across from him was responsible for everything. He hadn't gotten his revenge with the killing of Koslov. Instead he'd helped the man who'd planned it all by killing off the only thing that stood in his way on his climb to the top.

"Now, Kamal, calm down and let's talk about this rationally," Demetri said. He must have been able to read Kamal's thoughts. "You are understandably upset by this turn of events, but I think I have a way to make it sit a bit better for you."

Kamal dialed back his anger. He wouldn't do anything stupid on the spot with no way to back his actions if they were questioned, especially by the organization Demetri would now be an influential part of. "What do you have for me that will make up for you using me as an unpaid pawn in your scheme?"

Demetri smiled and this time it looked genuine. "Ah, well, you can't say you weren't paid for the job. As I recall, the contract on Koslov was worth over one point five million euros." Demetri reminded him of the money that was sitting in an offshore account just waiting for Kamal to make use of it.

"I didn't get paid for the kidnapping."

"I can arrange to make fair recompense for that job, and I also have an offer to make that would be much more lucrative for you in the coming years than the odd jobs you perform," Demetri said. He refilled his shot glass, prompting Kamal to swallow his own and offer his glass.

"I'm listening," Kamal said as he sat back in his chair.

"I'll need someone here in Sarajevo. I don't know many people that are capable of holding their own here that I also trust to be loyal to me." Demetri made his position clear, even though he'd not actually offered Kamal the job. If he wanted, Kamal could become head of the local Russian mob.

"I'm not Russian, you know that, right?" Kamal pointed out the one flaw in Demetri's plan. As far as he knew, no one that wasn't a national held any position that high in the organization.

"You don't have to worry about that. Believe me when I say my comrades are impressed with the man they know only as The Ghost. They all agree having such a man firmly in the family would be best for all concerned."

Kamal thought on it for a moment, but then realized he was not at all a *family* man. "I have to decline your offer."

"I don't think you understand exactly what I'm offering you here, *rodak*," Demetri said with a scowl on his face at Kamal's refusal.

"I understand perfectly what's on the table, but right now I have some plans of my own. I was going to contact you soon to tell you that I might need to be out of the game for some time."

"Are you retiring?" Demetri asked.

"No, not retiring. I just might need some time to work on a project, maybe six months, maybe a year, depending on how much resistance I encounter," Kamal said, hoping he'd need the time but not holding his breath.

"And if you don't need this time off?"

"It's not something I want to think about. If my plans fall through, then I will still be at your disposal, but I cannot take the position."

Demetri thought about Kamal's answer for a time while they both drank their coffees. "If not this position, then maybe you'd consider coming with me. A man as formidable as yourself would make a good second for someone like me," Demetri said.

Kamal finished his coffee and then his shot. "I have something I have to do before I can even think about your offer." In the end he knew he'd still say no because Demetri would have to pay for his actions, but for the time being Kamal would let him think he was considering it.

"Can I ask what sort of project you're taking on that will take so long?" Demetri asked, curious.

"No," Kamal said simply as he stood. Shaking Demetri's hand, he ignored the man's annoyance at his curt answer. He didn't even glance in Hamza's direction on his way out, his mind was already on the plans to make before he could go claim what was his.

Chapter 20:
Give Him What's His

Kamal sat in his car on the street outside of Orhan's gated complex. He'd made an appointment to see his former lover, but now he felt the old revulsion at seeing Orhan in person rise along with the bile in his throat. He wondered if Orhan ever thought about the last time they'd seen each other. Putting his head back against the seat, Kamal closed his eyes because there was no suppressing the memory of that fateful night when it came knocking at the back door of his mind.

Kamal swung the chubby-cheeked three-year-old who greeted him at the door up in his arms and kissed his cherubic face. The boy giggled and squirmed in his arms to be let down. Kamal set the kid down, but allowed him to take his hand and drag him through the small wooden structure that had become home for so many of the displaced families from their village after the war had ended.

"Come see, Mal," the little boy said excitedly. He stopped in front of a structure built out of colorful blocks and looked up proudly at Kamal.

"Wow, Mali, that's really something. Did you build that all by yourself?" The boy nodded and giggled. "Well that deserves a treat, I think," Kamal said as he pulled a rather large chocolate bar out of his pocket and handed it to Zijad who took it with the greedy hands of a toddler.

"No chocolate, it's almost his bedtime and the sugar will keep him bouncing all night." A voice that still grated on Kamal's nerves broke up the happy moment between man and child. Selma swooped in and took the child's treat from his unwilling little hands. "You can have a piece tomorrow." The child's mother put the bar high up out of his reach before returning to her work in the tiny kitchen.

Kamal smiled at the little boy who looked as if the world had just ended. "You can eat the whole thing tomorrow, but this should tide you over until then," he whispered, slipping a small chunk from his pocket into the kid's mouth. The child threw his arms around Kamal's neck and noisily chewed the sweet treat. Kamal stood and carried the boy to the couch where he sat waiting for the boy's father to finish getting ready to go out.

When Orhan emerged from the small sleeping quarters smelling of soap and hair still a little damp, he received a disapproving look from his wife that Kamal caught but Orhan ignored. "Kamal, I didn't hear you come in," he said, picking the child up and giving him a quick squeeze.

"I was a bit early," Kamal said, a little embarrassed at his eagerness to begin their night together.

"You're always a bit early," Selma said snidely, "I suppose you won't be home tonight then?" The look she gave Orhan could have killed a lesser man.

"You know you prefer me to sleep off my drunken stupor elsewhere, no need to pretend you're bothered by it," Orhan said with a smile and a peck to her cheek as he handed her their son.

"I just don't know why you have to go every weekend." Selma took the boy and set him back near his toys in the corner.

"That's none of your concern, woman," Orhan said, letting her know she'd stepped over the line. It wasn't a woman's place to question her husband, especially in front of company. Selma shot Kamal a nasty glare before she turned away. "Let's go, my friend, we have much to catch up on."

Standing, Kamal followed Orhan to the door but he didn't miss Selma's muttered, "How much could you have missed when you saw him just yesterday."

"I don't think your wife cares for me much," Kamal said as they walked the well-worn path to the edge of the little makeshift town.

"She's been nagging me about having another kid and I told her it's too soon so she's taking it out on everyone she can. You're just a convenient target," Orhan said. Kamal shrugged, but the fact that Orhan's wife wanted another baby weighed on him heavily. "Stop looking so glum, let's go get drunk."

There were no bars in the camp as alcohol was still something hard to come by, but there was one place where the men gathered and one or two of them always had *rakia* to sell. Orhan and Kamal entered the building that had been left vacant by the resettlement of the family who had occupied it previously. There were chairs and a few makeshift tables set up in the empty space and it was crowded as usual. They found a spot and sat cramped in the corner. Orhan and Kamal both pulled out their ration cards and pooled the ones they thought their families could do without to buy half a liter of *rakia*, more than enough to get them both drunk.

Time flew by as Kamal swallowed the liquid that made his insides burn and listened to the lively chatter that filled the small space. When their drink was mostly gone, Kamal felt the familiar lust brought on by the drink and the man pressed against his side. He turned his head to watch Orhan as he laughed and exchanged jokes with some men at the table next to them. He was beautiful. Kamal was sure he would never see anything that compared to the man he loved. He slid his hand onto Orhan's leg and gave it a squeeze.

"I need to piss," he said, a little louder than he'd intended, interrupting the men and getting more laughs than the joke. He stood unsteadily, putting a hand on Orhan's shoulder to steady himself.

"Your friend is drunk," Meho said. He winked at Kamal to show he meant no malice in the statement.

"I know, I should probably go out with him so he doesn't stumble off into the woods and get blown up again," Orhan said. The men in the room all laughed but it was no joke, the woods around them still held undetonated mines that made it dangerous to navigate in the best of conditions. Orhan stood and helped Kamal make his way through to the door.

"I didn't need a babysitter," Kamal said as the cooler night air hit him in the face.

"I know, but the way you're looking at me is driving me insane. I was afraid if I sat there a minute longer I'd jump into your lap and get us both beaten." Orhan led Kamal around the back of the building and then down a narrow path to another abandoned shack. He pushed Kamal up against the rough wood and kissed him. Kamal kissed back but then pulled away.

"I really do need to piss." Kamal turned and pulled his dick out, letting the urine flow. He groaned at the release of pressure in his bladder. He finished and tucked it back in, but he'd barely finished buttoning his pants before Orhan had him locked in his arms once again. Kamal dipped his head and took Orhan's mouth gently, and Orhan opened to allow Kamal to explore his mouth with his tongue. "Fuck, Orhan, we shouldn't do this here," Kamal said after he'd gone lightheaded from the kiss.

"Just something quick, please, Kamal, I don't think I can wait." Orhan bit his full lower lip and then let it poke out in a pout that drove Kamal crazy. "Please?"

Kamal looked around them, it was late and there was no one in sight. He pushed Orhan back until he rested against the building where just before he'd pinned Kamal. Dropping to his knees, he looked up as if worshipping the man that stood over him a moment before he pulled the button and zipper to open Orhan's jeans. It was crazy, but so was the need building in Kamal's own body, he'd take this one little risk but he'd make it quick.

He swallowed Orhan's cock and rolled his balls, knowing what would get his lover off the fastest. He was so engrossed with his task he didn't hear the footsteps nor did he heed the warning tugs on his hair from his partner. One second he was right where he wanted to be, sucking off the man he loved, and the next....

Kamal came to with a groan. He wasn't sure where he was or how he'd gone from kneeling in the dirt to... Kamal tried to move his hand to the spot that throbbed at his temple but the resistance to his movement made it impossible to accomplish. He stilled, but then when he realized he was bound, not only his arms but his legs too, he started to struggle before the pain in other parts of his body even registered.

"Look at that, he finally wakes up just in time. It's as if he knew it was your turn," a voice said somewhere off to the side, but when Kamal tried to turn toward it the pain stopped him.

"Go on, if he'd pay to suck your cock, I'm sure he'll love getting it up his ass," another voice said.

Kamal finally fought through the stabbing in his brain to raise his eyes. They met Orhan's blue ones that were shiny with unshed tears, tears he couldn't afford to show if he didn't want to end up in the same position as his lover. Kamal's sluggish brain had already cottoned on to the fact Orhan had lied to make it look like the blow job had been Kamal's idea and Orhan had only let Kamal do it because he'd paid him. Kamal was hurt by the betrayal, but on a deeper level he understood Orhan's need to hide what was between them.

"I can't believe you didn't know your best friend was a faggot," a familiar voice hissed from behind him.

Kamal screamed as something was shoved up inside him with enough force to rock the small table he was tied to. He tried to bite back the sound as he was brutally assaulted until the man behind him came and pulled away quickly. Kamal whimpered, but then another scream was forced from him when a boot connected with his balls that hung at the edge of the table.

"Do it now or we'll take turns seeing if you're lying about not taking it up the ass like him." It was Meho, the man from the bar. Kamal couldn't believe that Meho, a man whose life he'd saved more than once, would do this to him but proof showed itself when he stepped up into Kamal's line of sight to push Orhan closer.

Orhan's expressive eyes told the whole story of what was about to happen without him even having to open that mouth Kamal loved to kiss so much. Kamal watched as Orhan unbuttoned his pants, his mind screaming that it couldn't happen, there was no way Orhan would go through with it just to hide what he truly was. Orhan had always gone further than Kamal was willing to keep his secret, but this…this was too far. Their love had to mean more to him than that.

"Please, no," Kamal whispered as Orhan disappeared behind him. He felt Orhan's hand on his ass, much gentler than the man before him as if he was trying to soothe Kamal. Then the cock that was nowhere near as hard as it needed to be to penetrate him slid between his cheeks.

"What, you can't get it up?" a voice jeered.

"I'm not a fag, fucking a guy's ass doesn't get me hard," Orhan shot back in his defense, but his hand worked his flaccid flesh until it firmed up.

177

"Please, Orhan, don't..." But it was too late. Kamal let his mind drift as the only person he'd ever loved violated him.

"I'm so sorry," Orhan whispered when he'd spent himself inside his former lover and slumped onto his back.

Kamal cried silently into the table top. His body might recover from its rape, but he already knew his mind never would.

A knock on the window brought him back to the present and Kamal rolled down the window with an unsteady hand.

"You can't park here, move along," a man dressed in a security guard's uniform told him.

"I have an appointment with Gospodine Ferhatović. I'm a bit early so I thought I'd wait here rather than inconvenience him by showing up too soon," Kamal said.

"What time is the appointment?"

Kamal looked at his watch and cringed. "Ten minutes ago."

"Well, you better come on then. Just pull up to the gate so I can check you in," the guard said before walking back across the street.

Kamal drove to the little gatehouse and presented his identification card. He got a visitor's badge and was told where to park. It seemed a bit formal, but knowing what the family had just experienced with the kidnapping of their son, it didn't seem out of the ordinary. Kamal parked off to the side as he'd been instructed and took a few deep breaths to calm himself down. He could do this, he had to do this if he wanted to take back what belonged to him. Getting out of the car, he walked up the steps to the front door. He rang the bell and waited until it was opened by none other than Orhan himself.

Orhan smiled as his eyes swept up and down Kamal's body and then settled on his face. Kamal's eyes did the same. Orhan had aged fairly well, only a little weight around the middle and his graying hair gave away that he was past his prime. Orhan extended his hand, but Kamal just stared at it for a long moment before he shook his head and made no movement to take it. Orhan's smile faltered as he dropped his hand to his side.

"Well, I guess you should come in then," Orhan said as he stepped back to admit Kamal into his home.

"You sure?" Kamal asked when he finally found his voice to speak.

Orhan chuckled. "I guess I figured if you were here to kill me you wouldn't have made an appointment."

Kamal followed him through the house and into a smaller sitting room where coffee had already been set out on the table for them. "Have a seat." Orhan gestured to one of the chairs. Kamal sat as he looked around at the pictures on the walls. His eyes stopped on one that was placed prominently in the center of a grouping of old photos. Anger welled up when he recognized his own young face staring out at him. He and Orhan stood together, arms around each other's shoulders, smiling at the camera. Orhan noticed where he was looking. "That was right before the war started, remember? I look at that picture every day and it reminds me of how much I miss you."

Kamal's head snapped around back to Orhan. The look on the other man's face made Kamal angry, so angry he had to stop himself from punching that look right off his face. "I didn't come here to talk about the past or about you and I. I came here for one reason and one reason only, so don't try to make it sound like a social visit because it isn't," Kamal said harshly.

"What reason could you possibly have to come here if it's not about something between us?"

"I came for — "

"*Otac*, I need to send someone to get my medication, I'm almost out," Zijad said, interrupting Kamal as he entered the room.

Kamal turned to look at the boy as he stood unsurely in the doorway. His stomach clenched in anger at the sight of the pale and stretched look of the skin on the boy's face. He looked like a ghost of his former self; even under Kamal's care he hadn't faded the way he had in the few weeks he'd been back home. Kamal's hand itched to grab the boy and shake him back to life.

"Zijad, what are you doing in here?" Orhan stood just as Zijad's eyes shifted to Kamal, blocking his view of his father's visitor.

"I couldn't find Mama or Lila and I need this medicine now," Zijad said in a lifeless monotone.

"Give me the paper and I'll see that someone goes to fetch it right away," Orhan said, but his tone was uncaring and left no doubt in Kamal's mind that he saw his son as nothing but a nuisance.

"Thank you." Zijad stepped closer to hand off the paper, but his eyes strayed to Kamal for a brief moment until Orhan spoke again.

"Go back to the cottage, you shouldn't be out and seen in your condition," Orhan said.

"Yes, *Otac*," Zijad muttered. He turned to leave, but not without a last glance at Kamal. If Kamal didn't know better he'd have said those expressive blue eyes were pleading with him for help, but he knew that was just wishful thinking, the boy had no idea who he was.

Orhan sat back down on his chair with a heavy sigh. "I don't know what to do with him anymore."

"What's wrong with him?"

"He's not functioning. He's on so many drugs that he's basically turned into the drug addict they called him out as." Orhan poured coffee into the cups and sat one in front of Kamal. "He's weak and can't handle what's been done to him. I'm ashamed to call him my son."

"Did he tell you what he went through?" Kamal was curious as to how much Zijad had revealed of his time in captivity with him.

"I've not heard all the details, but he's told the police. They didn't believe him at first, what with all the people coming out to say that he was partying and then those videos, but then when he saw a trauma specialist she concluded he was telling the truth. You and I both know that he was taken, but the proof will never see the light of day."

"Why not?" Kamal asked, not denying he knew Zijad had been abducted.

"I can't go to the cops with the video, it was part of the deal." Orhan waved his hand as if dismissing the subject. "I don't want to talk about it. He wasn't good for much before and now he's utterly useless."

Kamal cleared his throat and sat up straighter. "I guess if that's how you feel, you won't be upset that I've come to take him with me," Kamal announced confidently.

Orhan's face was a perfect mask of confusion. "What the hell are you talking about?"

"I want the boy, he's mine."

"You've lost it, Kamal," Orhan said with a shake of his head. "We both know he's my son. Look at him, there's no doubt about that."

"I didn't mean that I'm his father. I meant he belongs to me and I want him so I'm going to take him."

Orhan stood so he loomed over Kamal. "I think you better leave," he said. The confusion on his face was replaced with anger. Kamal stood and thought about just going to find the boy and taking what he'd come for, but then the look in Orhan's eyes changed his mind. There were too many people on the grounds for Kamal to get away with taking Zijad since it seemed likely Orhan would raise the alarm if he tried. Kamal nodded. He let Orhan lead him to the front door, but before he could shut it, Kamal turned on him.

"I took him once before, just remember that," Kamal said, letting the unspoken threat hang between them in the air as Orhan finally grasped the meaning of Kamal's words. Realization dawned on Orhan's face and he opened his mouth to say something, but Kamal cut him off. "You have my number. Use it if you decide to return what's mine before I come back to take it."

Kamal walked to his car and drove away without looking back.

Chapter 21:
Taking What's His

Kamal locked his apartment door after he'd moved the last load of his belongings down to the *kombi* he'd bought. Walking down the stairs for the final time, he had no regrets at having sold the place. It was time to move on with his life and he knew his next stop would decide a lot about which direction it would go. He got in the *kombi* and checked his supplies to make sure he had everything he needed to do the job. Satisfied that he was as well-prepared as always, he set off across the sleeping city.

Parking the very noticeable *kombi* down the street from where his intended target lived, he made his way through the neighborhood on foot. When he approached the gated estate, he waited for the guard to make his circle of the perimeter on the outside of the fence, then followed him as he came around again until they were at the back of the property. He surprised the guard and knocked him out with one well-aimed hit to the back of his head with the butt of his gun. The unconscious man fell forward onto the ground where Kamal left him.

The fence was easy to scale alone, but he knew he'd have a heavy and ungainly package on his way out. He found the back gate that was locked securely from the inside and picked the lock so it wouldn't slow his escape. With that done, he turned his sights on the estate he'd been surveilling for the past few weeks. He knew where his target should be and made a beeline to the small cottage at the back of the property when the rotating search light left him with a darkened path. The guard posted in the front of it was playing a game on his phone which fell almost silently to the grass when

Kamal knocked him out in a similar fashion to that of his coworker. He dragged the heavy body around the side of the little building and propped it up against the wall.

He entered through the front door. Doing so made sure he could disable the only camera in the cottage before it caught his image. He knew he had little time to secure his package and leave before the guard at the gate would return from his own little walk along the front of the property to check the cameras. The cottage was only one room and a bathroom, his target lay in the middle of the bed under a pile of blankets. Kamal hurried over to the bed as he pulled the needle out of his pocket. He'd had a hell of a time figuring out what he could use that wouldn't cause a reaction or overdose with the medication he knew his target was currently taking. Lucky thing most Bosnian doctors were paid shit to do their jobs and weren't above taking a bribe to hand over sensitive information on their patients.

Kamal pulled the blankets back slowly, but he need not have worried since the action got no reaction from the sleeping body. Injecting the mild sedative into the muscle of the boy's thigh, he then wrapped him in a sheet and put him over his shoulder. As he turned to leave, a sharp bark rang through the air. A small dog had slipped through the crack in the open front door and was now growling at Kamal. With no hesitation at all, Kamal lifted his boot and stomped down on the dog's head. It didn't kill the animal instantly as was evidenced by its weak whine, so Kamal brought the heel of his boot down once more and the dog went still and silent. Kamal let killing the dog Orhan supposedly loved more than his son give him a small bit of satisfaction before he left the cottage.

He waited once again for the light to make its pass, but then he took off in a full-out run for the gate, leaving the house behind just as he heard the alarm raised. Kamal almost stumbled as his feet hit the pavement only meters from his *kombi*. With no time for finesse, he threw the boy into the backseat and drove away as quickly as possible. He'd known it was going to be a tight getaway but it had been a closer call than he would have liked. He drove steady and slightly under the speed limit until he hit the main highway where he could increase his speed enough to put some distance between him and the scene of his crime. Settling in for the two-hour drive to the cabin that was a few kilometers north of the small mountain village of Bakići, Kamal smoked and hummed along to the radio.

Kamal dozed off as he waited for the boy to wake, feeling the exhaustion that his physical exertion, combined with the stress of his quick flight, had wrought on his aging body. The cries from behind the hood snapped him back to attention. He stood and walked over to the mattress he'd put in the corner. It wasn't the same cabin, but Kamal had set up the living room exactly the same, complete with shackles for his captive. He waited until the cries grew louder and then finally died down to low murmurs. Kamal carefully got down on his knees so he could hear what the boy was muttering.

"Please not again, please, please, god, not again," Zijad repeated over and over.

Kamal touched the boy's chest in the way he'd done to soothe him before, but Zijad screamed and tried to move away. He fought the boy's head movements to remove the hood, but left the blindfold in place for the time being.

"Don't touch me!" Zijad screamed when Kamal put his hand back on the boy's chest.

"Shh, Mali, and quit struggling against the cuffs, you'll hurt yourself." Kamal rubbed small circles on the rapidly moving flesh beneath his hands.

"*Šef?*"

"Yes, Mali, it's me. Now calm yourself so we can talk a bit," Kamal said. He waited a few moments until the boy's breath came at a more natural tempo. "There, that's better, now we can talk about what's happening."

"He hired you to kill me, didn't he?" Zijad's chest hitched and he sobbed loudly a couple of times before regaining some control.

"Who do you think would hire me to kill you?"

"My *otac*, he thinks I'm disgusting and weak and he wants to get rid of me," Zijad said, managing to control his tears.

"Listen to me, Mali... Zijad, no one hired me this time," Kamal said. Zijad stilled completely under his hand. "You have nothing to fear from me. I will not kill you or harm you in that way."

"Why?"

"Why won't I hurt you?" Kamal asked with a smirk on his face.

"No, why did you take me if no one is paying you to?" Zijad's face scrunched up in confusion.

"Because I wanted to."

"But...You can't just kidnap people because you want to." There was a tremor in Zijad's voice that he couldn't hide.

"I can do whatever I want, but I'm going to give you a choice." Kamal wanted the boy, but he wouldn't keep him prisoner forever. He wanted the boy to want to be there for reasons he couldn't explain to himself.

"I don't understand," Zijad said quietly.

Shifting, Kamal uncuffed the boy's hands, then he lay down next to him on the mattress. "I'm going to detox you off those pills you're on because they'll kill you, Mali. Once that's done, you'll have a decision to make."

"What decision?" Zijad's hands found Kamal's shirt and he had fists full of it clutched in his grip.

"I'll tell you when you can think clearly without the drugs. Do you remember the rules?"

"Yes, *Šef*," Zijad answered breathlessly.

"Good. Then we'll sleep and tomorrow we'll begin," Kamal promised.

It didn't take as long as Kamal had thought for the boy to go through the painful process of ridding his body of the effects of the drugs he'd been taking. Kamal had been prepared for the vomiting, the bad moods, and the listlessness to last for many weeks instead of just the three it took for the boy to start eating more food and keeping it down. When he began asking Kamal why he had to wear the blindfold every ten minutes, Kamal knew it was time to end the wet nurse act and have a very important conversation with the boy.

They'd just finished their rather late evening meal, Zijad kneeling next to Kamal so he could feed him, when Zijad asked once again, " *Šef*, please, why do I have to wear the mask?"

Kamal sighed as he stood from the chair. "Come with me, Mali." He walked into the living room, not even checking to see if the boy had followed because he was sure Zijad would. He settled on the couch and waited for Zijad to once again kneel at his feet. After lighting a cigarette, he just sat for a moment and looked at the naked boy. This was it, the moment of truth, but he was hesitant to ask the question. "You have to wear the mask until I get your answer."

"Why? I don't understand, *Šef*," the boy said, his voice riding the line between a whine and annoyance.

"Answer a question for me, but you need to think on this very hard because there will be no going back once you've decided one way or the other and I will decide if the mask stays on or comes off," Kamal said.

"What's the question, *Šef?*"

Kamal reached out and touched the boy's cheek. His reaction was the same as it had been before, he leaned into the touch and his posture relaxed just a bit. "Do you want to stay here with me or go back home?" Kamal had to push the words out from his throat where they seemed to want to stay. Once he asked the question there was no going back; his question, like Zijad's answer, was irreversible.

Zijad pulled his face away from Kamal's hand and pursed his lips a moment before asking, "What does staying here with you mean?" Kamal saw that question as a good sign. The boy hadn't asked to be taken home immediately which meant he would at least consider what Kamal was proposing.

"I guess it wouldn't be too much different from the time you were with me before," Kamal said truthfully. He'd liked the way having the boy under his complete control had felt and he wanted that feeling back.

"I don't want to sit around for days in a hood or have to listen to..." Zijad began, but stopped to swallow hard. "Is anything negotiable?"

Kamal thought about it. He hadn't intended for the kid to wear the hood or spend his time chained to the wall. He'd hoped he wouldn't need to resort to that to keep the boy, which was why he was giving him a choice. "Not much is negotiable, but I don't want to keep you prisoner. If you're here of your own free will, do I need to keep you chained up?"

Zijad didn't answer him for a long moment. "Can I think about it for a bit?"

"I told you to think hard about it. I'll give you until morning, but then I will expect an answer."

"Thank you, Šef," Zijad said. Then he did something unexpected, he laid his head in Kamal's lap.

Kamal got hard instantly. It had been a long three weeks and even Kamal wasn't sick enough to abuse someone who had been in the shape the boy had been in. No matter how much he'd wanted to, he'd held himself back, but now...The boy was well again which meant Kamal didn't have to stop the urges welling up inside of him. He put his hand in Zijad's hair, gently petting him for a moment, but then his hand clenched into a fist. The boy's breath hitched, but as Kamal tugged on the hair at the back of his head it sped up. Kamal yanked the boy's head up roughly and Zijad moaned.

"I've missed your mouth, Mali." Kamal ran his thumb over Zijad's bottom lip, letting the boy's warm, moist breath wash over his skin. He had really missed those lips, and having them around his cock was the only thing he could think of as he stared at them. Just as Zijad flicked his tongue out to touch, Kamal jerked away. Pulling the waistband of his sweat pants down, his dick sprang out, eager for the attention it had been starving for. "Mali..."

"Yes, Šef," Zijad breathed out.

Kamal took that as assent, not that he really needed it, but.... He pushed the boy's head down, finding no resistance when he did. Zijad took him in deep, drawing a low groan from Kamal he was helpless to stop. Lifting his hips so the boy gagged, Kamal held him down, enjoying the way the boy didn't struggle against being choked until he needed to breathe and that turned Kamal on even more. He finally relented and let Zijad breathe, but only a couple of deep inhales before he pressed him back down. He repeated his actions until the boy started to whimper. Kamal grabbed his head with both hands to hold it fast while he fucked to completion. The orgasm was so intense Kamal's vision got fuzzy around the edges and he went limp against the couch, releasing his grip on Zijad's head. The boy licked up his mess and then laid his cheek against Kamal's bare thigh. He whispered something too low for Kamal to make out.

"What was that, Mali?" Kamal asked. "Speak up so that I can hear you."

"Thank you, Šef," Zijad repeated a little louder.

Kamal grinned.

Zijad was sitting up in the corner of his mattress with his knees drawn up so his chin rested on one of them when Kamal woke up. He studied the way the boy was just sitting there silently, as if in deep thought, and wondered what his answer would be.

"Good morning, *Šef*," Zijad said before Kamal even made it known that he was awake.

"Morning, Mali, did you sleep well?" Kamal lit a cigarette from the pack on the table in front of him.

Zijad shook his head slightly. "I didn't, *Šef*, I was thinking too much to sleep."

"About what?"

"You know what, and I think I have decided," Zijad said, sounding exasperated at Kamal's question.

"Watch the attitude, boy," Kamal warned.

"Sorry, *Šef*." A smile played at the corners of Zijad's lips.

"Zijad." Kamal used his tone and the boy's name to warn him that he was treading a very fine line.

Zijad's head snapped up at Kamal's admonishment. "You want me!" he shouted. He pointed an eerily accurate but trembling finger at Kamal and in a much more civil tone said once again, " *You* want *me*." He dropped his hand back to his knees, but his head stayed defiantly up like he'd be staring Kamal down if that mask wasn't in the way.

Kamal finished his smoke and stubbed it out before he got up and went to the boy. He sat on the mattress, but didn't touch Zijad. "Tell me your decision, Mali," Kamal ordered.

"Admit you want me," Zijad demanded back. Kamal sighed, at least the boy wasn't asking for him to tell him he loved him or some other sappy shit Kamal couldn't do.

"I want you. I thought I made that clear when I stole you out from under your *otac's* nose." Zijad's shoulders relaxed, as did his face, and he nodded. He bit his lip to try to stifle the small cry, but it escaped in a soft whimper. He laid his head on his knees and rocked on his butt. Kamal finally tried to touch him, but he flinched away, giving what Kamal thought was his nonverbal answer to the question.

"I'll take you home," Kamal said as he started to stand. "NO!" The scream stopped Kamal and he settled back down to see if the boy would say more. "I want to stay with you, Šef, please you said that I could choose. Why would you lie to me? Please let me stay," Zijad pleaded.

Kamal's mind was finally at ease for the first time since he'd seen the picture of the boy in Julien's file. The way all the thoughts in his head usually haunted him from a thousand different angles stopped and narrowed down to just one, the boy was his. He reached out and grabbed the sides of the boy's head, hands flat against his hair and skin. He used his thumbs to raise the blindfold off Zijad's eyes. Bright blue, wide open and shiny with tears and fear, Kamal thought they were the boy's best feature.

"You're mine now. I own you. Do you understand?" Kamal asked, as the boy's eyes roved over his face. The look was so intense it felt like the boy was trying to devour him through it.

"Yes, Šef," Zijad said.

Chapter 22:
Epilogue – A Day with Zijad

Zijad awoke, as always, a few minutes before his alarm went off. He shifted to his back and stretched. He'd wait until the alarm went off before getting out of the big soft bed. His mind wasn't at peace as he waited, but there was nothing to do for that; the beeping was a welcome sound because it meant he could start his day. He got out of bed and made his way to the adjoining bathroom where he took a quick shower and ran through his well-choreographed morning routine.

In the kitchen he checked the schedule he'd memorized quite some time ago and made a face. Oatmeal for breakfast, he loathed oatmeal. He got out the pan and the box of oats and fixed the much hated bowl of mush. A glass of milk accompanied his meal which he dutifully gagged down as quickly as possible just to get it over with. He cleaned his mess in the kitchen and went back to the schedule that ruled his life.

After his hour of meditation on his knees in the corner of the living room, he cleaned the master bath, changed and laundered the sheets on the bed, and vacuumed the rugs. He didn't mind the busy work that kept his eyes from straying to the clock to watch the minutes of his day slowly creep past. His routine was so well set that he finished just in time for lunch which the schedule told him would be a turkey sandwich and some chips.

After consuming his meal with more relish than his breakfast, he cleaned the kitchen once more and then went once again to his corner. Another hour of silence later and he knew free time was next on the list. Free time usually meant reading, but the books he had were all ones he'd already read. Sighing, he picked out his favorite amongst them and took it to the cushion on the floor of the living room. The mat was positioned in front of the patio doors so he could bask in the afternoon sunshine as he read.

The book couldn't hold his attention and he found he spent more time staring at the wall clock than at the well-worn pages. Then his eyes would dart to the door as if in anticipation, but he was always disappointed. He rolled over and spent his remaining free time staring at the ceiling. When finally his free time changed into outdoor time, Zijad's spirits lifted. He enjoyed outdoor time the most.

He entered the large fenced-in back yard from the patio. He found his football and spent a good hour or more dribbling it around the yard and doing tricks. Sweaty and breathing hard by the time he got done, he used the outdoor shower to clean the sweat off and then the grass that clung to his bare feet. Zijad took the stairs up to the deck surrounding the large above-ground pool and dove in, swimming the length before he surfaced. He floated on his back because he liked the way the sounds around him were muffled when his ears were submerged. Sometimes he'd drift to the edge of the pool and tap his foot in time with his heartbeat and wonder if that was what a baby still in the womb would listen to through its long days of gestation. It was somewhat soothing to think so and it brought a smile to his lips for the first time that day. After he was through with the pool, he lay on the deck to let the sun and light breeze wick the moisture from his skin.

Supper was more of an affair. Zijad fried himself some of the already prepared *ćevapi*; while they were in the pan, he diced a small onion to accompany his meal. He also made a salad of tomatoes and cucumbers with green onion and a dollop of sour cream. When the meat was almost done he put his *somun* on top to warm. Zijad ate heartily, as his appetite had benefited from his exercise. With a pleasantly full belly, he cleaned the kitchen for one final time that day.

Two hours on his knees in the corner seemed too much for him to bear. Instead of sitting still and letting his mind rest, he fidgeted. He watched the clock and the door, praying for it to open. He looked at his fingers, trying to focus, but then a hangnail caught his attention on his left ring finger and he lifted his hands from his knees with the intention of picking at it. Stopping himself before his finger met his mouth, he put his hands back into position with a sigh. The day had dragged by just like the four previous ones, he wondered when his wait would end.

He lay once again on his mat on the floor of the living room. He had two hours of television time, but there was nothing on. He reached down and itched his lower belly. For reasons unknown it caused an unintended and unwanted reaction. His cock plumped up and he glared at it as if he felt betrayed by his own flesh, having to stay his hand when it unconsciously reached for it. Breathing in through his mouth and out through his nose, Zijad tried to calm the urge to jerk off. His body was covered with a sheen of sweat by the time his dick went back down. His head lolled to the side so he could see the time, still an hour and a half left before he could prepare for bed and then the blissful nothingness of sleep.

He picked out a movie and put the disc in. With no memory of what he'd chosen, he lay there and absently watched the flickering images on the screen until he could finally leave his spot. He took a long soaking bath, making sure to wash his long hair with extra care. Then, after going through his night time ritual on autopilot, he climbed into the big bed alone.

Zijad was sure he was dreaming. The big hard body pressed warmly against his back was just his mind giving him what he craved during his waking hours, nothing more. He let himself sink into the feeling as the body moved rhythmically against his and then finally, oh, he loved the first moment of penetration. The feeling of being possessed left him breathless with its meaning. He may not ever know what it felt like to be loved, but he was owned, which he was sure in those moments felt just as good. Rough whiskers brushed the tender skin between his shoulder blades and he commended his mind on being able to replicate that sensation so well as he shuddered.

"*Moj mali mačić,* will you not wake up to welcome me home?" The boss's gruff voice startled Zijad out of his mind and into the moment. He was home! Finally, after what seemed like an endless wait filled with uncertainty, his boss had come back to him.

"Yes, *Šef*, I'm awake now. I thought you were a dream," Zijad murmured sleepily. He bowed his back so his hips pushed out, giving the man behind him better access to push in deeper., Zijad felt the hard cock fill him completely before he stilled. The man's big hand wrapped around Zijad's own straining length, making him moan out in pleasure.

"Must be some dreams you have, Mali," the boss said with a chuckle. He used his calloused hand to stroke Zijad slowly, tormenting him with what he knew he'd most likely not get, at least not this time, but later, maybe... "I missed fucking you, Mali, I always miss this," the man said. He let Zijad's dick go so that he could grasp his hip. He fucked Zijad with long measured movements that would draw out his own pleasure while Zijad whimpered, because he knew he couldn't find his own without the command.

Zijad tried to think of other things, but all he could think of was the man behind him. The boss had taken ownership of him on the day he'd made his choice to stay. With only a call to his father to tell him he was fine and not to look for him, Zijad had cut all ties with his family and the outside world. The man was his whole world now, had been for the past year and Zijad had never been happier. The boss was a rough man and he showed no mercy, but he always made Zijad feel as if he mattered. The man saw him, and thought about him when he was away. Even if it was just for his ass and his mouth, Zijad was wanted.

Zijad's wandering mind had not helped his lustful body which had begun moving wantonly against the boss who growled a warning. Zijad stopped his rocking when he felt his orgasm bubbling up to the point of no return. He whimpered, and then even though he knew it would do no good, he begged, "Please, *Šef*, please..."

"Please what? What do you want, boy?" The boss shifted and nailed Zijad's prostate, making him cry out instead of answering. "Oh, you want to come?" He hit the spot a few more times after his taunt. "No, you don't get to come yet, Mali, so hold on because I don't want to have to punish you after just getting back."

"Yes, *Šef*," Zijad said, but in his mind he weighed whether it would be better or worse in the end if he ended up punished for coming. Deciding to hold on when the boss's thrusts picked up, he knew it would be over soon. He could feel it when the man spilled his seed deep inside of him, and Zijad moaned along with the boss because he loved that his body pleased the man so much. "Thank you, *Šef.*"

"Mmm, Mali, that was a nice welcome home," he said as he crushed Zijad to his chest for a moment. "Now go."

Pulling away, Zijad sighed at the lost connection when the cock slipped from his body with his movements. He crawled to the bathroom and started the water in the big tub. With patience and effort, he used the toilet which helped his dick deflate while he waited for the tub to fill. The boss came in just when Zijad was shutting off the water, he must have timed how long it took to fill because he always showed up at exactly the right time. He picked Zijad up off the floor and sat him in the warm water before he climbed in behind. Zijad lay back against the man.

"Did you miss me, Mali?" he asked as he always did. His hands ran over Zijad's chest and arms, making him shiver.

"Yes, *Šef,* I always miss you. I'm so lonely here without you," Zijad said truthfully. He ached to touch the boss's skin but left his own hands on his thighs. He knew the rules and wouldn't push so soon after the man had come home.

"I know you're lonely, but what would you have me do? I have to work."

Zijad knew that was a lie, he'd seen the man's bank records for himself when he'd stolen a peek at the computer screen, but he wouldn't say that. "I know, *Šef,* I'm fine. I make do."

"Sit forward so I can wash you." The boss gave him a gentle nudge and Zijad did as he was told, letting the man wash him with a soapy cloth. He liked the boss's tender touches almost as much as he liked the punishing ones. The man poured water over Zijad's head and Zijad enjoyed having his hair washed even though it had been unnecessary after he'd done it the previous night. "Your hair is getting long. You look like a girl from behind," the boss said, a playful lilt in his voice.

"You can cut it if it pleases you, *Šef.*" A hand twisted roughly in his long locks and pulled his head back.

"I think I like it this way, makes for easier handling," the man decided. That grip in his hair used to frighten Zijad, but now he only felt his dick harden in anticipation. "I can see you like it too." The boss gave a pointed look at the head of Zijad's cock which stuck up out of the water.

"Yes, *Šef*," Zijad said breathlessly. He liked the idea of the boss controlling him with his hair, something the man did often even when it had been shorter.

The boss chuckled as he released his hold. "Go do what you need to do while I finish up in here."

Zijad's schedule never changed, even when the boss was home, though it did get interrupted whenever the man wanted use of his body. Zijad crawled out of the tub and went about his morning routine. He left the boss to his bath and went out to prepare breakfast for them both. He was only allowed to stand when his chores made it a necessity, otherwise he crawled about on his hands and knees. Donning an apron that would protect his naked body from any grease splatters, he put the coffee pan on the stove to boil the water for the boss's coffee while he scrambled eggs with shallots and fried sausage.

The man sat down on the only chair at the table. Zijad had set his plate, his coffee, and a glass of juice on the table just moments before and was kneeling on his pad next to the boss's chair. "This looks good, Mali," he said as he set up his laptop. He ate a few bites and sipped his coffee before offering a bit of eggs he'd scooped up with bread to Zijad. Zijad opened his mouth and wrapped his lips around the man's fingers, sucking them gently as he took his food. He chewed while thinking about how much he'd missed this simple act while he'd been alone. Taking his nourishment from the man's fingers like a helpless child or a cherished pet made Zijad's chest swell with emotion. The boss lifted the glass of juice to Zijad's lips and he drank.

After cleaning the kitchen, Zijad went to his corner while the man finished his work on the computer. Zijad was thankful his chores were light that morning because he hoped to finish early enough to get the boss's attention for a bit. He swept the floors, cleaned the bedroom and dusted, then looked at the clock and saw he hadn't finished with enough time to play with the man before he began preparing lunch. With a heavy sigh, he went to make the meal. They ate the same way as they'd eaten breakfast, but instead of letting Zijad go to his corner, the boss called him to the couch. Zijad crawled over and knelt at the man's feet.

"I've got something for you." The boss was holding a gift bag he'd pulled out from under the table. "Here, open it and tell me what you think." The man handed the bag to Zijad.

Zijad took the bag. This wasn't the first time the boss had brought him a gift after he'd returned from one of his jobs, but Zijad always approached them with some trepidation. The first such gift he'd received had been a pair of nipple clamps the man had used to make him cry, the second had been a pillow that was covered in the softest material that he loved to snuggle against; Zijad never knew what to expect out of the man's presents. He pulled the bag open and looked inside, eyes lighting up at what he found. He took the device out of the bag and stared at it.

"It's one of those book reader things," the boss said when Zijad just turned it over and over in his hands. "I asked the guy at the store to help me get some books on it. I told him some of the books you have and he downloaded a bunch that were by the same people or that were sort of the same — "

"Thank you, *Šef!*" Zijad exclaimed. He threw his arm around the man's waist and laid his head on his lap. He could feel the tears pricking at the backs of his eyeballs. It was the best present he'd ever gotten. It wasn't the most expensive, of course, his father had never let him want for anything, but this was better. The man actually knew that Zijad loved to read and even what he liked to read, it had to mean something that the boss would know those things. Zijad was overcome with emotion.

"I knew you'd like it. If there are books you want, you can tell me and we'll download them for you." The man petted Zijad's hair. Zijad nodded that he understood the gift didn't give him access to the internet and he didn't care, he'd have new books. The boss patted his head, the signal he was done with Zijad clinging on him, so Zijad sat back up on his knees. "Okay, you go read a book, I have things to do for a bit." The man stood.

"Yes, *Šef*, thank you again, I love it," Zijad said as he crawled to his mat.

"You're welcome, Mali."

Zijad watched as he walked out the door and then across the lawn to the little shed at the back. He unlocked the padlock and disappeared inside. Zijad had no idea what was in the little building as he wasn't allowed in there, but the man always spent a couple of hours out there on the day he returned home from a job. Zijad powered up his book and browsed through the titles. He was so excited, he started reading and lost track of time. He thought that was the reason for the boss's angry look and terse command for him to heel.

The apology was perched at the end of Zijad's tongue, but the man cut him off. "Over the bench, boy," he commanded.

Zijad knew not to argue, that only got him an extra sore ass. He went to the bench and laid himself out for the man to do as he pleased. The crop fell across his ass and left a sharp pain that made him cry out. The crop always hurt more when his ass had a few days to forget its sting. Another fell just above where the first had landed.

"Tell me what happened while I was away," the man demanded.

"Nothing happened, *Šef.*" Zijad wracked his brain trying to think of something that would have made the boss mad, but nothing came to mind.

The crop fell again and again before he asked, "So there's nothing you want to tell me, huh, nothing at all?"

"N-nothing, *Šef,*" Zijad stammered.

"What did you do yesterday?" he asked after he hit Zijad four more times.

"The schedule," Zijad sobbed out. He'd started to cry somewhere around the fourth hit, but still he couldn't think of anything he'd done wrong.

"Did you eat the oatmeal?" He landed one blow.

"Yes! I h-hate it b-but…" Another strike cut off his words.

"What did you do last night?" The crop smacked down again.

Zijad thought about his evening of waiting and being distracted from everything *but* the waiting. "I fidgeted during meditation, I'm sorry, *Šef,* I couldn't hold still. I prom — " This time a volley of blows landed quickly, one after another, and Zijad screamed out his pain.

"You are lying to me," the man growled. "You're supposed to tell me when things happen, not hide them because you don't want to pay the price for them."

"I got an erection!" he cried. The man's words had sparked the memory of himself lying on his mat with a hard-on. He hadn't even touched it, but he hadn't reported his slip-up either. He wasn't allowed to get hard while just lying about when the boss was gone. Morning wood was fine because no one could help that, but his mind had be preoccupied and he'd lost control over his body when he should have been more attentive.

"Yes, Mali, you did. Why did you get hard? Were you thinking about your young lover?" His voice dipped dangerously low to put the fear into Zijad.

"No, I was waiting for you, I was thinking about you," Zijad protested. The man hit him two more times. "Please, Šef, I'll do anything for you to believe me, give you anything." He made the offer knowing he had nothing to give that the man wouldn't take when he wanted. Zijad heard the crop hit the floor just before he was pulled from the bench by his hair. He stood facing the angry man. His dark eyes, so dark Zijad had a hard time discerning between the pupil and the iris, were so piercing it felt like he could see right into Zijad's mind.

"Anything?" he asked.

"Yes, Šef, anything," Zijad whimpered.

"Would you give me your life if I asked to take it?" His eyes bore into Zijad's as he waited for his answer.

Zijad couldn't keep the smile from his face. The man was clueless if he didn't know the answer to that question, but Zijad answered it nonetheless. "No."

The man's face twisted in anger. "NO?"

Zijad let the anger wash over him, but it didn't sway him. "I can't give you what doesn't belong to me. My life is already yours."

Author Notes

First I want to thank those that were always there for me as I wrote this book. Morwen Navarre, Tonna Saunders, Jamila Lindsey, Chrissy Quinn and Lisa (for reading even though she hated Kamal badly enough to want to kill him). Without all my wonderful supporters, I would have given it up when it got hard to deal with the darker stuff.

This story idea came to me one night when I was thinking about the things politicians do to get into and then stay in power. I knew I didn't want to write about a politician but I wondered about what one would do if he was forced to deal with a kid who would make him look bad in the public eye. Then Kamal stepped up because that's how the characters in my head work, they sort of start talking to me one day and there you have it, I'm stuck with a hitman whispering dark things into my ear.

Kamal had a story to tell but I didn't want to tell his back story, it's too dark and depressing. It did however make for an interesting twist in a story where a politician's son was kidnapped, tortured and then released back to an uncaring father who just happened to be the very man that betrayed the kidnapper years before. To me, figuring out how Kamal would deal with knowing someone he'd once loved was about to be kidnapped by someone like himself wasn't easy. Kamal was a hard man to keep a bead on. He shifted from someone I thought might find a heart to someone I knew had no empathy left for anyone. It made him cold and hard to connect with but it also made him fascinating because he chose to become the man he did instead of finding a way to cope better with the traumas of his past. Kamal is a monster, incapable of tenderness unless it serves his purpose in some way. He's probably the only character that I've ever written where I could honestly not find one thing I liked about them.

I got a lot of feedback on how the readers wanted to know how Zijad was coping, what he was thinking and feeling, but I chose to tell the story from Kamal's point of view for a couple of reasons. The biggest reason I chose not to delve into Zijad's head was because I didn't want the story to become too emotionally driven by his reactions to his situation. I did know what was going on with him but the story's focus would have changed had I switched point of view to include his experiences. The last chapter is really to satisfy the readers need to know that he's at least okay in the end.

About the Author

C.L. Mustafic is a born and bred American mid-westerner who mysteriously ended up living in one of those countries nobody can ever find on the map in Europe. Left with too much time on her hands – let's be honest here it was the lack of television channels in her native language – and too many voices in her head trying to fill the silence, she decided to give her life-long dream of writing a novel a shot. After finishing the first one she figured she may as well do it again because as she flipped through the channels in the vain hope there would be something interesting on she came to the realization that there are only so many 90's sitcom reruns one can stomach before they are compelled to throw themselves in front of a bus. So now between shuttling kids back and forth from various activities, risking her life on the insanely narrow, busy streets of her new home town, she loses herself in her own made-up world where sometimes things get a little freaky.

About the Publisher

ForbiddenFiction.com is a publisher devoted to writing that breaks the boundaries of original erotic fiction. Our stories combine intense sexuality with quality writing. Stories at Forbidden Fiction.com not only arouse readers through sensations, but also engage them emotionally and mentally through storytelling as well-crafted as the sex is hot.

ForbiddenFiction.com is also designed to be a social reading environment. You'll have fun even if just reading the latest post each day, yet you will have the chance for so much more. Readers and authors can be part of ongoing discussions of specific works and individual authors as well as more general topics.

Sign up for a FREE Membership today at <u>ForbiddenFiction.com</u>

www.ingramcontent.com/pod-product-compliance
Lightning Source LLC
Chambersburg PA
CBHW072057170626
46813CB00004B/1387